SAMS IN A
DRY SEASON

Books by Ivan Gold

NICKEL MISERIES
SICK FRIENDS
SAMS IN A DRY SEASON

SAMS IN A
DRY SEASON

Ivan Gold

BOSTON 1990

Houghton Mifflin / Seymour Lawrence

For information about permission to reproduce selections from
this book, write to Permissions, Houghton Mifflin Company,
2 Park Street, Boston, Massachusetts 02108.

Library of Congress Cataloging-in-Publication Data

Gold, Ivan.
Sams in a dry season / Ivan Gold.
p.   cm.
ISBN 0-395-52281-1
I. Title.
PS3557.035S36   1990   90-37474
813'.54 — dc20   CIP

Printed in the United States of America

BVG 10 9 8 7 6 5 4 3 2 1

The poem on pages 132-33 is reprinted from
The Avenue Bearing the Initial of Christ into the New World
by Galway Kinnell, © 1954 by Galway Kinnell, published by
Houghton Mifflin Company, Boston.

This is a work of fiction, and all the characters
in it are fictitious.

To my wife and son

Acknowledgments: the church basements; Dan Wakefield; Writers Room at the Artists Foundation in Boston; Peter Halperin; the necessary grace.

Contents

If I change
You change

Vivekananda

Still Drinking
after All
These Years

JASON SAMS, in danger of losing his job (not ready to admit it was already lost), deemed it high time to return to the literary wars. It was 1976, year of the tall ships, two hundredth anniversary of the nation's founding; impossible to ignore (in Boston, in March) signs of impending celebration, but the prospect of pervasive pageantry depressed him less than the knowledge that his best efforts were unlikely to keep the Englishwoman from finessing him out of the job.

He was entering his eighth year of marriage, father of one and author of two (in marked contrast to Fiona, divorced dam of seven, perpetrator of six), forty-three and intermittently aware that alcohol had become less useful to him than once it had been, at some indeterminate period in his life. He knew there might well come a day (comfortably in the future) when he would elect to give it up entirely.

(And once he returned from New York, where he must venture soon to talk up his new book, as yet barely on the drawing board, he intended to put together an extended piece of abstinence, long enough to launch, at least, the project that would signal his return.)

Even the impending loss of livelihood was less disturbing

than the recollection of how *nice* he'd been to her in the dog days following her arrival in July of '75, when no one in authority had been in town, let alone on campus, and (fresh off the plane) she'd called him from the Creative Writing Department office, to which she'd taxied directly from Logan, and burst into tears right on the phone in her confusion and loneliness.

Delighted to be summoned from whatever it was he had been doing, moved further when he laid eyes on her (about ten years his senior, no harm in that; his cock and he much taken by her earthy, ample, Colleen Dewhurst qualities), Jason saw her settled into the nearby Howard Johnson motel and then helped her, over the next few weeks, find a university-owned apartment not far from his own. He squired her to neighborhood pubs, gave her a hand moving in when her stuff finally arrived, and when her back went out he drove her to and from the supermarket in his beatup Valiant and finally to his own house for dinner, carefully arranging the pillows and extra chair on which she might prop up her leg (for *he* knew better than to underestimate a bad back, even if she didn't), setting her up in his own favorite chair at the head of his table in a manner that recalled to him both his grandfathers, or any imperious patriarch presiding at a seder. His wife, battered by years of proximity to his habits, still wildly hopeful that their "new life" in Boston would bring new meaning to their lives, busted her butt in the kitchen and turned out a masterpiece, a flawless novella of a four-course meal. His four-year-old son said impossibly witty, insightful things at dinner and otherwise (incredibly) behaved himself, when he might just as easily have staged a repetition of the antics that had sent John Cheever scurrying into the night the previous academic year. But Fiona managed to ignore the kid and even had the balls to send the chicken tarragon back to the kitchen for fine tuning, while blowing literary smoke Jason's way and framing keen questions about the head of the English Department and other notables (to which, long since smashed on his own Chivas and his own Bordeaux, Sams returned — callow fucker that he was — keen and humorous and self-compromising answers).

Nevertheless he drove her home, turning her over to the doorman in the posher quarters she had found by then, in genteelly seedy Brookline Mansions.

He remained at her disposal through August and into September; by late September the bigwigs were in place and the new term had begun, and as the visiting star-for-a-year she settled in right from the beginning, socially and pedagogically, for he heard nothing further from her. A victim (all his lousy life!) of misplaced compassion, Sams finally felt, by mid-December, her ill wind blowing through the fog, adding its particular peril to the boozy miasma in which he passed his days.

The limey son of a bitch! Himself once the visiting star for a single semester (filling in for a distinguished drunk who had begun academic year '73–74, taught a class or two, then vanished), he was now in his second year of discharging the duties of backup person to the hotshot of the moment, a safe (he had thought), reasonably well compensated, untaxing gig he would have been content to continue for as long as they would have him or until his ship came in, whichever was soonest; but Fiona was after the job now, and not (from what he'd further heard) from love of teaching or a need for money but because she'd fallen for some West Indian poet putz and needed the promise of a job in order to renew her visa; what could be simpler than to go after some version of the position she already held, stepping with Ms. Dewhurst's own terrible grace over whatever bodies might litter the road?

Not without resources, Sams primed himself with a few pops of Jack Daniels and a Rignes beer and got on the blower to the Sunday *New York Times.* They accommodated him with three first novels to review. He was sick and tired of writing book reviews, even (or especially) for the Sunday *New York Times,* but the point now was to see to it that the brief bio accompanying the ephemera contained not only his literary bona fides but also a thunderous plug for the half-ass creative writing program (as weren't they all) in the half-ass university that was about to discharge him.

This much unfolded as planned: "Jason Sams, the author of *Just Desserts,* a book of stories, and *Slow Dying,* a novel" was further described as Visiting Lecturer in Creative Writing (Fiction) in the Graduate Creative Writing Program at the University of Greater Boston, and in the days after his review appeared the doddering Shakespearean scholar took to nodding at him in the hallway, and the philologist who specialized in New England place names allowed that he hadn't read a novel in thirty years, and Sams' omnibus pan had done little to alter his habits. Surely someone in the administration or at least high up in the English Department must have seen the review too, and too bad his class of six that semester was totally uninspired, or he would have solicited testimonials from some or all of them regarding his preternatural ability to elicit the best prose (fiction) they had to offer. But to a man (and one snide woman) they were obtuse and talent-free, so he let that aspect go.

*

In mid-February the Joycean scholar who chaired the English Department, new to the position and also to the U of GB, suggested lunch. Jason accepted, recommending a frugal Greek place in the square, not far from where he lived. Between the chairman's invitation and their meeting a week later a Sunday *New York Times* appeared, and there on the cover of the Book Review was Fiona, Visiting *Professor* in the Graduate Creative Writing, etc., assessing Doris Lessing at considerable length. The *Times* had to have bumped someone else to have given her the new Lessing on such short notice; holy shit (if he had doubted it before), was *he* ever overmatched! He thought he might share this rueful insight with the chairman over lunch, while not neglecting to make his own strong case for keeping the job: he was (unlike the Englishwoman) an experienced teacher of the unteachable, had done the thing at Columbia University and at Bard College before arriving at the U of GB, and (not that this necessarily mattered, nor did contemplation of it always bring him pleasure) could point to moderately successful young writers publishing out there at this moment who had obviously benefited from his guidance.

He would of course endeavor to steer clear of the fact (although it informed their every word to each other) that he and the chairman had known each other for almost twenty-five years, and that the chairman had written a delighted review of Jason's first book some thirteen years earlier for (of all places) the Sunday *New York Times*. Now married to a young woman who had been his student at the university he had recently been lured from, father by his first marriage of two teenaged boys he saw every other weekend (his ex-wife taught English at Radcliffe), the chairman had aged well, retaining all his curly locks (unlike the thin-topped Sams), a becoming salt-and-pepper now, as was his neatly trimmed beard; had published two collections of scholarly essays with university presses and was readying a third; to Jason (who had read all their mentor's fiction and nonfiction with considerable profit and pleasure), the chairman's work seemed to owe a great deal to Lionel Trilling's, while managing to sidestep entirely the master's readability. Sams had not loved the chairman, as he still loved a few of the friends he'd made way back then, and in fact had not known him all that well during their undergraduate years. But they had been at Columbia at the same time, shared whatever the class of '53 had shared, and beyond that were both New Yorkers, from orthodox Jewish backgrounds long since repudiated, and so the present situation, the chairman inheriting both Jason and his problems, was indeed perhaps a trifle *fraught,* as Trilling might have said, although not nearly as fraught, in Sams' opinion, as the chairman, with his love of complex Jewish suffering, liked to make it appear.

In the beginning, while Sams still attended faculty functions (for the free booze, and for the opportunity — which eluded him always — of advancing his career), the chairman would seek him out and drape an arm across his shoulders and say to whatever third party happened to be passing, "You see this guy? He's one hell of a short story writer!" (The chairman had not been enamored of Sams' novel, but neither, for that matter, was Trilling, or the *New York Times.*) "We were classmates at Columbia, can you beat it? We even took Trilling's Austen-Dickens-Wordsworth course together! And he wrote well then! 'Silent Generation' my foot, eh Jace?" With these facts and opinions public record, any temptation toward favoritism the chairman might have felt was clearly compromised, and at that point, if he judged the company receptive, and even if not, the chairman would fire off a brand new Jewish joke, which invariably glazed Jason's eyes and strained the corners of his mouth, while he wondered what idle nincompoop continued to grind the damn things out, and how the chairman managed to have instant access to them.

I've known this guy forever (Jason heard), *and now that you know it you can rest assured I won't be doing him any favors. In these corrupt times, in this city corrupter than most, in this university corruptest of all, led by an iron-fisted president (with a palace guard of wildeyed satraps) who summarily dismisses his enemies and appoints his cronies to high administrative posts and what is worse does not scruple to anoint anyone who strikes his fancy a "professor" and inflict same at budget-busting rates on some unsuspecting department head (and you may rest assured I will resign my chairmanship and my position both before I allow such a thing to happen in my purview), all the while shooting off his mouth with an incredible mixture of chutzpah and cant about the need for belt tightening and the quest for something he calls "excellence," some few of us in a position to do so must combat the prevailing tone.*

Jason was with him up to here (although there were times he found himself wishing that the president and his hand-picked band of merry psychopaths didn't scare the shit out of him, and that he and all the powerful freaks had come to be fast friends), but did such scrupulosity mean you had to bend way back the other way and shaft people you knew, whose work (if nothing else) you once respected in a former life? *Hah,* lansman?? Was it so written in the Talmud?

The chairman was an inch or two talller than Jason and (even had he not been wearing the expensive tweed topcoat) considerably broader; couldn't blame him for these physical advantages, but who else was there to hold responsible for

the writer's weird feeling of being bested from the start?
"Dutch treat?" the chairman said as he walked up, ushering
Jason into the restaurant. To the employee it was an ill omen,
although he had chosen this particular place to guard against
just such eventuality. This was not New York, he was not
lunching with a publisher or some other seeker after his
favor, he would not be starting off with a martini (which
he never otherwise drank), getting ready to be courted.
Would such a wooing, he wondered, ever befall him again?
Minus (unthinkably!) booze, if so.

"Absolutely, Frank. I wouldn't want to get stuck paying
for everybody's meal."

The fine gray eyes perused him, weighing the irony; Sams
was reminded that the chairman had the knack of shrugging
with his eyes.

They did not have to wait long for a table.

"So how's Jennifer? How's the kid?"

"We're well. How's you and yours?"

"Fine. Martha just got a job at Wellesley. The boys are
in great shape. I've got the usual physical complaints. We're
growing a bit older, Jason, have you noticed the signs?"

Sams had noticed the signs. He was not ordinarily reluc-
tant to discuss even the most intimate of his various mal-
adies, the prematurely engorged prostate as well as the
arthritic shoulder, honing a standup comedy routine he fantasized one day delivering in several cities (having discovered at long last his true vocation), spun precisely around
the nonfatal diseases of middle age (or at least his), and the
not always optimally successful treatment of same by the
(generally) goodhearted souls of the medical profession; but
the context was wrong, the audience was wrong, he could
afford to give nothing away, he realized sadly, so merely
nodded in agreement.

"What do you usually have?"

Jason sold him the shish kebab lunch, and the chairman ordered a glass of white wine. Sams would take tea. It was his nineteenth day of dry, which should have alerted him to danger. Four or five times before he had put together nineteen days, only to drink on the twentieth. It was as if he feared making twenty days because then he would have to face the twenty-first, and three sober weeks would put him over some mysterious hump, after which he would be shut off from alcohol forever. He had drunk through his thirties and into his forties, turned over cars, bought unwanted real estate, wrecked friendships and otherwise wreaked havoc with his social life, but had also screwed up his professional life, thereby weakening his one remaining rationale, that too many important American writers since Poe or even further back to a few in Increase Mather's time had been roaring drunks, making it quite clear that art and alcohol went hand in hand; furthermore, as the great writer must suffer for the sake of his art you always had the exquisite hungover remorse of the morning following the insane behavior of the night before, if you happened to recall it; so, with all this in place, what had gone wrong? How many years now since he had written anything worthwhile, or completed anything at all, while his drinking continued unabated? How many more false starts lay in the stars as he continued to insist on up-to-the-minute memoir as the whole of his vision, obliged to watch the amazing vicissitudes of daily life daily upstage him? Even his last published work (he had come to understand) had booze for its subtext, as tiny birdlike shrink Fanny Wallenda had pointed out to him in Woodstock, in '72, that time she tried to send him to AA; someone, usually his befuddled writer-narrator, was tossing one back on almost every page as he messed up his fictional life, or someone else's, or collapsed over his fictional typewriter keys. Maybe that was why so few people had had any but the most perverse admiration for *Slow Dying*, his autobiography cum novel, and maybe booze was also why its author would wind up verbally (and only that, thank God, to date) abusing his wife, when he finally found one, and was maybe even getting ready to abuse his son, as Wallenda had outrageously suggested, which even more than her bringing up AA had caused their rupture.

But by 1976 enough of him had become ready to consider the loss of alcohol from his life, if loss is what it turned out to be. Hoping for answers, he'd read straight through William James' *Varieties of Religious Experience* until he found what he was looking for: "The sway of alcohol over mankind is unquestionably due to its power to stimulate the mystical faculties of human nature, usually crushed to earth by the cold facts and dry criticisms of the sober hour. . . . it is part of the deeper mystery and tragedy of life that whiffs and gleams of something that we immediately recognize as excellent should be vouchsafed to so many of us only in the fleeting earlier phases of what in its totality is so degrading a poisoning." Twenty years already of whiffs and gleams, and this time he had dug his Antabuse out of the medicine cabinet and put himself on the pill, around the seventh day of abstinence. Antabuse was the bizarre medication (but not a degrading poison!) that caused deathly discomfort to anyone who went ahead and drank alcohol despite the pill being in the system; Jason had never required personal proof of its efficacy, always going off it a safe three or four days prior to getting bombed, planning ahead, although he often wished he'd had the scientific courage to see whether they were fobbing off a placebo, on him in particular, since they must have known that what they were dealing with here was one gullible bastard, which if they doubted for an instant, go ask Fiona. But he found it easier if not braver to put his trust in the written accounts of those pioneering alcoholics who had, in the drug's early days, experimented themselves into the grave.

"I saw your review a few weeks back," the chairman told him, leaving it at that. "How's your own work going?"

"Slowly," Jason told him, exaggerating in his own behalf. "The teaching goes well. I suppose you heard that Fiona's chasing my job?"

The chairman looked forlorn. Then he looked like a man on the spot, who did not relish having been driven there.

"It isn't exactly your job, Jason. Fiona's become a candidate for the position, yes. That's one of the reasons I asked you to lunch."

Another being your profound affection for me, Sams thought, tearing into his meat, watching the chairman sip his wine.

"Well, no one informed me it was up for grabs," he said, as lightly as he could.

The chairman sighed. "I heard this yesterday," he said. "This Jew goes to work every day, and every day at lunchtime he looks into his lunchbox and shakes his head and moans. One day, when he seems particularly upset, his coworker asks what the problem is. 'It's tuna fish again,' the Jew says. 'Every damn day, tuna fish.' The other guy says, 'So why don't you ask your wife to fix you something else?' 'Wife, what wife?' the Jew says. 'I make it every day myself.' "

Jason screwed up the corners of his mouth. "That's good," he said, relieved by the absence of shvartzers in the story, or any other ethnic set, for an uncomfortable number of the chairman's tales were powered by the humor of the still-scrambling, as they felt or thought they felt the breath of the group right behind them on the ladder. The joke had seemed a little rushed, coming earlier than usual in their colloquy, as if the chairman feared that if he waited a second too long, this afternoon, all opportunity for joke telling would be well behind them.

"What is it, though?" Sams asked. "Homily for the day? Bearing some pertinence to my situation?"

The chairman remained patient. "Nothing that unsubtle, I hope. The job isn't up for grabs, exactly, but if you keep it much longer you become a candidate for tenure, and that's not the way these creative writing positions, which were meant to rotate, are designed."

Rotate on this, Jason thought. He said, "I'm not after tenure, Frank. I renounce, I abjure tenure. I agree with our fascist, union-busting prez that all tenure is good for, excepting his own, is to lock mediocrity in place. All I had in mind was to keep the job a little longer, until Jenny and I figure out if we even want to stay in Boston."

Baldfaced lie, of course; Jennifer loved Boston, had loved it from the moment they unpacked Jake's stroller and she pushed him for the first time through the unfamiliar streets of the South End. He had hoped (as he hoped every time he and the chairman met) to sound calm and reasoned, unneedy, nonpetitioning friend addressing friend; why did an angry wheedling almost always overwhelm him?

"You put me in a tough position, Sams," the chairman said, mournful and offended.

"How do I do that, Frank?"

"Because I'm obliged to tell you that, as of this moment, Fiona has the inside track."

Thunk; the sound of a drunk's heart sinking. There went the rest of his day.

"Why is that? Because of the tenure crap? Because her book review wound up on page one?"

"Give me a break, Jason. You must be aware of a few of the problems you ran into this year."

His heart dropped further: he was aware of them, indeed he was. But they were his problems, his alone. That someone else presumed knowledge of his inmost fears and failings, and judged him for them, began to tap his rage.

"What kind of problems, Frank? Or should I say, who doesn't have problems?"

"You really want to know?"

"If I'm about to lose my job to some conniving hack with no teaching experience, I'd like to know the reasons, yeah."

"I had lunch with her last week."

"Looks like she scooped me all around.'"

The chairman almost let this slide. "She called me," he said evenly. "She told me she's giving a reading at Harvard next week from her novel-in-progress. If she reads at Harvard, that's points for us. The next is her sixth or seventh book. Most of them have been favorably reviewed, on both sides of the Atlantic."

"Have you read any?"

"One or two."

"Then you know what flimsy crap they are." (A year or two down the road Sams would discover he had served as model for a spineless character in Fiona's most recent, a departure from her customary overpopulated chat, a prose narrative dense and symbol-strewn; but this anticlimax, when it rolled around, would scarcely bother him at all.)

"Very possibly. But she's *known*. She'll make a good

backup next year to Elkin or Barth, whichever one we land.
The fact is, Jason, to put it bluntly, you're a very good
writer who's a book or two behind."

"A book or two behind?"

"One more full-length published work would have vastly
improved your chances here."

Jason did not argue the point. The enormity of being a
book or two behind on top of all his other problems would
not come home to him for several days. (When it did, he
would realize that as an exact contemporary of John Updike
and Philip Roth, writers as gifted as they were busy, and
both with an oeuvre that dwarfed Fiona's, he was more like
ten or fifteen books behind, and he almost picked up the
phone at that point to call his almost ex-chairman to share
this delighted discovery.) There in the Greek restaurant he
was more immediately exercised by the thought that Elkin
or Barth, successful fiction writers and academics both,
could be lured from their lives for a year only by a salary
immensely larger than any he could ever hope to command.
All he could find to say was, "How about being able to
teach the goddamn stuff? Does that count for nothing?"

"She's been running two fiction-writing workshops now
for a semester and a half. I haven't heard any complaints."

"Frank, I've got letters from students over the years insanely grateful for the help I gave them. I can show them
to you, or to whomever. I can have a package put together
by tomorrow."

"That might not be a bad idea. I can hardly not mention
that I've . . . received some negative reports about you
from your present class."

This was definitely news. A severe pain struck him in the
belly. He grabbed at a passing waitress and ordered a beer.
As she began writing the order, he added a white wine; only

then did he throw an inquiring glance at the chairman, who shook his head no; but Sams allowed the order for both beverages to stand.

"Can you be specific?"

"They say you often seem depressed in class. You schedule conferences, don't show up. Sometimes you haven't read their work before the class meets. You've missed office hours. On at least two occasions you've come to class unsteady on your feet, smelling of alcohol."

"An exhaustive list. How many of them contributed to it? More than one?"

The chairman shook his head. "It all came from the same source. I'd just as soon not betray a confidence."

"Couldn't be my cabdriver, he's not there often enough to smell my breath. Not my screwball; he's in love with me as I am. Has to be the music student. Her last two stories were overwritten garbage, and I told her so."

"I'd rather not say who it was."

"Who's to say who's depressed, for God's sake, Frank? Is she a psych major too?"

The chairman sighed. "She merely described the situation, Jason. I apologize for the medical diagnosis, which is mine. I trust you won't be vindictive now that you know who told me."

"Shit no, Nelson," Sams said. "What can I do to her that comes close to what she's doing to me? What's a fucking job between old friends? Do you always put such credence in apparent candor?"

"I didn't say I trusted her. I hoped for some degree of clarification from you."

During this last exchange the beverages arrived, and Sams, scarcely hesitating, gestured with the wine glass toward his old acquaintance and drank off half the wine. Before it blew his gaskets out, almost before he could taste it, he chased it with a gulp of beer.

"You want to hear my side?" He ticked it off on his fingers. "I'm trying to sneak through the back door to rip off tenure. I write much too slowly. I drink far too much. I went to college with the chairman and have been using this circumstance ever since to sniff after unmerited favors. Whereas all that's happening now is I've been beaten out of a job by a better woman. Or by a pair of better women. Give me a hint, Frank: how the fuck do I defend myself?"

The chairman looked away; rebuked, exasperated, neither of the above. Sams imagined Frank Nelson thinking, *This asshole has not the slightest inkling how the game is played.* He felt he had to move quickly. He stood, fished out his wallet, dropped a twenty on the table. "I got to run. Look, I know there's nothing personal in all this, Frank, you're only doing your job et cetera, but I wasn't supposed to drink because of this pill I take, and I'm probably better off moving around. So see you later. Keep chairing."

"Are you all right? Your face looks very red."

Jason waved this off, hit the air, and felt much worse.

Nothing to do but outrun them, the booze and humiliation both, and before he turned comatose (should he feel that state approaching), seek out medical advice. He was still too angry to be really frightened, although the prickling had started in his face and body, needles everywhere, and he had the chairman's word for the state of his complexion. But until he got to look in a mirror, half an hour later, he had no real conception of that crimson hue.

There was the matter of his heart. It had surged and moaned even before his untimely imbibing, never ever peaceful in the chairman's presence (critic, larger sibling, implacable foe; yet no doubt about it, when Jason first learned the chairman was coming to the U he *had* expected special treatment, some sort of inside track), and had flirted even more with whoop-de-do today as it listened to its owner being terminated, or (in euphemistic academe) exposed to the likelihood that his contract was not going to be renewed. But this, now, was something else, his heart going all out in the hundred then stopping suddenly to smell the flowers; this, now, brought home to him that he might not survive this latest, booze-induced error: no mere blackout here, no eating the clam dip at some party for Norman Mailer with his hands, no sudden perspective on life (as he tried to escape the MP's) from the roof of an off-limits Japanese whorehouse, no racing through London streets from Soho toward Hampstead trying to outrun tomorrow's hangover only gradually aware of the bobby running right behind him, no sleeping through pickup time for theater date with beauteous Danish psychotherapist in New York pulled gently down upon her own couch and fiddled with the first time they met so there had gone *that* promising relationship, no slicing up both thumbs and bleeding heavily into the salad he was preparing for eat-in dinner with statuesque sculptress of erotica, giving her a chuckle when she arrived, and bandaged thumbs be damned, becoming stoned on Old Overholt and making pawing passes . . . therapist and sculptress both responding from a long gelid way off to subsequent remorseful calls . . . no compassionate trip to Montreal with redhaired Wisconsin naif to not merely pay for termination of pregnancy he had caused but offer up God help him moral support and the night before the procedure she wanted to go bowling but they had no shoes small enough to fit so she threw gutterball after gutterball in stockinged feet then the surgery which unfolded while he was back at the hotel getting smashed and cheering Koufax as he mowed down the Minnesota Twins, then the morose (for him; she happy as a lark) boozing trainride back and once safe in NYC never calling her again . . . running into her accidentally two years later in a liquor store on Second Avenue and having the temerity to say hello and feel stunned and hurt because she took one look and dropped everything and fled, no raging stupor at the cocktail party in Woodstock at the ranchhouse with the German shepherd and yellow birches belonging to the eight-fingered opera singer who lived down the hill the Sunday afternoon his infant son had had his face torn open not by the shepherd but by the visiting Scots terrier the kid had been eyeball to eyeball with in the grass on the hot day just as the J&B did its paralyzing thing so with Jenny out of it from terror a bare acquaintance a virtual stranger drove the kid the ten miles to Kingston where their pediatrician calm gent with a penchant for checked jackets with wide lapels and wide loud ties got the right Indian surgeon off the golf course, the one who stitched Jake up leaving just the dueling scar, no careening off the Masspike trying to pass a pickup in a snowstorm nearly blind from drink descending and spinning to certain slo-mo doom but instead landing upside down in a soft hill of snow, — this here now was fucking *serious,* and irrationally assuming that a cardiac event was less likely to occur in the presence of someone he knew, he ran down the steps and into the liquor store he was passing, the one run by the Golden Brothers, which happened to be the one he used.

"Why hello, Mr. Jason, haven't seen you for . . . what? three weeks or so? How've you been keeping?" said Israel, younger Golden brother, a man Jason's age. "Looks like you've been spending some time in the sun."

"Am I that red, Iz? How red am I?"

"You're pretty red. I guess if you're not in pain you're all right, but you should use a sunscreen the next time. What can I get for you? Quart of Jack Daniels? Fifth of Chivas? Six-pack of Rignes?"

The brand names enhanced the tingling, elicited a dangerous thump from his chest. These guys would sell their "degrading poison" to any rummy with the price. Couldn't Israel see how agitated, fucked-up he was?

"Nothing, just dropped by to say hello." But on the way out he grabbed a Diet Pepsi from the case, chugged it down. Dilute! He threw a dollar on the counter, didn't wait for change. The square was full of students, some (for all he knew) his own, past and present if not future; they were lightly clad. It was a warm day for February, but the chairman, cautious as ever, had been overdressed. Jason wore khaki trousers, his thin black jacket from Filene's, and beat-up sneakers, uniform for all seasons. He took a tissue from his back pocket and wiped away the sweat. Just let me survive this, Lord, Whomever, and I promise You, never again!

That helped, it seemed; he received assurances from somewhere that his agony, while unabated, would once again not do him in. TAKE TO YOUR BED, SHMUCK, GRAB FORTY WINKS BEFORE SHE BRINGS THE KID HOME TO CARRY ON HIS PRESCHOOL REVELS. He made his way back to the apartment, studied himself in the mirror (enormous pupils, face still lobster red), took a long leak, stole a Valium from Jenny's emergency stash, crawled under the covers on his side of the queen-size bed, put on the all-news station and actually dozed for a while.

"So what came of lunch with Frank Nelson?"

"I believe he fired me."

"You lost your job?"

He couldn't look too long at the shock, the incredulity, the outright fear. Where's your faith in the drunken scribe you wed, o Mountain Lady?

"I think so, yeah. They're going to give it to Fiona next year."

"Migod!"

"Yeah. She's a great conniver. Look, I'm teaching through the end of April, and the paychecks keep coming in through May. After that I ought to be able to pick up a writing course in each summer session. And we still have a few thousand left from selling the Woodstock house. So we're all right at least through the end of the year."

"By which time you'll be done with your book." The declarative sentence, with its real or imagined ironies, pissed him off, then made him happy, as if she had seen the news presented in *Publishers Weekly,* or had plucked it from an astrologer's chart. He knew he had given her that precise assurance every year since 1970, the year they left the City and, still childless, moved to Woodstock, and she'd believed it once, as he'd believed it himself, delivered as it had always been in one or another madly looped omnipotent moment.

"I can't say finished, no. But getting there."

"So tell me again why you're going to New York?"

"To announce my return to the literary wars."

"And you can't do that from here, by phone, because . . . ?"

His guilt, her (beyond doubt now) blunderbuss irony, finally lit the fuse.

"Look, what's the problem? Why does it piss you off every time I go anywhere or do anything by myself?"

"I can't think of very much we do together. But that's not the point. It just seems we could save a little money if you phoned your publisher and agent, that's all. You needn't be so defensive about everything."

From his room their young son, a lover of syntax, had taken in these last few lines. He stuck his head around the door.

"You needn't fight," Jake pointed out.

"Butt out, shorty," Jason said, pleased.

"You don't have to talk to him like that. He doesn't have to be dragged into the general hostility."

"Ah, Jesus. Spare me the jargon, will you? If you think we need more money, why don't you get some kind of a job?"

"And what would you do with Jake? Phone him every hour from New York?"

"Look, I'll be gone two or three days at most, and I repeat, it's not a pleasure trip. I need to *see* Mitchell, *see* Ralph, and maybe I'll drop in on my folks while I'm there. I'll be back here soon enough to partake of the misery. Why is it all so hard to fathom?"

He watched her anger, watched her grapple with a few zingers, choke them back, then walk stylishly down the hall to patch up the scion's view of life. While admiring her forbearance, he wondered with real curiosity what her riposte would have been, for neither of them down the years had been above taking pleasure in lunatic wrangling. But he was reminded that she had learned this and that at the Ramakrishna Vedanta temple just across the street, had picked up from old Swami on several Sunday mornings useful tips about the peace to be found in not rising to the bait. He sometimes envied her what she'd managed to learn about right living, and wished, from time to time, that he too had used the place more wisely, had brought a less jaded psyche to the temple. It was he who had found it (not that it took much finding, located diagonally across the street from where they lived), but Jenny, retreating now to the kitchen, Jake in tow, was the one who had ultimately profited.

Meanspirited shit that he was, did he begrudge her even that?

He thought of his own first encounter with Mahananda, back when he and Jenny had been living in the university-owned apartment for just about a month, back in the winter of '74, Sams girding up on a hungover, snowy Sunday morning for the three-block drive to buy them both cigarettes and pick up a Sunday paper. He backed the decrepit Valiant into a snowbank in front of the temple, and no amount of engine gunning or jockeying back and forth or positioning under his rear wheels the piece of thick, corrugated cardboard he found in the trunk made the slightest difference, his car was doomed to live in that snowy hill forever, and since it blocked the thoroughfare, going about his errands on foot was not an option, either; the day was ruined, utterly changed. In exasperated rage he gunned the engine yet again, sending black billows of smoke onto the snow, great particles of soot, and it was then he noticed the man in the saffron robe looking calmly down at him from the portico at the top of the exterior stairway. It was seven-thirty in the morning.

For reasons he could not have defended, Jason assumed that the brown, noble-looking man in the strange outfit, with jet-black hair and eyes, cheekbones carved from iron, spoke not a word of English, so he launched without further ado into an elaborate pantomime, pointing to his vehicle, to the blackened snow, scratching his stocking cap and gesturing at his ears and shrugging by way of apology for all the noise he'd made, and then, since the man still gazed at him uncomprehendingly, he ran through it all again, indicting now with vigor the guilty snowbank, but this time, despite himself, tacking on the words, "I didn't see," to which the swami finally replied, "I know."

A shudder went through Sams; he refused to believe he had heard what he had heard. Fighting the urge to act it out again, he kicked at the snowbank, shook his head, and clarified, "I didn't *see*," to which Swami nodded his assent and repeated, "I know." Then he vanished into the temple, and just when Jason had begun to despair of ever seeing him again he emerged at the head of a queue of four young men. Not the same quartet of course but just as rosycheeked and bulky as the four who had detrained one night a few weeks earlier after Jason, plastered and raging, wending his way home from a solitary pub crawl through Cambridge, messed up the left turn off the bridge (illegal in any event) and wound up bumping along the gravel bed toward an oncoming trolley; those four had picked up his car with its three flat tires as if it were a bale of hay, deposited it neatly in a parking space, and never looking at him once, returned to the train, which proceeded on its way. Humiliated but relieved, Sams had proceeded to a nearby pub, ordered a beer, and phoned to tell his wife he'd be a bit delayed. These four temple acolytes were less abrupt; one even murmured a word or two of sympathy, and it took just two of them to lift the rear of his vehicle free of the snow, and after asking him to put the car in gear, they pushed it free.

For weeks he remained shaken. He had always believed that some necessary ingredient was missing from his life; but that he would be needing an Indian guru at the advanced age of forty-two (hair a distant memory, wild reddish beard already flecked with gray) came as a stunning surprise. It was clear to Jason that the man had absorbed him in a flash, had offered comment not on a car in a snowbank but on Jason's blindness to life itself, especially damning in the light it cast on the humorous arrogance of such a one harboring plans (however vague) of literary performance. At the same time, there'd been a touch of hope in what the man conveyed — standing there in his orange gown at the head of the stairs he had clearly been holy, able if he wished to help this drunk blast through all the deadends he'd wandered down in the previous twenty years, able to restore to him the modest gift that once there was.

At last he took himself to a Sunday service, on a week in which Swami was discoursing on "Pain and Suffering." He understood, through the dark Bengali accent, no more than half of what was said, but he found this soothing and appropriate in a communication (through a chosen intermediary) from the Hindu Gods (who were, after all, everybody's Gods: "Truth is One," read the quote from the Vedas painted on the wall, "men call it by various names"), experiencing particular pleasure when he was able to tease the meaning out of phrases such as "eunuch devil up meant" (unique development), a phenomenon unfolding, in Swami's ultimately upbeat view, quite often in the world.

At the end of the service he took his place on the receiving line and watched the Indian couple just ahead of him prostrate themselves and kiss the ground at Swami's feet; when his own turn came he made the more modest gesture of greeting and respect he'd seen others make, touching his hands together lightly in front of his chest, and the swami did likewise, apparently aware that their paths had crossed before. He reached out and touched Jason's beard, remarking that he'd recognized him through the shape and color of his beard. Then he proceeded to confound Sams with a professor of astrophysics he'd met in Amsterdam on a pilgrimage the year before. Jason, less devastated than relieved by the error, barely disabused Mahananda of this notion.

He described the service to his wife, thinking they might go together one Sunday morning. She expressed little interest at the time. But a year or so later, out of the blue (another Christmas looming, a difficult season), she suggested they go. Jason, for whom Vedanta had been more or less settled by Swami's faulty memory, had not gone back since "Pain and Suffering." They chose two of the straightbacked chairs at the rear of the hall. Up front, behind the dais, dwarfing smaller icons, was a lifesize photo of Ramakrishna, the ascetic founder, wearing only his loincloth, seated in the lotus position, smiling his gaptoothed smile. At five minutes before eleven the twangy, haunting music began, and promptly on the hour the swami materialized on the dais, having arrived on little cat feet, with only the most alert and nonmeditative of the congregation having noted his slow passage down the aisle. He made profound obeisance to Ramakrishna, bowed a little less deeply to the likenesses of Buddha and Vivekananda, the disciple who had taken Vedanta abroad, offered up a prayer to inner peace, and the music picked up its pace and volume; a middle-aged white man played the cello, an ascetic-looking Indian youth in a flowing white shirt banged the drums, a soulful black woman elicited sound from a strange, long-necked instrument, and a man so large he was obliged to twostep sideways down the aisle played a splendid piano and in a sweet thundering tenor led the faithful in Sanskrit hymns. At her very first service Jenny (to Jason's surprise), clearly enraptured, made a yeomanly effort (using the transliterated Sanskrit) to sing along.

In Apple Creek, where she was born and raised, her family had always sung along on Sunday mornings. In later years, in a certain mood, she'd mock that music, screeching out "Amazing Grace" or "Precious Memories" in so eerie an Appalachian Baptist voice that a listener's hair might stand on end. The songs, or the way she sang them, conjured not Christian love and salvation but abject dread of hellfire and backbreaking work in the tobacco fields. At seventeen she fled for good, making her way to Cincinnati and from there to the relative sanity and safety of New York, where after a bizarre flirtation in her middle twenties with Scientology (as practiced by a lonely Lesbian in the adjoining apartment) from which Jason, as he liked to recall it, saved her, her need for religion, or spirituality of any sort, went into eclipse, to surface briefly in connection with her impending marriage to the New York writer, when the idea of conversion to Judaism seemed to move her, and she acquired several books on the subject. But her husband-to-be (guilty, lapsed observer), with a dead-earnest joke or two, dissuaded her from that.

In Boston, eight years later, Vedanta won her (its gentle acceptance of other faiths, its steady path up the mountain), and was hers to embrace. For a long while she attended weekly, and involved herself in temple business. By writing and directing plays for the kids to act in (in celebration of the founder's birthday, Buddha's, Christ's), she tempted Jake (no joiner, but a ham) into occasional participation. Mahananda, delighted, applauded them both, mother and son. He knew who they were.

When Jake finally arrived (no instant family for Jenny and Jason Sams: come late to the game, twenty-eight and thirty-six, both on the rebound, fatigued by their histories, brought together by physical passion and the enormous differences between them, they were prepared to reap at once the fruits of matrimony, but wound up instead three years later with fertility experts in their bed, the last in a long line of whom was a genial walrus of a man who leaped for joy when he brought the thing to pass), Jenny, while she was concerned about what faith or credo their first-born (so long in the making) would have to sustain him, also — with Jason in the tank most days — had other things to worry about, not the least being how they had come to be living in Woodstock in a country fastness not so different (with all due allowance for its artsy-craftsy, secular surround) from the place she thought she'd left behind; and, in the absence of much money, how they would ever get out. In Manhattan she had studied hard to be an actress, survived the wrenching, risky training of Strasberg's Actors' Studio, worked in several plays off- and off-off Broadway, did some radio and television work, eking it out with a parttime job at a publishing house, which was where she and Jason had met. As messy as her private life had sometimes been, she would have described herself, meaning it, as having been happy in New York.

The progression to meeting and marrying Sams, to putting her own aspirations in the theater on hold, to buying the Woodstock house (their rustic L-shaped "summer home") by spending all the advance he took on a book he did not seem willing or able to write, then giving up (after a subtenant's fire gutted their New York apartment) her life in the city she had come to love, was hard for her to trace, a deadly mix of stubborn decisions (his) and mountain passivity (hers), along with a touch of bad luck, so that when the chance arose to sell the property and move with their two-year-old son to Boston, even her husband, unrelievedly gloomy by then and saucing daily to collapse, was somewhat touched by her delight.

But Boston had not worked out either, for him.

No more nor less a lush there than he had been in Kyoto, London, Barcelona, Malmö, Woodstock, or Manhattan, and growing no younger, he was nevertheless able, on certain days, to blame geography, still waiting, as he had been since the fire, for the summons back to the imperial capital, the city he was born in and the one he loved. Living in Boston was like exile on Staten Island, banishment to the wrong end of the Verrazano Bridge, the spires of Manhattan tantalizingly visible, but not there for him until the sentence was served.

Why, you could squeeze the nuts of Boston Central in a fist, the theater district and Chinatown and the financial district and Boston Common and the main public library and the street of art galleries and the street of shame and the big department stores and the fancy hotels and the two count 'em tallish buildings and the State House and City Hall all cheek by jowl, more or less, welcome to Tinytown, the big time glinting in the morning light a ferry ride away, and when the hour struck he'd board that ferry, follow the yellow brick road, assault the City's battlements another time, and win!

One other fairy tale, "The Shoemaker and the Elves," had not worked out for him: in Woodstock, one night, drunk out of mind, as on what night of the four years had he not been, maybe a few, he waited for Jenny to retire before he put a fresh ream of typing paper outside the door of the screened porch, knowing he was being foolish yet more than half expecting the little buggers to knock out the novel he was already late on, not necessarily a best seller but something in his own inimitable and increasingly subtle early-middle style, and he would share with them quite happily whatever royalties and rights accrued, have a miniature Olivetti custom built by one of the two million craftsmen in town or lay in a generous supply of miniature pencils and pens, whatever the bastards would be most happy with, but it rained hard toward dawn, and whatever they'd done while he dozed was washed away.

But New York itself was no fairy tale: he'd *lived* there, been *born* there, triumphed there, or come close enough; only boozy idleness delayed the summons.

So. In the words of the Hindu hymn, dashed off by chief disciple Vivekananda (talk of your prolific gents — died in his thirties with uncountable volumes, chapbooks, hymns, and broadsides behind him): "No One But Me To Blame." He was blowing his life all by himself, covering up with sneers directed (for the moment) at Athens on the Charles. It had become his wife's beloved city and would no doubt always be his son's: the kid had thrown his favorite bear emphatically into the back of the U-Haul by way of farewell to Ulster County, no love lost there, the wound beneath his eye still suppurating — country life was much too dangerous. Jason hoped the child's scattered memories of Woodstock, even the traumatic ones, would not trouble him for very long. Forgetting was a useful gift. Fresh start. Daddy's route around his banishment.

Back on a ten-day dry (without the assistance, thank you very much, of Antabuse), Sams received a call one Tuesday afternoon in early March of the bicentennial year from the book editor of the *Boston Globe,* exploring his interest in doing a book review for the Sunday paper. She did not seem to give a hoot one way or the other, merely discharging an obligation to an old college buddy of Jason's, Dan Wakefield, who had given her his name. It took Sams a good few moments to realize he was speaking with a woman, so profoundly had cigarettes and/or booze altered her voice. He knew by now it would do him not one ounce of immediate good to write a book review for the *Boston Globe,* or anyone else; his job at UGB was definitely gone, but since (whatever his misrepresentations to the chairman) he and Jenny had no plans to move in the foreseeable future, in all likelihood he would now have to scramble to land some kind of teaching post at Brandeis or MIT or Boston College or Boston University or Harvard or Radcliffe or Wellesley or one of the junior colleges that proliferated in the area. Thus there might be some ultimate utility in publishing something or other in the local "paper of record" as they called themselves, and he resolved not to be put off, whatever amount the lady with the raspy voice put forth, when he asked "out of curiosity" what doing a book review for the *Boston Globe* in 1976 might pay to the reviewer. He was rendered temporarily speechless nonetheless when she gargled out the sum (with more than a suggestion of take-it-or-leave-it in her voice) of thirty dollars. Well, what the hell, he was not in the game for the money, if in it at all, not the money he might earn from writing book reviews at any rate, and he ended the dead air by agreeing to produce for that sum eight hundred to a thousand words about the book she would send him, a second novel by a young New York writer on the way up whose first book about growing up tough in the Bronx had earned considerable applause. Sams had not read the first novel but remembered the reviews. It had sounded to him like the early work of James T. Farrell transposed from Chicago to New York, but this assessment from afar may well have been unfair, and there was no reason to expect that a writer's second book would necessarily resemble his first. Jason thought he might stop by the public library in Copley Square and glance at that first book, then decided against. For the *New York Times'* $250 a pop and 1500-word assignments he had at times been moved to a degree of conscientiousness, skimming, at least, a writer's earlier work, but for thirty big ones he would do what he'd been asked to do, no more.

On Wednesday of that week he met with his writing class, and despite his assurances to the chairman, which he'd believed to be true when he made them, said to the four students present that a certain amount of discontent in the room had come to his attention, and he could only wish that those having grievances had brought them directly to him rather than deal with them in such a way as to put his job in jeopardy. The three men, who had been nodding off, sprang awake and regarded Jason and each other with enormous interest, while the woman blushed and turned almost as red as Sams himself had been not that many days before.

The lecturer obliged her to meet his eye and then — with nothing to prove, nowhere to go — dropped his gaze and let it go.

The book arrived in the next day's mail. He took it into the room he used as a study and shut the door. He opened the package with something like anticipation. They had sent him, alas, bound galleys, not the book itself; there went the resale possibilities. He had several weeks in which to do the job. He was off to New York on Friday morning, and being the sort of writer he was, without a lighter side, which is to say with no untortured manner to bring to bear on lesser tasks like book reviewing, the chances were he would get none of what would turn out to be the final eight hundred to a thousand words written before he left, and not many right after he returned, either, not until the deadline neared (at which point, terrified by the prospect of failing even at this, drained of perfectionist tendencies, he'd get his ass in gear). But he could begin to look through the thing tonight, do some light typing, make some jottings on its pages.

Four hundred pages in galleys, the book turned out to be, as he had feared, a sequel to the first. Jason did not find it gripping. We all have our material, baby, the young writer must have told himself: I shall build Yoknapatawpha right here on the Harlem River.

He shut the door against the noise (young son amok, wife noisy on his tail), but there was no way to lock it. He felt obliged to try to get at least a portion of the review, as it would ultimately stand, out of his life. Given his track record, some inroad into the unopened bottle of Johnnie Walker Red would be required. Too bad, of course: he was better than halfway to the magic number, nineteen days;

but the literary life or life in general was a minefield of difficult choices. Someday he would absolutely kick the habit, but today was clearly not that day, nor did it seem likely this would be the week, nor (so far as he could tell) the month, or year.

Using the jacket copy, he banged away on a quick summary of the novel's business, followed by a necessarily brief account of the author's career, to be eventually followed (for the time being, he left blank space) by his considered opinion, made a rough word count, then indulged himself in a bout of self-congratulation, and was almost ready to rejoin his small (but choice) family; whatever had been going on out there had apparently been resolved, for he grew conscious that he had heard nothing for a while but the clacking of his typewriter and the scotch spilling into the glass and the roaring in his brain and now and again rock music from the stereos in the frat house just across the street — for some reason they always set up their enormous speakers facing the street, facing his fifth-floor windows. Some days and nights this would enflame him, and he would imagine himself roaring over there and raising hell, or he would phone the university police and now and again they might send a car; but tonight it all meant nothing. He was just touching up his opening paragraph, working on a perfect final line, sipping scotch, when the door sprang open and his son, wearing a broad grin, charged into the room.

"Hi, Dad! What's up? Drinking? Can I have some?"

Jason's anger, particularly when sloshed, was usually disproportionate to the circumstance that set it off.

"How many times have I told you to knock before you barrel in here?"

The child's smile vanished (it pained his dad to see it go), but not his sense of logic or language or irony: he stepped into the hallway, closed the door softly behind him, banged on the door and bolted into the room.

"OK? I knocked, then barreled."

"You're too wise for your own good," his father said.

"Why are you going to New York? Can I have some of what you're drinking? There's too much smoke in here."

"What I'm drinking tastes lousy, and it's bad for your health."

"Then why do *you* drink it?"

The obvious reply occurred to him: Fanny Wallenda's reply.

Lately she had been popping into his thoughts with disconcerting frequency. She had weekended in Woodstock in the summer of '72 in a cabin so laden with cats and chachkas that she had to tell her brand-new youngish spouse to go and take himself a hike when (as a favor to a few) she practiced her profession there. An Armenian ex-friend of Jason's (their rupture the result of a ferocious quarrel Sams could not for the life of him recall the genesis or substance of; a plague of Armenians in his life those days!), a writer she'd helped through a crisis by playing Willy to his dark and beetlebrowed Colette, locking him into the empty office next to hers in New York City (where her real practice was) for four hours every weekday and tossing away the key until he wrote the book he'd contracted to write, this Armenian friend pushed his tormented buddy to give her a call: She'll help you out, you fool, she'll get you over the hump, and Jason, responding to the love in his old buddy's voice, as well as to his own distress, had given her a call.

That had been error number one. Error number two, and one far greater, had been lending her copies of his books.

He had squeezed himself into the tattered wing chair on

six successive Saturday mornings, watching through a window as Hans, stoopshouldered and adoring, made his way down Tinker Lane past fly-by-night headshops, Breslers' Pottery, the Espresso Tavern (on the patio of which Sams loved to idle away the afternoons and drink). No ailurophile, Jason put up with the three giant beasts rubbing against his legs, and settled in to get the business:

"Led me dell you zomezing, now I haf vinished vith your verk. Your verst book vaz aggzezzible, though nod verstrate, dezpide vad Lionel Drilling had to zay on ze cover. Your zecond book is far verse. Id is nod liderajure, you understand, id is nod about love und zex und loss und zadness. Your verst-person narrator . . . you understand vad means zubdext?"

Jason thought he did.

"Zen ze zubdext is dringk. Dringk, drangk, drungk. Your noble is nod a noble bud a cry for help. He is an algoholic, this Jazon Zams. Und zo are you. You must go to AA."

Shaken, he had replied, "You're talking bullshit, Doctor. Maybe I have a dram or two too many from time to time. But I'm not about to piss my life away chasing God in church basements."

"Zo? Zen if nod AA you must come zee me in ze zity. Two times a veek. I can no longer zee people on my veekends here. Id iz nod fair to my husband. Zoon id vill be fall, vad zen?"

Then ta-ta, Sams thought.

"I don't see any way of getting to the city twice a week, or even once."

"Ride. You are too busy. If I may ask, vad is the age of your zon?"

"Two months."

"Do you beat him?"

Jason came close to springing from the chair. "No."

"You are zhocked, I zee. But belief me, you vill ruin nod just your own life, und the life of your vife, bud alzo your zon's."

The life of my wife and of all mankind is death, Jason had read years before (during a lost drunken year in Malmö, God knew why he was in Sweden, or why he had read there what he'd read), in mad dancer Nijinsky's diary, and it had stayed in his memory. Her litcrit he could handle, but she had gone too far with the Cassandra stuff.

"My son was a gift. He'll grow up fine. What are you, a therapist or a fortuneteller?"

"Vor algoholics is nod much to foredell. The disease ends in madness, jail, or undimely death. I know you are angry. Bud I am obliged to eggzbrez my conzern."

"Sure," he relented. "Let me have the week to think it over."

He hadn't seen her after that.

"I don't know why the hell I drink," he told his son.

"You're not drinking, are you?" Jenny said, entering the room.

"I was, some, to get the review under way. Only a couple."

"Half the bottle's gone!"

"Well it wasn't full when I started."

"You're so full of shit!" she wailed.

She had recently begun attending meetings of Al-Anon, he knew, seeking support from others whose lives had been darkened by alcohol, and these meetings had sharpened both her courage and her sense of despair.

"Look," he said, still feigning patience, "I'm trying to get a handle on it."

"How? By drinking half a bottle of scotch?"

"I've been dry for long periods, lately. Or haven't you noticed?"

"So from a daily drinker you've become a binge drinker! How many points do you want for that?"

"I'd better finish packing."

Sams straightened his papers, switched off the desk lamp, rose, and with colossal dignity, hardly staggering, squeezed past the pair of them and made his way to the bedroom. He flicked on the television set to await dinner and the seven o'clock news, a quarter of an hour away, and remained unconscious until one in the morning.

At one, rising stealthily, he finished packing, drank a beer, and longhand, on yellow foolscap (keeping a carbon), wrote a brilliant letter to Bill Broder, his old friend in Sausalito. That cost him another beer and four cigarettes, but he remained clearheaded enough to leave the envelope unsealed. (The morning light might bring some heavy editing, destruction even, and the repeated resolve to write his letters sober.) Then, feeling queasy, he returned on tiptoe to hover by the nuptial bed. His sleeping wife, acknowledging his presence, turned her back.

For some reason the gesture moved him to warm thoughts of her, although he knew better than to try to wake her for any carnal purpose. Back when they were busy trying to make the babe she had woken *him* in dead of night according to her diabolic cycle, basal temperature, suppositories, jottings in a book; she'd put up then with a certain amount of boozy intercourse for the sake of the larger purpose, and they had fucked by the fire's dying embers, and she claimed afterward to know the exact moment she conceived, and Sams, in due course, came to think he shared the memory.

For he too had been implicated: spent a freaky night in the Chelsea Hotel in New York, flogged the bishop (with official sanction) with the help of a new glossy *Penthouse* the following morning into a Mason jar that had lately held his mother-in-law's blackberry jam, sealed the jar (having lost the lid) with aluminum foil and a rubber band borrowed from a painter who lived down the hall, inadvertently inverted the jar during the subway ride so that the dour Ph.D. whose lab was located in the bowels of New York Hospital spilled a portion of Jason's vital fluids on his fingers, and responded with outrage and disgust. Summoned a chastened Sams to the microscope.

"Sluggish little bahstahds. Indifferent motility. Come have a look."

He squinted and peered; the tadpole-like things seemed to be getting around OK, given that they had no place to go.

"You smoke, I gather?"

By what means had he gathered that?

"Smoke some."

"Drink 'some'?"

"I drink, yeah."

"Given your habits, you're lucky they're alive at all."

"Editorials apart, what's the prognosis?"

"How the blazes would I know? You heard me say they had a little life in them, didn't you?"

Exculpated, Jason ascended into a glorious Manhattan afternoon and was soon situated behind a miniskirted au pair of nineteen or so pushing a wicker stroller with twins in it; given the smallest encouragement, he would have followed her twitching butt to the ends of the island.

Standing alongside the queen-size bed that had followed them from New York City to Woodstock to the Hub, watching her breathe, more than a little drunk, he remembered his first visit to her hills, a five-day pause in the summer of 1968 on the tail end of their coast-to-coast honeymoon, swinging back to New York by bus and train and rented car via visits to friends in Chicago, Sausalito, and Tucson, plus a stopover in New Orleans (where he saw his novel, still a month away from official publication, on multiple display in a bookshop window, and imagined he would soon be laying claim to his moment in the sun). Loyal bride, she warned him they were headed into a dry county, and in Huntington he had laid in several quarts of Jack Daniels Green Label (never heard of it before, a new, exotic drink to him) and six six-packs before venturing into the land where the stop signs were pockmarked with bullet holes, and abandoned strip mines uglified the hills. He remembered kindnesses: the flower-patterned, scented rolls of toilet paper laid in (Jenny told him) just for him, in the listing outhouse over at his sister-in-law's hundred-acre spread, where they'd gone to spend the night, and he watched the sun go down behind a gnarled apple tree, alone at the end of an empty field; but he recalled in particular the August afternoon when he sat with a huge plate of food on his lap, surrounded by her kinfolk on the sloping lawn outside the house of her mother's brother (now also *his* Uncle Boyd), in the shadow of the wooden Baptist church in which Boyd sometimes preached, and he, breaking a lengthening silence with an irony too weighty for the circumstances, remarked on the convenient proximity of God's house to Boyd's avocation, thereby providing the opening the patriarch Sherman, her mother's father, already in his nineties then, had clearly been waiting for. "And what might *your* persuasion be?" Sherman asked, more silence ensuing while Jason, a forkful of green beans halfway to his mouth, thought it over. His new wife couldn't help; he doubted she had uttered more than ten words during the entire five days, struck almost dumb by this first sight of her family since she and Jason met two years before, and she had finally succumbed, with a discomfort painful to watch (but this one he didn't want to lose), to his frightened insistence that she leave her place in the dangerous West Forties with no front door on the building and the Scientology freak nearby and move into his small garden apartment near Gramercy Park. At last he had answered Sherman with the truth, "I'm Jewish," and the old guy had nodded, as if enlightened and relieved, and said, "There once came a Jew through these parts nigh sixty years ago, toting a mess of pots and pans on his back," and family members chuckled along while Jason, merchant manqué in his heart, grinned maniacally and felt accepted, or at least somewhat less misunderstood.

But being misunderstood, he reflected sadly, climbing stealthily beneath the covers, was a substantial part of his stock in trade. And a good part of the rest of it (although he took perhaps excessive pleasure in contemplating his productive career as Hindu astrophysicist in Amsterdam) lay in being misidentified.

She had carried radiantly, distending a little more each day her Property of NY Knicks T-shirt, and a bit before his time Jake slid forth under his father's astonished scrutiny trailing an umbilical cord as thick and green and endless as a jungle vine, with a cock red and erect and almost as big around as his head, harbinger no doubt of standoffs to come (if Freud was to be countenanced), to be dealt with in their season.

Pillows the right height, settled in, he admired the back of her shapely head, stroked her long blond hair ("Could have been as good/as Woodward, with a touch of luck/Though he no Newman,/nor was meant to be"), and wished for her (and for his sleeping son, and while he was at it all mankind; up yer kazoo, crazed Russian leaper!) a biblically long and very happy life.

Advancing
the Career

TOWARD MORNING he dreamed of himself and Al Seamans and a couple of willowy ladies not their wives at sea in a lifeboat that cut through the fog and foam like the sixteen-horse outboard Evinrude he had tooled around Lake Mohegan in one long-gone summer, the year his father let him run it for the first time. Al stood in the prow, hand in breast like George Washington crossing the Delaware. They were headed toward a not yet visible shore, and the moment of awful sadness when Al would pick up some other craft and return to his eternal life. Allowed back for one lousy day, and Jason was glad to see him, and said so ("Thank you for choosing to pass your limited time with me, Tott, rather than with any of the other better-known authors who were part of your stable and never dished out the shit you had to take from me"), and Al, eyes straight ahead, waved a disclaimer and in a voice hard to hear above the sea roar said, "You were always my favorite, Tott, writer and friend," but it was clear to Jason his late editor was not the least bit unhappy about returning to the dead. "You know, you really ought to write about your life as it is now, Totteleh," the drunk suggested, but Seamans smiled gently and said, "I'm not the writer, Tottenyu," and then the mist rolled in and claimed him. Sams was alone, tempest-tossed, the women having vanished long before.

It was a dream he dreamed with variations maybe three times a year. Fitting, he groggily noted, to suffer through a rerun on the morning of his journey.

He thought he had woken for good in the predawn, but as gray light filtered through the window shades he dreamed or imagined that his name broke away from his body. For a time he watched calmly as it hovered just above his head, impressed by the boldness of the type, wondering how much time must pass before it decided to return. Just as the thought crossed his mind that he could reach up and bring it back, it moved south and slightly higher, undulating now over his midsection, but remained, he estimated, well within his reach. When he decided the game had gone on long enough, he half sat up in bed and went for it with his nonarthritic arm, but the thing juked left, wafted right between the TV rabbit ears, continued on an upward course and disappeared, into the whiteness of the ceiling.

He felt bereft. In a moment he was stunned to discover that the name was gone from memory. His grief then was greater than any he had ever known.

World news startled him awake: a plane in Rome, or was it Seoul, exploded on a runway. He bolted up to shut off the radio and reset the alarm so his wife could sleep another hour, and then a thin metal plate began slicing through his head at a forty-five-degree angle, which was how hangovers, returned after a long absence, had lately manifested themselves. For many years he had not suffered from them no matter how much alcohol he had consumed the night before, absolute proof to himself and to whomever else might need it that while on occasion he might drink too much, you could certainly not put a goddamn label on it, "alcoholic" or other. Lately, however, the hangovers had returned. He misplaced the dreams.

His right hand covering his right eye, he vacated his side of the bed and went to the john. He relieved at length his swollen bladder (still saddened by the trickle, the fading memory of strength of flow; but his jolly proctologist had assured him that voiding at all these days, given the size of his prostate, was miracle enough), went to the kitchen and put the coffee on. He took a long, very hot shower, letting the water beat on the back of his neck, which brought some relief to his head. Dawdling over coffee and cigarettes, Jason hoped his bonny Jake would wake and roar into the kitchen, so he could bid him a sober goodbye. But the child slept on. At seven-fifteen he left the apartment, stopping at the corner convenience store for the *Boston Globe,* the *New York Times,* two packs of Merit cigarettes, a Kit-Kat, and a package of honey-lemon Halls.

The Green Line chugged in as always in its own sweet time, packed to the rafters, bouncing its riders around nonetheless, outrageous system if you'd ever ridden the underground in Montreal or London, which he had, or in Moscow or Washington, which he hadn't, but without the leisure to wait for a less crowded car he forced his way on with his overnight bag and newspapers and stood crushed in the doorway until some rearranging at the next stop found him a post to cling to, after which he employed various stratagems until Park Street, where the doors opened to disgorge people from both sides of the car. At Park he went down a flight of stairs and waited for the Red Line, which would take him directly to South Station, if *it* ever arrived, but he didn't panic, having wisely left himself an hour and fifteen minutes to negotiate the distance between his house and Amtrak, being the kind of person who avoided cabbies where he could.

No elbowing or jostling to board and find seating on the Paul Revere, South Station being the starting point for New York City and beyond. He settled himself into an almost empty smoking car, lit up, and took a look at the *Boston Globe*. The *New York Times* he'd save for later on. He had kicked the habit of the all-day-sucker of the *Times* (one of the not inconsiderable perks of living out of state), yet was far from hooked on the *Globe,* where misspellings and in-felicitous usage and front-page photos of cute kids flying kites or ice fishing as the season required and photos of interesting shadows cast by churches and photos of the latest fire (arson in Boston and environs virtually a profession, usually landlords trashing their own buildings with or with-out people in them for the insurance dollar; hard to com-prehend!) were the order of the day and the obituaries (known as "deaths") were often cheek by jowl with the comics page and were so listed (DEATHS COMICS) although you couldn't count on this, since nothing was ever in the same place twice, but he lived in Boston now, hard as it was to believe and accept even after two years, and there was a whole lot of business going on in the streets and elsewhere most days to do with blacks and whites and buses and schools and court orders which would no doubt one day soon affect him (or "impact" him, as they had started to horribly say) and his wife and especially his kid although it hadn't yet, so he took a brief interest in the headline SOUTHIE PROTEST PEACEFUL TODAY (no buses carrying black kids trashed, that seemed to mean), skipped over KIS-SINGER LASHES CRITICS (the best defense, ah Henry?), PLAYBOY CLUBS HOP TO JAPAN nearly drew him, but CUBANS EXECUTED BY FEMALE FIRING SQUAD IN AN-GOLA carried the day, close as it was to being the obverse of his childhood fantasy, SAMS CAPTURED BUT NURTURED BY SVELTE AMAZONS, who in due course would transport him to their Surgeon-Queen, who could, through a secret procedure, detect true royalty in a commoner. Turning now to sports, he found confirmed that Peter Gammons was a very good writer, so chances were he would not be wasted at the *Globe* for very long, covering Red Sox spring training today, and the hope that sprang eternal despite the previous year's agonizing World Series loss to the Cincinnati Reds, Gammons devoting perhaps a bit too much space today to the bizarre and wondrous pitching motion of Luis Tiant. Sam's fingers blackened under the weight of the news.

Was "Hicksville" excessively unkind? He scanned the ink-free *Times,* which at once informed him that the Dow had climbed above 1000, unknown parties in London had bombed Harrod's, Patty Hearst's credibility in her kidnap-ping case had been impugned, a peanut farmer from Georgia was making the run for the president, Cuba was once more a threat to the well-being of the United States, and he could have followed with interest any or all of these, and still had the obits ahead and sports and Broadway and books, and again be hooked on the *Times,* his peak reading experience in Woodstock and Manhattan, so he laid it aside and looked at his watch, much too early for beer to be available in the club car although coffee and sandwiches would be on sale but he had brought his own sandwiches and didn't feel like trudging through four cars for indifferent coffee, and thinking then of his mother's percolated coffee available in the tiny kitchen on the Lower East Side where she had lived in the same apartment for thirty-five years with his father still out there laboring six days a week and loving it and resting on the seventh day and Jason considered that both his parents were old now (seventy) and likely to be cheered were he to drop in on them unannounced after discharging his other business although it was not his usual procedure not to call them first but a little planned spontaneity might do them all some good and he thought of his remaining friends who were few if any apart from the widow of his editor now two years gone and also forfeited perhaps forever was the right to drop in on short if any notice at the townhouse of his former buddy who had flipped out entirely and precisely at what may never now be known although Sams would wonder ever after what had caused the rupture whether it was his foul ingratitude in re the flying Wallenda episode or an allegedly shabby performance at the college where he had taught creative writing for a year and also of all things Japanese literature in translation with a flask in the desk in the office he shared with young Brandenburg dapper Jewish specialist in Native American lore and taught well enough in my own opinion but Demirgian who had arranged the gig for Sams to replace a tenured poet on a Guggenheim evidently thought otherwise and thus felt his own job or judgment or integrity was somehow in jeopardy or compromised who knew exactly let us say one of the above but a finally exploded Armenian rage that the drunk got the girl and the beauty of impending fatherhood while he. No question I was smashed that night and hollering and perhaps putting down college teaching as a man's life work with

insufficient irony but when had he known me during our
eight years to be entirely sober why we had been hollering
at each other that long the Jew and the Armenian hollering
was the cherished heart and soul of our relationship so what
made that night different from all other nights why now
precipitate a quarrel during dinner with me and pointedly
pregnant Jenny on what became literal eve of son's arrival
this dear unmarried friend to us both and until that moment
or so she and I believed Jenny one of his favorite people in
the universe which troubled me in no way if you can believe
it pleased me in fact since I loved them both the hillbilly
and the dark crazy writer with the townhouse the three of
us dining at some joint in Shandaken on the last night of
the term she had been to my last writing class we were both
going to sleep in the room I rented on campus I taught the
last Japlit course in the morning and she was scheduled to
come to that one too but here we were some high decibel
I had thought usual and friendly quarrel escalating suddenly
and suddenly I feared the demented son of a bitch who
wasn't drunk but brought his face close to mine and hers
and roared his rage and the evening was abruptly over jointly
shaken we went to bed and her waters broke at three A.M.
three weeks early as they might have done even had Demirgian never lived and I drove furiously to Woodstock and
scoured the house for lollipops why had they told us at
Lamaze class in Kingston she'd need to suck on lollipops
nowhere to buy them at three A.M. for in her panic and
obsession she really thought she had to have them and I was
no longer sure myself throwing more clothing on us both
took time against the chill Woodstock night and looked
around the deserted village green at that hour for some
zonked-out hippie who might have lollipops secreted on his
person so didn't get to St. Benedictine emergency until

three-forty-five where they knew she was coming I'd called her doctor popped her into a wheelchair and in less than half an hour although Jenny would never believe it was that short a time I squeezed her hand as per Lamaze helpless before that pain a son was given and I saw his slimy entry and a hardon from the getgo not much the worse for early arrival just a touch of jaundice but they kept him in a private solarium wearing giant sunglasses where he looked like King Farouk and was it two days later or three I drove him home to his own barnraised room kind handy friends had carved out of our bedroom in the queer L-shaped two-room shack in the queer town our summer home turned year-round residence bought with the advance extracted in a rage from Al driving my son home in the Valiant my father bestowed upon us not yet the wreck it would become moving five or ten miles an hour the infant bundled across mother's lap I couldn't believe it stealing wild glances at the thing swathed in her lap and doubting what he saw. Forty years old and yet to find himself, how could J. Sams so abruptly have become a *father?* Listen God he thought at God (good Jew that he remained) I know we have been trying for four long years to bring this thing to pass she and I and assorted fertility geniuses and You, screwing by the numbers and sometimes with true passion just the same my sperm no doubt as sluggish as my muse but mountain bride in touch at last with all the good news within herself and now this Jacob storming the citadel lying here across her knees I ain't sure I'm ready for this Lord a volume or two yet to write and myriad sights to see plus new drinks to drink with new brands of beer with new lovely labels on the market every day hollering thus silently to his Lord of the time until his wife said sharply would you please keep your eyes on the road you're endangering the three of us by all these goofy glances at my lap

So kept his eyes on Route 28 thinking life would certainly change now but maybe for the better with the chance to stop the bullshit settle in and do the work and get responsible missed the Woodstock generation by a year and most of the sixties drunk in Europe and here but now it's two years into the seventies time to get serious asshole but booze would remain in the saddle for the next four years

The ticket-taker on the Paul Revere safely past he pulled out the flask same flask I kept in Brandenburg's desk drawer at Bard heap good container for firewater eh? but the Indian expert made no moral judgments had no sense of humor either a peyote freak to boot and I remembered suddenly buying the flask in London at a little shop in Highbury Hill when living in a basement room cleaning out the outside drains once a week to keep the rent low just a guinea a week but GI Bill just $110 a month then sharing the kitchen with a dour Englishman named Mr. Love and pretty dour himself until one day Mr. Love got pissed at our mutual silence or at something else and pointed out the kitchen was included in *his* rent not mine I apologized and became a trifle friendlier he backed off and let me use it all within range of the shouts from Arsenal Stadium soccer games he never attended although the flask had been to Boston Garden for a Celtics game last season but could never warm to the locals after so many years pulling for Clyde the Glide and Dollar Bill and mighty Willis the once and future NY Knicks although Bill Russell of course and lisping Hondo were amazing to watch it held half a pint or so and by now the snackbar

must have started selling beer to chase the brandy with no
one yet sitting within five feet of him not even after Providence which he would one day visit but for now enjoy once
more the statehouse splendid even through the unwashed
window out the righthand side Vedanta's other New England temple on a hill out there somewhere to his left one
pop and then content to doze or sleep

His literary agent third agent first male had carried him for
years a gentleman said to be tough in the clutch and Jason
hoped to test this one day soon since he had not yet made
a dime for the man not that Mitchell needed his money to
get by and once he had fully apprised his agent of his book-
to-be he would mosey downtown for his appointment with
Ralph the overworked editor who had inherited him when
Al Seamans died and do the same for him although he had
already raised them both on the phone and fumbled out
some thoughts about which they had expressed cautious
enthusiasm Jason Sams here on the line once a prince of
promise six years silent but now BACK if you took his word
with an exquisite novella or outline for same or germ of an
idea for an outline on what may unfold or in fact already
had with appropriate fictional safeguards to a writer and his
editor who become too close confusing life and art and even
doubledated for God's sake and when my Armenian
bombshell fled for good and Seamans was headed west for
a bookfair I gave him this extra mission and he dutifully
looked her up reporting back on her health which was good
what a dumb thing that had been for me to do in my then
frame of mind for now I could suspect her of diddling him
as well as the rest of the world not from disloyalty but he
would have had no choice at all if such a thing had been for
her a top priority ah harking back to the good old days

when he and I first met with no Armenian flame in sight
and all that publishers' money to burn back then in the early
sixties and he signed me through my first agent with what
seemed then a tidy sum solely on the basis of my first book
which had not sold at all but won awards and the sum grew
tidier as the author followed the editor like a puppy as Al
moved laterally up the ladder to how many different houses
had he lugged the growing MS out of fear and loyalty and
for the couple of bucks accruing and it seemed to make
sense at the time no one was hurt by it the rest were only
businessmen if you find an editor who loves you and your
work as well in fact scarcely distinguishes between the two
how could you not stick by such a person through whatever
vicissitudes collecting more money also in part to impress
your father who had worked with his hands all his life except
your father never believed for a moment it would last or
even that it was happening to his son in the habit as he was
of stuffing me with money large sums and small even unto
a twenty-five-cent piece one time on my way back to Woodstock from a New York visit when Sams made the error of
saying to his dad he was going to pick up a *New York Times*
to read on the bus trip back stuck a quarter in my hand old
guy never believed for a moment it would last if it was even
happening and he was right

So sent Al in '67 having already pursued her twice himself
and got his ass kicked twice and gradually lost the habit of
phoning the west coast twice a week and still the drunken
prose unfolded in some raging spiral never would there be
a finish to the melodrama and his cataloguing same until
finally one balmy night of a New York spring Sams just
recently returned from abortion and baseball and bowling
in Montreal his despair at its most exquisite I had to tell Al

I can't finish Tott there is no finishing and no going on with
it either at which point Seamans the late editor and as it
seems with hindsight great and gifted friend separated him
gently from the final box of manuscript pages taking cus-
tody as he had taken off without comment and by mutual
consent earlier chunks as they came off the press in order
to prevent Sams' excessive endless tinkering no doubt reading same but keeping his counsel this time saying gently to
his goodbuddy in distress It's over Tottenyu you're done

You shittin me? ah how Jason wished it true

It was

In two weeks time a letter which he still must have somewhere Were you to put this here restore time sequence for
the poor reader's sake drop the book within the book sweet
as I know it is to you and I love it myself but it doesn't
belong and not a word altered anywhere or added by me
you may have to write a few new transitional lines and
everything I've said here is suggestion only Tott you understand it runs exactly as it is if that's your pleasure and a
fine book that way too but the author had to trust Seamans'
sense of the marketplace had to trust *something* after all the
house-hopping and apparent faith and had no objection
whatsoever to selling well so let the changes that were not
changes stand for all he knew they left his book enormously
improved and then Jason waited and then went off to Europe
for several months with his wife of a year and by the time
they returned Al had made the jeté to his final eminence
with Sams' book ready to roll at the penultimate place and
a respectable place it was so now it was not with any ease
Jason contemplated an uprooting and this time sought the

advice of his second agent when he finally got her on the phone and while she was aware as was the entire relevant universe of the closeness and importance of the tie between this writer and this editor she advised him to stay where he was advice to which he gave his best boozy agonized attention and seemed to accede to in the following manner

Drank Jack Daniels alone all day chased by Ballantine ale not the double Dickels they usually drank when they drank together at Max's Kansas City or at Peter Luger's or at Jason's place or Al's place in the West Village for this event he invited Al to his own garden apartment shared now not with his heroine but with his wife where Al had been perhaps a hundred times before to hear now his irrevocable decision on whether he was going to make this final leap or stay put where Al had most recently been where the book was already in galleys and pub date set and where while they did not love him madly nor his book either they promised fair and decent treatment as well as a generous advance on his next if not the three-book six figures Al had tossed around while saying what only he the son of a bitch would dare to say Tott if you don't come with me I'll have to reconsider going myself so the thing was well out of hand before Seamans ever arrived at his house Sams as drunk since early morning as he had been on his wedding day which unfolded out back in his own garden with Seamans the beaming best man I was out of control from the outset but could mask it for a time until abrupt unraveling sudden nonstop venom you haberdasher you you furrier you failed lawyer failed ballplayer it being fact that before he found his way into publishing Seamans had the kind of work record publicity writers in the fifties loved to ascribe to writers just getting published as for example Mr. Sams is a soda bottler or was for a few weeks one summer in Atlantic City a shipping clerk later a coach cleaner on the Penn Railway before finding his way to his twenty minutes of literary notoriety but Al's work record was similar and more genuine especially impressive and endearing his tryout with the baseball New York Giants as a first baseman all this now Sams' raging prelude to the spate of grievances I have become a laughing stock throughout the industry thanks to my inappropriate loyalty and two-bit greed and a figure of contempt let it stop here you go your way Al and I go mine which is to say STAY PUT and maybe I can redeem what little is left of my reputation and maybe one day and that soon restore my book to its rightful shape which is the one it had before your half-ass tinkering and Al's face working close to tears or an uncharacteristic rage of his own rising finally from the chair where he had taken all this in endlessly rising to his six four until the drunk felt fear right through his craziness I guess I have your answer Tott moving unsteadily to the front door departing without looking back although saying goodbye to Jenny who stood immobile in the tiny kitchen stunned silent by her new husband's fresh insanity

Some sleepless days and nights tossing and moaning alone by choice on the couch amazed into profound remorse by his error until four or five days later compelled by the supreme need to undo the harm and loss or try it might be reversible finally with enough beer and brandy in him to make the contrite mumbling call to the new editor-in-chief who was inclined now to caution and Sams couldn't blame him for that I feel like shit Al it wasn't me it was the bourbon talking I still want you to have the book if you're still interested as it is of course not as it was sure you want to sleep on it let's talk sometime soon and certain for a few days that this time he had gone too far but the final leap is made the book although already at the printer's somehow moved over to Seamans' apparent pleasure but I can see from his face in unguarded moments that things have changed and there is no further talk of multiple-book and six-figure contracts from any quarter

And it bombs despite full-page ads and a few good reviews in important places and a paperback sale that earns him not a sou and an early-morning call to Sams' unlisted number from a film producer with an Armenian-sounding name so probably *was* one promising Sams the moon beyond the generous option fee and the chance to write the script but when nets and grosses enter in he refers the gent to his second agent who is on top of all this and the Armenian is heard from no more

And of course there was the killing review in the daily *Times* right smack on his pub date having risen early picking up the paper not opening it until back in his apartment and scanning and coming back to bed but neither his wife nor his mother-in-law's great hand-stitched Appalachian quilts piled high against the New York autumn stop the shivering

On the order of Look what Jason did Mum blew his nose right into the doily in the sticky unduplicatable prose of the wraith who will mask this revenge on poor old Sams with obfuscating objectivity but the wraith will know and the drunk will know he (the novelist) should have never insulted him (the critic) three weeks earlier before he even knew who he was although it might not have mattered since he knew to which reviewer his book had been originally assigned and it was not the creepy fellow blocking access to the bar

at the party at Luchow's for old friend Leonard Gardner's
new novel *Fat City* so a few gratuitous remarks on critics
or shall we say rather hack reviewers who muddy the waters
and he must have thrown in agents too although he had not
the smallest notion that the plumpish gent with whom the
hack reviewer chatted was or was said to be one of the better
agents in town and since he would himself soon be looking
to switch from agent two to one more accessible and less
acclaimed well he ruled out that gent didn't he but anyway
all reviewers and all agents parasites on a noble calling loud
and manic and shit shit why hadn't he remained off in the
corner appearing to listen to the syndicated fathead drunk
and building his case if it wanted building but well you see
his wife a once and perhaps future woman of the theater in
profound much too intimate confab with Bert Lahr's son
and Sams was already too looped to trust himself intruding
and besides all that the point was his glass was empty and
access to the bar blocked by the soon-to-be-anointed Cultural Correspondent of the *NY Times* but still a book reviewer and by the fat soft body of the well-known literary
agent and Sams would never remember exactly what he said
nor why he chose that moment to say it but certainly loud
and offensive to someone with a mind to be offended and
somehow with hardly any time at all remaining the wraith
clearly had the clout to wrest or request Sams' book from
the bumbling one with whom he alternated space although
the bumbling one already had his lead composed on the
order of As long-awaited second books often do it often
disappoints yet here and there are sections of such masterful
appeal I found myself feeding the toast and buttering the
cat or some such inane kindness the bumbling one being a
friend of Al's in that they attended athletic events together
but it fell out as it did the wraith doing some quick home-

work thumbing through Jason's first so as to better imitate judiciousness cum crocodile tears it saddens me to have to report that the usually astute Trilling's faith was here misplaced followed by dismissive disgust and perhaps worst of all in the opinion of the butchered one himself everything accomplished in less than the allotted two full columns highly unusual for the daily paper but there it was some other book creeping in for pleasant capsule review in the last few lines of the second column so I picked up the *NY Times* on Sams' publication day and wound up shivering uncontrollably for several hours followed by years of rage and silence before he would ever hear of Vivekananda and Noone But Me to Blame

Put the arm on a distracted grieving Seamans just then separating from a wife for portion of advance on my unimagined next and plunked it down on the Woodstock summer house since every writer on the way up or down should have a summer house and not long after eking out his one-year parttime work at college across the river courtesy Demirgian by composing soon-to-be-abandoned fragments and peddling same as true beginnings of new work to Seamans who had to go to the mat with his superiors to get the writer these further incremental sums and did so not from naiveté or lingering guilt over the failure of their collaborative tome as was easiest for Sams to assume but love

Then up and died now as Richie Havens sang in his first great record died in broad daylight on a fucking golf course at the age of thirty-seven in February 1974 as Jason would learn when he made it back from his new job in Boston and what a commute it had been to tell his wife the story of careening off the pike in heavy snow believing his life was done love but landed softly and stand here before you chilled and sobered to tell the tale at first undistracted by her stricken face then unaccepting of her news

So flogging now an idea left over from the days when Al still lived Al having expressed jocular interest in it once or twice himself if just to set the record straight why goddamn it Totteleh not just *your* version should be out there misleading the unwashed so in fantasy they would each do half a book describing the absolute truth about their bumpy and splendid association to be published of course between the same set of covers what an irresistible idea what was the point of truth if it could not be refuted on the spot

which could no longer happen

So I will do it myself that is to say my version of events will have to do for both whatever target it shall present to the vindictive wraith who has of course been waiting lo these seven years to do me in again this time even on public radio Sams working away steadily and stealthily in order to be done in in several media by the cultural correspondent of the *New York Times* will you tell me please the point? have another drink and show the bastard produce not a word although more likely he has forgotten me entirely as has most of the rest of the world not altogether to my disadvantage so will do Al's version also transforming the whole into high art

Barely into Connecticut but very hungry why wait before consuming just a little on the early side his Hebrew National salami sandwich not failing to note as always that the meat was smaller in circumference and tasted not nearly half as good as the same-name brand was and did in New York

and was this legal? were there no outraged or disgruntled
Jews besides himself trapped in Boston or Brookline not for
one second fooled ready and eager to join forces class action
suit and raise a stink? So why do you keep buying it? the
chairman might with reason have inquired as per his tuna
fish joke, which is to say, what the devil are you hoping
for? my parents on their infrequent journeys to Boston are
more than eager to bring with them the real thing and the
rest of his heart's desire, the "specials" (jumbo franks) and
the sour pickles from the barrels on Essex Street Jennifer
and Jake too right from the start a fan of such items so my
parents had it all in tow when they barely remembered to
alight from the Amtrak on their most recent visit a story
he has raised some chuckles with from friends but is still
flabbergasted by when he tells and retells it to himself and
ravenous suddenly Jason devoured the ersatz Hebrew National on decent rye dressed up with lettuce and a German-
style Gulden's good enough and the jar of Claussen pickles
near enough to the barrel finishing up with a Bosc pear and
Delicious apple and two more jolts of Courvoisier from his
flask and one of two cans of beer from the snack bar he
finally went to buy and slept most of the rest of the way
waking somewhere in the Bronx or was it Queens to Manhattan's stirring profile, arriving in New York only half an
hour late at the no-longer-new Penn Station in fine fettle if
still a degree tipsy stuffing the other beer into his weathered
bag and untroubled by the blustery day set out on foot at
a good clip to meet agent Mitchell at his office in the East
Fifties and Mitchell shook his hand and treated him as if in
fact at any moment he was capable of producing some splendid masterpiece this treatment no more nor less than his due
but watch out you don't settle for it.

*

They had been friends for many years, even though his earnings over that period on the order of forthcoming three dollars from the *Boston Globe* returning to the agency barely the postage it would cost to send on his pittance and what of it? Mitchell was doing very well of late and did not complain. Mitchell genuinely mourned Al and whenever they met he and Jason traded memories of that receding time. Why would he contemplate changing agents? No one had asked him to. In the Japanese restaurant right below Mitchell's office Sams ordered raw fish and kept the edge on with a Kirin beer and when that was gone a Nippon beer as he elaborated more fully on the book-to-be but Mitchell's greyhound face revealed little as he sipped his Perrier and lime and finally said, Certainly it sounds interesting Jason but these days we need more than an outline before we can move I'm afraid the sixties are over when the money flowed and Al and the rest of the free spenders are gone now or altered in their habits but one hundred pages would likely stimulate some interest somewhere shake loose the advance you need assuming that is you see it as nonfiction since of course if it's a novel you're still under contract to Al's last house and yours. How far along are you? The idea stage? I see. Well, as the elderly Tolstoy is reputed to have said (before slamming the door) to the would-be writer who had trekked across the frozen tundra to seek out the Master's words of wisdom, Ecrivez!

Minute I'm back in Boston, Mitchell. I never could write well on the road. They tell me at UGB that I've fallen a book or two behind. You also think?

Behind what?

*

To commemorate which supportive remark Sams ordered his third beer an Asahi this time the real reason being as he assured old Mitchell to better recapture the rapture of the bad old days in the Far East when these three brands were all there were and he drank all three as well as Akadama Red Jewel wine and Akadama white but Mitchell soon excused himself to return to the literary wars departing only after putting all they had consumed on his tab and leaving his alcoholic but supremely gifted client a little latitude on that same tab should Sams need to drink and think for a few moments or a few hours more.

"Give my best to Jenny. And call me, if there's something I can do."

"Thanks, Mitchell. Say hello to Frieda and the kids. And thanks again for everything."

Alone, Sams looked around the nearly empty room, taking in his surroundings, hoping to file them away; but damned if he could find very much if anything to distinguish the interior of the place from the interior of any other fancy restaurant, whatever its cuisine (except for the raised rooms with the straw mats and low tables for the convenience of the Japanese and others wishing to remove their shoes and adopt a semi-lotus and dine Japanese-style, more or less), and he concluded (not for the first time) that he was royally screwed if the resumption of his calling depended on his having learned to respond with any degree of lyrical or scientific precision to his physical surroundings. He was simply no damn good at it, ceding the territory gladly or otherwise to those with a painterly eye or the gift for the telling detail. But neither, he assured himself, was he one of those bareboned "minimalists" who had parachuted onto the scene (or into his consciousness: for his most recent birthday his mother had presented him with an unsolicited subscription to the Book Review, and he would have to have been even more stiffnecked than he knew himself to be to toss the publication without even a cursory glance) just the previous Monday; he supposed that now, by and by, he'd have to take a look at this Raymond Carver if only to remain hip to what was happening or see if there was something he might learn from Carver, a device worth ripping off, or merely, feature this, Jason, read the guy for pleasure and moral instruction. He did observe of course the two young handsome Japanese waiters in black pants and bright white jackets swooping here and there, changing tablecloths, laying places, readying the restaurant for dinner, managing to ignore Sams and wish him gone while at the same time honoring his right to be there and his wish for privacy. He was tempted to summon one or the other of them with the peremptory "Chotto!" not to order anything but to flabbergast with seeming fluency, find out where in Japan the young man hailed from, then say his own little piece in Japanese about where he'd lived twenty years earlier when he too was in the motherland, what his profession had been then and what, let us say, it remained (novelist, *shosetsuka*, he loved the word), and when the kid seemed to grow genuinely interested despite the press of his duties and strung together a few rapid sentences Jason knew he should have understood but no longer did beyond a few stray words, he would feel the customary sweat spring to his armpits and brow and the usual sharp sense (beyond mere embarrassment) of remorse and self-contempt for (down the years) his countless wasted opportunities.

So he spared them both the difficult encounter, but his mind reeled, only in part (he imagined) from too much alcohol in too little time, but more from a glimpse of what his True Subject should have been, or what it was — not the forced, attenuated pseudo-memoir (I Know You, Al?) he had just finished describing to Mitchell Busch and would shortly be obliged to reinvent for his would-be editor Ralph Maduras, a man he scarcely knew, but his vanished life as a young man in the Far East, from the moment in 1954 when the troopship bore him and a few thousand others to Yokohama harbor, and he came topside and saw the sampans glistening in the morning sun. Then the trainride to Zama through alien countryside, the strange and lovely language briefly heard then glimpsed on billboards from the sparklingly clean train windows, knowing even then that he would be obliged to learn the lingo of this green and sun-filled planet. Then the midnight shifts at Camp Zama, those splendid second breakfasts at eleven-thirty P.M. for signal people going to work at that peculiar hour or for troopers staggering back from a debauch in town and about to go to bed, no one working in the mess hall seemed to care, hardly any chickenshit at Zama in those post-Korean years. (And, as he prepared himself to abandon this sanctuary in the East Fifties and face the wicked streets of the city he still loved more than any other, more even than Kyoto, more than his beloved London, it seemed important to record somewhere that he had never in his life, day after day, eaten as well as he had eaten for those two years in the army, especially at the smaller mess halls in Japan, and that he would spend the next twenty-three years of his life if not the whole of it trying — at four-star restaurants, at a greasy spoon in eastern Kentucky, in his own kitchen — to duplicate the taste of the pork tenderloin that came his way every Tuesday evening at Camp Otsu, near Kyoto, to which he was lucky enough to be transferred a few months after reaching Zama and where he would receive, a year later, his separation from the army. He would come tearing back from town, if that was where he was, or even catch a train from neighboring cities, if it happened to be Tuesday, to catch the evening meal. He'd also loved the setting of the camp, nestled at the base of a mountain, and he rarely strayed far from magnificent Lake Biwa or sacred Mount Hiei during his civilian year.)

He had written about it some, but not yet got it right: just that pair of army/whorehouse stories, as he disparaged them now, that had appeared thirteen years earlier in *Just Desserts,* plus the first chapter of a novel (that went no further) purporting to explain how he came to be clinging to a chimney on the steeply sloping roof of an off-limits house of ill fame in Hama-Otsu, with two MPs awaiting his inevitable descent in their jeep below. But he had touched nowhere yet on his overseas discharge (or the reasons for it), his thirteen civilian months, his daily life in the village of Yamashina near Kyoto when he still had it all ahead, a kid of twenty-three, a fiction writer, not yet utterly dependent on the sauce, although how much truth there was in that he wasn't sure, for he could remember while still a trooper himself recumbent in the middle of the road leading back to the shack he rented near the base composing haiku as his live-in lady Keiko tugged at his hand and he even remembered what she may have said, "Gerrup! You stinko!" smiling now as then at the harsh but accurate judgment, not only busy writing haiku but studying his old friend the Big Dipper, knowing damn well that one of them was upside down, and not long after that commencing the bureaucratic chase to the Kobe consulate and something or other else that had to be done in Osaka, finally nailing down the paperwork to assure somewhere down the road his receipt of the modest booty (but it went some distance then) of the

GI Bill, and then the abrupt ascension right there in the company orderly room (where he happened to be standing when his orders came through, awaiting company punishment for the rooftop episode) into civilian life, and a simulacrum of the writing life, and the scholar's life, but a rake (he knew now, looking back) was all he'd ever been, or not even that but a lush, sleeping only now and then on his own futon on the tatami in the six-mat room he rented for a pittance in an inn on the old Tokaido, using the room most days just long enough to type a bit and get a buzz on and let him not forget as if he could twenty-seven was it days without a shit unable to master the squat nonflush communal toilet in the inn and approaching some sort of local record they enjoyed telling him at the Baptist Hospital in Kyoto where he sought relief, and where they sorted him out with strong medicine and the use of their western-style toilet, after which he found the good tutoring job in the Tudor house right up the hill from where he lived with its "normal" toilets galore or else used the facilities back at Camp Otsu which he wondered why he had not done from the start. Must have been all the go-native crap, why he'd even bathed in the public bathhouse for a while, weathering the stares, until he took to showering at the Tudor house or at the western-style cathouse just there at the bend in the road leading into Kyoto. He even tried smoking the local brands, even Shinsei, which could tear your head off, more powerful than the Turkish cigs that did in his mother's father Joe, after whom (in Hebrew, anyway) his only son was named, old Joe who owned and drove the seltzer and soda truck that serviced most of the Jewish Lower East Side in the late twenties and through the thirties and into the forties carrying the heavy crates up however many flights of stairs as long as he was able, and then his sons Jason's uncles did the same for a time, cigarettes that did him in in conjunction with the bolts of schnaps he put back several times a day . . . you rummy and cigarette smoker, Sams judged himself; no one but me to blame.

Finally, with a hacking cough in place, Jason went off the local economy and asked one of his few remaining army buddies to pick up Luckies at the PX with what was left of his mustering-out pay, as well as the jockey shorts he couldn't find, at Daimaru or anywhere. But he was happy with Japanese food, had never eaten so much fish before or since, especially happy with the breakfasts delivered by the innkeeper or her daughter every morning to his room with a bow and winks and chuckles all adding up to appropriate respect for the shosetsuka-in-residence and his odd artist ways. The bowl of rice and the two hardboiled eggs and the bowl of tea and the incomparable miso soup: never the smallest variation, the single constant in his life.

When the job in the Tudor house ended he moved to a western-style house in Shimogamo, a quiet suburb in the northern part of Kyoto, on the same street, he was told, where Tanizaki Junichiro lived, and Jason thought he might have glimpsed the master once, but the main attraction of the house apart from its two western-style toilets was how close it was to the school for missionaries where he studied the language on the GI Bill (the school he'd managed to get VA-approved all by himself). He sublet a room with use of the kitchen from an army captain not long back from Korea who'd fallen in love with a *musume* downtown only days after he'd sent for his wife, who was already on the high seas. Young Jason, wary but willing (no more than a PFC on the day of his discharge, and without combat skills), succumbed to the tears and advances of this jilted, raging spouse, an angular blond, once she arrived and took in the lay of the land. When the captain got wind of what was taking place under his very own roof he thanked Jason for his trouble, and the American woman, to her credit, did not stay very long.

So there he was in quiet Shimogamo drinking the best sake right out of the bottle and pecking fitfully at an old Underwood, a fake (in his own eyes at least), someone who knew who Tanizaki was and knew by name some of the foreign scholars (Americans mostly, some Indians) who attended or hung out around Kyoto University, listening to Beethoven in tiny coffeehouses, some gone the whole hog to kimono and geta and topknots but most with ordinary haircuts and shoes and western clothes like his own but almost all entirely fluent on the conversational level and also in some specialized scholarly mode, able to read with ease the language he would always have to struggle with, so what kind of game was he playing, hardly ever *heard* of Japan after World War Two ended and now living there, feigning an interest in its culture . . . why? But shouldn't sell himself entirely short, took in his share of temples and museums and famous gardens, could look for hours at the white zen stones of Ryoanji, shuddered with awe before the giant Buddhas at Kamakura and Nara, loved the ukiyo-e of Utamaro, Sharaku, Hiroshige, Hokusai, and most of the rest of the woodblock crowd, enjoyed kabuki if not Noh (and the ineffable koto, plaintive planking of the samisen) and the Kabukiza as well, the lavishly appointed Tokyo theater in which the drama unfolded (for Sams retained a lady friend in Tokyo, let us call her Masako, he still went by train to visit now and then, an utterly respectable and totally bilingual retransplanted Nisei he had met working in the Camp Zama PX, born in Vancouver, awkward, shy, reading *Crime and Punishment* — in English! — when he approached her counter, and who, over the next couple of years, would sometimes drive him bonkers by her sudden tears, unbroken intensity), he was crazy about Akutagawa's short stories in translation (but knew he could have read them anywhere), so hanging on there in the ancient capital writing badly while scrambling for English tutoring work and studying the language like a third grader at a school for missionaries, merely to go on getting drunk and laid, merely because in terror of "real life," "home"?

On other days it was just as clear to him that he was one unforgiving critic where his own behavior was concerned — so what if he never became the brilliant literary translator he had set out to be (for a time crazily regarding this rare and arduous calling mastered only after many years of incredible preparation by geniuses like Donald Keene and Edward Seidensticker and Ivan Morris and a few other true heirs of the great Arthur Waley as a "fallback position" for the vicissitudes of the fiction writer's life), he had in fact learned to handle the Kanji dictionaries and the Japanese-Japanese dictionaries and could read the daily paper and certain novels (although too often he felt himself in direct competition with them, that is to say, why bother trying to translate what his own talent once he got round to steady employment of it could surpass), and while he had no real colleagues of any description, which occasionally troubled him, he had learned the regional dialect well enough to become a fairly familiar face at a number of out-of-the-way temples and restaurants and bars and whorehouses in several Kansai cities (encountering a headshaven bonze one time at Higashi Honganji who, while cordial enough, professed — and Sams did not know to this day if the young priest was putting him on — never to have heard of the United States), returning finally from the zen fleshpots in November of 1956 with NSU, nonspecific urethritis, a drip that baffled the medics of the Eisenhower years. He underwent some painful treatment for it in New York, as well as a cystoscopy, which revealed nothing, and the drip hung on for years, moving eventually to his eyes, first one eye and then the other, that mysterious NSU again, but this time non-specific uveitis, and then the bug or whatever it was migrated from his eyes to his back, causing a kind of arthritis, all three things in conjunction familiar to some informed doctors as an entity called Reiter's Syndrome. Well, at least they had a name for it, one someone in his thankless profession could find some bitter humor in. All three problems went into remission by and by, to return in his forties as the far-too-early prostate troubles, true payback for his inexcusable behavior in the Land of the Rising Sun, and off pretty cheaply at that, having frequented the kind of places he had frequented, particularly after the army was behind him. Then it had ceased to be the more or less sanitary bars and houses of ill fame where American soldiers went but establishments in say the Gojo section of Kyoto where even thoughtful natives feared to tread, and now they were being sought out and visited by this pimpled foreigner, Ivy League grad, this sheltered Jew, immersing himself in, well, you just might not believe the depths to which he sank, or maybe they weren't that bad, but they certainly seemed so the next morning when he woke with a blinding headache in God knew what part of the city, or even which city, scarcely able to make peace with the esthetic shortcomings of the female human being who lay beside him.

Finally, one day, with the notion strong that he had just about outgrown this sort of self-destructive behavior, with a couple of good new English teaching jobs in place and more fluent in the language than he'd ever imagined he'd become, plus the government checks rolling in on time and his writing (a long story about basic training) finally going well, in real danger, after a year, of settling in and making something of the expatriate's life, he decided (it was a day on which the same street urchins he used to see almost daily in Yamashina, to which he'd taken the trolley for old time's sake, trailed after him just as they used to do when he had lived there, through the same unpaved streets, and tried out their English — which consisted of the single word "Hello," pronounced "Haro" — just once too often) he was not cut out for exile.

Yet later, on the freighter out of Yokohama, having had at least one difficult farewell, the face of his Nisei friend as she left his cabin the saddest face he'd ever seen (until matched or surpassed years later by the faces of his in-laws as the bus carrying their youngest daughter and her new-fangled husband pulled out of West Rightfork, Kentucky), watching the coastline of Japan recede, knowing already he would not be back, he realized that it had not been the kids and haro haro but something that happened later that same afternoon back in Shimogamo, when he walked along the bank of the Kamo River near where he lived and saw the Kamogawa turn red and blue from dyeing cloth and from the opposite bank a good long way off a cur began to bark at him insanely and did not stop until he dropped out of sight behind the river bank and did not stop at once then either. There was no way the beast could have picked up his scent across that distance; it had to have been the mere sight of the hated for-eigner that triggered that display. Well fuck you then, vicious distant dog and master; there must still be a few places on the planet where the welcome would be warmer.

But nearly went nuts in NYC in 1957 living again in his parents' house at the age of twenty-five (could afford no other), or standing around MacDougal Street in Greenwich Village waiting for his life to happen. On such evenings he felt profoundly the size of his error, and somehow got the Veterans Administration to approve his harebrained scheme to take what was left of the GI Bill off to the University of London to pursue an advanced degree in of all things Modern Japanese, which he followed through on, garnering an upper second, but his own agenda from start to finish was to write what was given him to write, and see the world, and prolong the years of his apprenticeship.

It took him only two years to get the degree, but he hung on in Europe for five; staggered home in '62 to face the music and vote for the first time in his life on native soil; watched the funerals of Kennedy and King and Kennedy again on a small Sony, crying and drunk out of mind; courted women, lost interest, or they beat him to it, published stories, taught writing, made friends, married, continued drinking, moved to the country, fathered a son; and by the bicentennial year could dredge less Japanese out of his head than he could have done after his first three months in Japan.

Now he was almost forty-four and had propelled two volumes of fiction into the public domain in an earlier decade, neither of which made a dime.

*

Had a teaching job but couldn't keep it.

Had a wife and son and (Peter, Peter, pumpkin-eater) hoped to keep them very well.

Had — saw no way around it now — a drinking problem of some magnitude.

Was a genuine fake. No one but him to blame. Self-critical to a fault.

What else was new?

He strolled downtown along Madison Avenue toward his next appointment, passing the sloping foundations of buildings so new he did not know their names. The smooth, angled bases spoke to him of inaccessibility, slippery footing, unscalable heights, but above those daunting beginnings the structures climbed straight into the blue with unimagined grace. What a hick he was himself, craning for a better look at New York City's newest skyscrapers, measuring these relaxed giants against the self-conscious pair back "home," the one a thin, blue, angled thing that created a fierce wind tunnel in the plaza below it and the other lifted straight from the blocky imagination of what they had recently come to call (Orwell, thou shouldst be living at this hour) the "exceptional" child. Well, his knowledge of architects and their manifold problems was nil, and he was dimly aware that some frantic construction of things tall and short (like malls and "markets") was going on in downtown Boston at that very moment thanks at least in part to the efforts of the flamboyant Irish sharpy mayor Kevin White who would turn the small town into a "world-class city" if he could, not neglecting to reward in the process his many friends; but Jason, even Jason, at last grew weary of finding fault with his adopted city, finally tired of the negative hum; so consciously shifted his attention to the street vendors (a new wrinkle — wasn't sure yet if he liked it — for NY's posher avenues) and the heterogeneous faces of the passersby. He was at ease in the streets, touching no one, knowing when to jump the "Walk" sign at the corners; in his mind not the slightest doubt that he was ambling through the streets of the fantastic city (mayor, Abe Beame, no bargain either) where he would live again one day, the city he had not stopped living in yet.

Six years away was not that long: entirely possible he would find himself looking into the face of someone he knew, or had gone to high school with, or even into the face of a relative, his father's father Chaim having sired fourteen children by two wives and old Joe no slouch with six. Sams felt closer to the aunts and uncles on his mother's side, some of whom had almost raised him, but it was highly unlikely he would encounter Uncle Al or Uncle Jim or Aunt Lil strolling down Madison Avenue late on a Friday afternoon (least of all his favorite, Aunt Lil, nine years his senior, his first babysitter, who would be getting ready for the Sabbath in the Bronx), and while he was more likely to run into his father's siblings, many of whom lived in pricey condominiums right there in mid-Manhattan, and he would know them if he saw them (if not always which was which), those cousins of his who were their issue could waltz right by unrecognized, since many of them he'd never even met. Someone in the Sams clan, usually one of his father's half-sisters (the ones who, through marriage, had done nicely for themselves), brought off a family reunion every couple of years; Jason usually ignored the invitations, but the previous year, mostly at Jenny's urging, they had bundled up Jake and driven to New York, checked into the Murray Hill East, and joined the clan at the fancy Chinese restaurant which could not be far from the corner he was passing by at that moment. The seven (or however many) sisters split the expense of renting the place and having it shut down for four hours of a Sunday afternoon while its kitchen and bar stayed open and catered to the whims and tastes of a couple of hundred "Chinks" and whiskey lovers and bombed though he had already been he remembered his wife remarking to Helen his cousin Eddie's wife that she could not recall the last time she had eaten so well, and Helen theatrically widening her mascara-heavy eyes, responding, "Maybe your menu will improve after Hotshot writes and sells a book," and overhearing this as he was meant to he tried to muster a few shards of indignation, but as he looked into Helen's shrewd and entirely vulgar face and bent to accept her moist smack on his cheek and recalled all she had in recent years accomplished with her life, he could not manage feeling in the least offended.

She had made herself into one of the clan's top entrepreneurs, right up there with the owners of women's clothing chains and coast-to-coast hardware stores and the inventor of gizmos without which rockets would not fly and the merchandizer of time and space, all the pious and sometimes philanthropic smug and self-made men of property who'd worked for what they had but Helen was gifted beyond mere hard work, and many of them knew it and admired her for it, even the ones who would not speak of what she did. She'd begun small with ads in the *Enquirer* and the *Star,* and before long came the need for a sizeable staff to keep up with demand, to despatch photos of the scantily clad and sexily posed young female strangers she bought in bulk accompanied by letters that brightened the nights and enriched the fantasies of midwestern farmers mad with loneliness or of urban crazies benignly focused on the erotic promises she dreamed up and sent in response to their dollars in the mail. Jason had never seen her prose, but knew he could no more emulate it than he could sit down and dash off a potboiler or create on demand anything at all that might make him a buck; but Helen sustained some of these postal relationships for years, until rich men grown old would send their particular ageless beauty trying to make her way in the big city as model or actress substantial sums and mink coats, some remembering her gratefully and generously in their wills. Was it pornography? Not to Helen: prudent mother of four, she saw her avocation as a public service, an attempt to fill a crying need. The one thing Sams knew (shocked as part of him was, the part Puritan to the core), it was his kind of scam, her continual reinvention of alternate selves: it was fiction, it was art.

Jenny enjoyed Helen also, and most significant perhaps Helen was married to Jason's cousin Eddie, Eddie son of Abie, who was Jason's father Julie's identical twin, and what a rat's nest there

Jewish salami ersatz or no and sashimi and Japanese beers war for attention and sudden double vision around Thirtieth and Lex both things happening as he sees blurred in the crowd the image of his other self, as so many times before on three continents surprised by him on a London bus or at a bullfight in Alicante or in a Barcelona honkytonk the two of them watching with like fervor the enormous black woman in G-string bump and grind belting out "Yo negra soy!" BUMP! "Soy negra, yo," GRIND! until Jason distracted and wearing some neatly trimmed version of his red beard by then but it had never mattered whether cleanshaven in London or skull-shaven in Malmö or young and arrogant and weakchinned on the fast train to Tokyo or in New York by and by encountering the face and form of his identical twin too bad they never spoke or once only outside the *systembolaget* in Malmö queuing up with the working class to buy booze at six-thirty A.M. the pair of them safe behind dark shades exchanging pensive looks long time no see amigo Jason might have said not having bothered to learn much Swedish his live-in friend of the time bilingual and all the excitement of mastering exotic cultures long past by then or said nothing bought his booze and cradled it back to the apartment and thought when the morning wine was almost gone a sickly sweet Portuguese white called Fragal what he would say when next they met the same question he had always meant to put to his cousin Ed but somehow never had Did you know back then which one was your father?

Because more than once in ancient times the twins had teased the crap out of him most vivid always the miserable rainy Coney Island summer when Julie and Abe worked together in the city all week at the junkshop the salvage emporium his father liked to call it no dummy his father although no reader either leaving their wives to fend for themselves Monday morning to Friday night and coming to Coney together on weekends no idea what age he had been but not much more than single digits alone in the house up on the chair driven to action at last by the flies' pathetic buzzing consumed as he was even then by idiot compassion freeing them

one by one from the sticky yellow spiral but his grubby
fingers not delicate enough or else some poison did the
damage watching horrified as most dropped stone dead or
struggled mortally wounded to the floor but he kept at it
doggedly for the few who tipped their hats at him and
buzzed farewell

His father walking in just then directly from the city Hi,
Sonny, what are you up to up there? his father Julie did not
often call him Sonny (but neither did his uncle Abe) so he
said to his father I am freeing the flies and his father said
That's a good boy Jacey in his father's voice and left the
room while Jason buoyed continued trying to handle them
more gently so they might not die between his fingers and
just then his father walked into the room and said What are
you up to now, Son, and Jason said I am still freeing the
flies from the flypaper and his father said That's what it
looked like you were doing but I couldn't believe my fucking eyes now get the fuck off the chair why do you think
the flypaper is hanging there in the first place your mother
keeps telling me how smart you are in school and how she
doesn't like you hanging around the shop even after you
finish your homework with your dumb cousin Eddie and
other foulmouthed riffraff but if you're smart in school
you're a shmuck outside and Jason descended carefully vision clouded by tears but grief maybe the least part of what
he felt or could then or even now describe.

One thing you could say about cousin Eddie one tough
hombre growing up was that he saved Jason from physical
harm in the streets around the salvage emporium more than
once and if occasionally he wasn't there to bale him out he
would afterward avenge him but Eddie was gentler now in
his forties (Jason's senior by six months) and somewhere

along the way had had something done about that childhood glottal stop whereby a word like "bottle" came out "bohul" and he handled Helen's windfall with aplomb and even pride no longer driving or even (merely) owning medallion and cab but now running several limousines and happy in his work which eventually meshed to a degree with hers when she branched out a little into visiting firemen looking for a good time on MasterCard which could well include a stretch limo from the airport but Jason did not know and did not care to know a great deal about this aspect of her trade

Helen with a fraternal twin sister living on the West Coast so you might say Eddie married one but there for the time it ended none of their four kids nor even (when the time came) their kids' kids being twins

Uncle Abe and Aunt Trixie lived in Miami now and time and separate illnesses had done their work so only the un-tutored would confuse Julie with Abie and Jason's poor mother Tillie's task to continue tolerating their daily half-hour phone conversation right around the dinner hour it had been going on for years even when they still lived in the same city working all day at the same job and having parted company only fifteen minutes before.

He stood outside the Cedar Tavern on University Place, in Jason's day a painters' bar, where you might find yourself bending an elbow next to de Kooning, or someone as em-inent, and it might have been a painters' bar still, for all he knew, but it was where Maduras had wanted to meet. The editor would be coming from three streets away.

Sams was some twenty minutes early for his five-thirty appointment with Maduras. He and Pisacano had not spo-

ken since Paul offered him the use of his loft a week or
more ago, Jason remembering only now that he did not
have a key, no way of getting in, if Paul had forgotten the
conversation, or happened not to be there. The temperature
was dropping quickly. Sams wore, as usual, his thin black
jacket from Filene's. He spied three vacant phone booths,
or doorless half-booths (three-sided treehouse on a pole;
contraption new to him), on the other side of University
Place. None were in use. He crossed the street and entered
one, where he discovered soon enough that someone had
taken a sledgehammer to the phone, while in the next, which
at first glance seemed intact, the receiver was missing, but
the third seemed to function, although his dime bought him
only a faint recorded message to the effect that he was still
fifteen cents shy of the toll. Could it now cost all of a quarter
to make a local call? An unexpected surge of affection for
Boston and its backward ways went through him, as he
reached into his pocket and pulled out the proper coin. Paul
might be out at this hour; he wished he had nailed it down
with a long-distance call the night before.

The phone rang, once.

"Speak."

"Father!"

"The peripatetic Boston scribe? Welcome to our fair city,
Father."

"I thought I'd confirm the arrangements for the evening.
Do I still have a bed?"

"A bed, a fridge, a john. All the comforts of home except
booze. I'm very low in that department. Given your habits,
it's safer to say I'm completely out."

"I expect to be sufficiently tanked when I get there."

"You high now, Sams? Your diction is too precise."

"What we got working here is just an ordinary day."

"Why don't you fall by now, before you pass out? I got fettuccine. I got dago red. I got a lovely person shortly dropping by to dine."

"Thanks, but I'm scheduled to hoist a couple with an editor, after which I'm having dinner at the ancestral hearth. Will you be there later on, and if not, how do I get in?"

"I'll be out. I'll leave both doors open."

"You're kidding. I'm calling from a block of ravaged phone booths a few streets from where you live. This is New York."

"Relax, Father. Pretend it's Berkeley. Although you got some unfortunate memories of northern California also, I seem to remember."

"These days they lock their doors in Berkeley."

"Then the world's become a fearful mother, Father, if the West Coast is paranoid. What's with an editor? You coming out of retirement?"

"That's the plan."

"Good move. I ain't being invited to dine out on *Slow Dying* as often as I was of yore. What's the subject?"

"Myself, my life."

"You're yanking my dick, Father. You did that one already! You want a movie, don't you? There's no backing for a one-character movie. Wait, I have misspoke myself, Warhol did it twice. 'Sleep.' 'Blowjob.' "

"You're still my favorite critic, Pisacano."

"I think my company's arrived. Later, Father."

"Looking forward to it."

On his way back to the bar he imagined that he'd had a glimpse of Life imitating Art, Paul graciously attempting to sound like the Pisacano character had sounded in Sams' seven-year-old pages, whereas Jason knew Paul's life had traveled on apace, had taken some turns for the worse (seven lean years for them both), his lodgings now in jeopardy for one thing, the church whose rental property he had inhabited without incident or lease for the past fifteen years suddenly deciding they needed the space, threatening eviction; his sundry careers as artist and architect and developer and in his own words *macher* and *tummler* lately unravelling, his purportedly carefree attitude toward "ladies" having altered thanks to the sexual politics of the time and his finally running into the one for whom he would have abandoned all the rest and all future possibilities, but not knowing this until she had put up by her own reckoning with one indignity too many and fled to Spain, where she remained unreachable . . . you put somebody in a book with all the love and wit and guile and shuddering insight you can muster and they refuse to stay put sometimes even if they're dead, for new data may surface even from the grave and sock you in the chops, my lad, or your own considered view may change, and so, and thus, Beware romans à clef, my son, the jaws that bite, the claws that snatch

He entered the Cedar right behind a portly gent he thought he recognized from photographs, Maduras having received some play in the press as discoverer and redactor of Matilda Bang, runaway bestselling author of *Fucking Is Free;* at least Jason thought it was he, took a chance and introduced himself.

"Ralph? I'm Jason Sams." He was pleased to watch a flowering in the pursy face.

"Of course you are! And I would have guessed it, too, had you not surprised me from behind."

"My usual approach."

Maduras regarded him oddly. "Good to see you. Shall we take a booth?"

A man Jason thought he recognized as Imamu Baraka was just then vacating a booth with a group of friends. Sams had known him once when he was still Leroi Jones, had drunk with him more than once, vaguely remembered long and impassioned conversations, less likely to have been about politics than women (say), or poetry. Of course he could not remember where or when, nor what in fact they may have spoken of, but he was drunk enough to risk a nod, a mumbled hello, although he might have predicted that Leroi would look blankly through him, elbow past. The past wasn't prologue, for Jason; his history was some spectral film he wasn't even sure he'd been awake for. So nothing personal in Leroi's snub; hardly one at all if they had met only once, or never; even called for, you might say, from a man with two sets of names, encountering a man with none; he remembered the morning's dream, his name vanishing into the ceiling. He and Maduras waited while the table was swabbed, then slid into opposite sides of the booth. A waiter immediately appeared.

"Evening, Mr. Maduras. What can I get you?"

"Evening, Frank. Jason, what's your pleasure?"

"A . . . double J&B on the rocks." Not the brand he usually drank, but his father's favorite, or the one his father usually had on hand.

"I'll have the same. I suppose I should eat something as well. Jason, will you join me in some food?"

Sams, very hungry, very logy, thought it over; then reminded himself that he had been invited to sup with his folks, as it seemed to him now, and they would no doubt want to ply him with a number of his favorite foods. Who said a drunk (or this one) was slave to instant gratification?

The editor ordered a medium-rare hamburger and a side of fries. "My next appointment is with a boozehound, a shut-in. I doubt she'll have a thing in the house by way of food, and it makes her very unhappy if you bring your own."

"Who's that?" Jason asked, although he already knew.

"I suppose I shouldn't say, but . . ." Maduras let fall the name of the woman Sams had been asked to replace at UGB in the dim, distant days of 1974, the name that got him out of Woodstock and into Boston, and so saved his life. He'd heard somewhere that she'd discharged herself from Smithers almost instantly and had holed up in her apartment, where she drank around the clock and pursued her vocation. He remembered the strange surge of envy he'd felt upon hearing the news.

"She doesn't go out at all?"

"Heavens, no. They say she scarcely leaves her bed."

"But she's able to write?"

"Some small dropping off in quality, a few opine, but I must say I haven't noticed it myself."

"How does one write books in bed?"

"A la Proust, I suppose, although in her case more à la Erle Stanley Gardner, since she dictates everything she writes."

Maduras' burger arrived, but he ignored it for a time; Jason imagined the fat man was eyeing him shrewdly.

"Suppose I ought to watch my own intake," he dutifully mumbled.

"Oh, I shouldn't worry about it. She admits to having been at it since she was fourteen, some fifty years. I don't imagine you've been drinking quite that long?"

Sams struggled to return the smile. "Not that long."

"Well, Jason, I'm an admirer of your work, as I'm sure you know. Glad to have inherited you, so to speak, after the fate that befell poor Al. All of us at the house are delighted to hear you're well launched on something new. Now, how can I be of service to you?"

It was a terrific question, and Sams wasn't sure he any longer had the answer, if he had had it to begin with.

"I think I explained when I phoned you what the book is about?"

"The relationship between you and Al Seamans, opening out to explore the relations between editors and writers overall? Is that reasonably close?"

"Right on the money."

"Strange phrase, that. How does the book appear to you in terms of size: something bulky, or more on the order of the 'blessed nouvelle'?"

Haven't the fucking foggiest, Jason imagined for a moment he had said aloud. The plot, or whatever it was, had sounded even more threadbare in Maduras' summary than in his own as he had sat in the Japanese restaurant not too many hours earlier mulling over his Japanese past and mourning wasted opportunities.

He drained the scotch and looked into the man's hooded eyes, gateway to his hooded head, mysterious place where lies and truth had the same valence, where Matilda Bang or King Kong or whoever it was could climb the lists and appear "literary" while the true poet was dead meat, and while Al had been no less a businessman than this character, he had also been more. Absolute bullshit (which now and again, in the nature of things, Al had had to employ) made Seamans wheeze and retch, Sams had seen it happen; you were lousy at lying, Tott, it was harder for you I think than hitting the curveball, which is what truly changed your life, as I did not fail to remind you the Night of the Great Insanity to my undying regret, and Jason remembered his other dream, of ferrying Al home across the choppy waters, and his keening grief, so what he was doing in this noisy establishment apart from getting bombed was trying to make a buck, he now supposed, an honorable attempt to support me and mine, despite Mitchell having already pointed out the unlikelihood of money changing hands without at least some fraction of manuscript to offer, and his more or less absolute certainty now that his agent had been right.

"Blessed nouvelle sounds more like it. A minor masterpiece, that sort of thing. What do you think of the idea?"

"I'd be delighted to have a look at what you've done so far if you're not uncomfortable with that."

"Probably I'd want to finish first."

"Perfectly reasonable."

"What are the chances of a small advance to get me through the next six months or so? I just finished with a teaching job, the writing is going well, and I'd hate to have to interrupt the flow by looking for another job."

"Hum. I'd like to be able to help, Jason, but my sense of it is that before I came aboard some considerable sums had already been advanced. Or is that incorrect?"

"That is entirely correct."

"I could double-check with Herman, if you like; he may have other thoughts; but he's the one who would have to approve anything along those lines."

Ah, Herman the German, imported publisher, very same chap who had lured Seamans from the penultimate house with various emoluments ("editor-in-chief" loomed large), whatever it took to overcome Al's resistance to assaying the leap to his final eminence, and a final leap it was, with barely time for either of them to rue the error before Al was carried off, and who the devil perishes while playing golf? Tennis, yes, but *golf?* Old ramrod Herman hating Sams' grubby novel with patrician passion, above all the other populist and vulgar writers Seamans brought with him, or signed up. Herman shutting off with unseemly haste Seamans' health insurance, thereby inconveniencing no end the late editor's loved ones. Or so had gone one sorry version of the tale.

No money there.

"Well, Ralph, since you're to have your own imprint within the house I thought maybe you could end-run Herman, if you catch my meaning."

"Ah, my naive and talented friend, it doesn't quite mean that, I'm afraid." Don't be afraid, Jason thought, harking back to e.e. cummings, who never went out of style.

"Herman the German whatever his literary leanings has authorized you to pick up the present tab?"

"I beg your pardon?"

"I'd love another double, Ralph, but I'm not sure I can pay for the one I've had."

"I see." But he could not see the daub of ketchup on his fat cheek. "Drinks on your publisher, of course. I wish we could be more helpful, Jason. Please do have another."

They'll pay to get you loaded, buzzed his ungrateful brain, but they draw the line at feeding you and yours. He didn't really want another scotch. When the waiter came by he ordered what he did want, a draft beer.

They parted on good terms, as he would later remember that evening, rising and shaking hands shortly after Sams had virtually *guaranteed* a finished book in not a day over six months, a swell, crafted thing as complex yet readable as one could wish, well worth the six-year wait (the deadline in his signed contract had been the autumn of 1970), which

Ralph professed himself delighted to hear. You lying son of a bitch, why would you believe me when this time, usually the cockeyed drunken optimist, I hardly believe myself? Yet all at once the dream was back, not sad at all, he and Al barreling through the surf, maybe headed over the bridge to Peter Luger's for a steak, and the idea seemed resurrected, absolutely whole, just the two of us, Tott, and one still left alive to tell the tale.

He was staggering as he left the bar, not in the best condition to turn up at his folks', but the hefty walk crosstown through several no man's lands might go some little way toward straightening him out enough so that by the time he arrived both diction and gait would be presentable and he would be invited without scolding to dig into the delectables he fully expected to find in the refrigerator, cornucopia of his youth, the true-blue New York Hebrew National salami and the pickles from the barrels along Essex and creamed herring and unsurpassed lox from Houston Street and the Rokeach's gefilte fish he preferred even to his late grandmother's homemade of a decade earlier although unlike the military's pork tenderloin he was still searching for it did not even occur to him to look anywhere else for her jellied calves' feet with a touch of gristle since the taste indeed the experience was so subtle and elusive he knew instinctively it could not be duplicated or for that matter described although his aunt Lil now of the Bronx made a decent facsimile.

Until it struck him suddenly that all such goodies were laid in by his folks to mark an impending state visit by number-one son they had been *notified* about, and what he was more likely to find having given them no warning was his mother's leathery boiled chicken of which heaven knew he was no fan but hell's bells if that was all there was then he would eat it, by gum, slathered in Betamte's or Gulden's or even French's whichever mustard was on hand and by rummaging find whatever ethnic stuff might still lie around in the thirty-year-old fridge from some earlier entertainment, a salami butt, perhaps, and be more than grateful for it.

Moving east, he passed almost immediately out of the range of taverns and bustle and NYU and Washington Square Park and guitars and drug sales (of scant interest, pure juicer all his life) and other signs of activity, passing empty warehouses behind burned-out streetlights on deserted streets, not too wasted to know more than a trace of the fear that had blighted his childhood, blighted for that matter that part of his adulthood spent back in the neighborhood, between lonely vigils on exotic continents, chasing God knew what, first-rate sake and pints of bitter ale, Papa's Fundador and the Nordic's aquavit, whatever was on hand, not yet Aqua Velva thank God, to Whom, as he saw some stirring in a doorway just ahead, this might be an opportune time to address a word or two, but it was just a bum shifting position, reaching for the sneaky pete, and only three posh blocks north of where he passed (so quickly did neighborhoods change) Al's parents still sat at the kitchen table only two years down the road from the event they could not possibly have made any kind of peace with mourning their only child now ashes goddamn it to hell why didn't they have more than one kid and why hadn't his own parents presented him with a sibling or two so he need not be saddled with what he now felt was too awesome a responsibility so that (thus freed up) he could drink himself to death or (if it was so written) expire in his own blood on a dark Manhattan street at the hands of muggers or of drunken bums (acting untypically in concert) and either way the paralyzing fear of doom would be behind him.

"Tott," he said aloud, "DO YOU KNOW WHAT SHE DID? Do you have any idea what the bitch did?" Things happened even after you departed, for when she finally found it she sent me a copy of *Slow Dying* while my folks were visiting Boston as chance would have it thank heaven my mom was out walking with Jennifer and Jake and we sat at the dining room table my pop and me while he downed a recreational beer and I kept the edge on as I could see him gearing up for How goes your work, Son do you need any money, Son, that deadly logical progression and to delay it just a bit knowing the agonized pleasure the outcome would give us both his hand going into his pocket and fetching out his wallet and peeling off fifties and twenties I went abruptly downstairs to check on the mail and never even knew what I was bringing back up in a plain brown wrapper amidst the junk and bills until back at the table I picked it up with sudden foreboding thinking the handwriting looked familiar but it had been years since I'd seen it and it bore no return address nor legible postmark so I opened the package and encountered my own book a bit dogeared but sense enough to keep it from his eyes and when I opened the volume its heart had been excised Tott I shit you not a neat hole about an inch and a half square from the middle pages to the end made with a razor or some artist's tool she was an artist all right as you know but it did not end there as what she cut out she burned THEN POURED THE ASHES BACK INTO THE SPACE and that might have done it for the average cunt but not Christa there was a tiny note in there this time I knew the hand, all the cutting and burning mere prelude to the message: HEART AND SPIRIT MISSING no signature no curse upon my house none needed.

Tott, to move her to this act, might we have gone a jot too far? Or you, perhaps, not nearly far enough, one "cunt" or "cocksucker" too many littering those pages, judicious cutting called for, but you too respectful of the sacred text? Where are you when I need you? "COME BACK AND EDIT MY LIFE!"

What's that you've got there Son he asked and I gulped my drink and there was still inspiration in it for I answered Nothing much Pop my fans still send my own book to me to autograph maybe I should start charging them for it like a baseball player har har and he said You're better off writing a new one Son only keep your mother out of it the next time she's still upset by the things you had to say about her in *Slow Dying* leaving me astonished by the comment, and its source.

They had shlepped themselves to Boston to visit him. They had come via Amtrak. Jason's mother loved trains. Jason's father was indifferent to trains, would have rather flown. Jason had arranged (he thought) to meet them at Back Bay Station in Copley Square, rather than at South Station, which was further from where he lived. He arrived at Back Bay with half an hour to spare. He went down to the tracks and roamed the chilly cavern. Right on time, the Colonial chugged in. Crowds of people disembarked. Jason walked at a good clip up and down the platform, consternation growing, looking for his parents. The platform gradually emptied. A conductor leaned away from the train, peering both ways. Once more their signals had crossed, it appeared, his mother and father were headed for South Station, if they were even on this particular train. Jason considered leaping into the Valiant and racing the train to South Station, but to what end? They would take a cab from there, as they usually did from the airport. As the Colonial began to pull slowly from the station, he headed toward the escalator. But he turned round for a final glance. He saw his mother appear suddenly as if propelled onto the platform, saw two large suitcases come flying after her, then his father hit the ground running and loped for a spell alongside the train, giving the conductor a piece of his mind.

The conductor had blasted his whistle and brought the train to a screeching halt. He looked chastened under the barrage.

Jason retraced his steps. "Hi, Mom."

"Did you see that, Jacey? What your father did?"

"Hello, Son."

"Hi, Pop."

"Conductor's supposed to wait until everyone's off the train, the shmuck." He spoke through an unlit cigar.

"Julie, you're such a stupid fool!"

"Shut your trap. We're here, right?"

To Sams this was not a persuasive argument, but he suspended judgment.

"What happened, exactly?"

"*After* they called out the station he decided he had to take a crap."

"Jeez, Pop, I live five minutes from here."

"When you gotta go, Son . . ." Julie went to round up the suitcases, which had landed a distance from the track. Jason beat him to the larger bag.

Then he threw his free arm across his mother's shoulders

and pecked at her cheek. It was not his customary manner, and seemed to surprise her, but Jason thought it justified by the circumstances. She looked much smaller than the last time he'd seen her. But she might have lost some height in the past five minutes.

"How goes it otherwise, Tillie?"

Julie, as always, had pushed on ahead. A gnarled and rolling gait, but still fast enough to outdistance any and all impediments to his life.

"I'm insane to go on living with this man."

"Nobody's insane. Let's just pretend the visit's starting now. OK?"

"I'll try, Jacey. But try to imagine living with an individual without an ounce of bowel control."

Sams could imagine. In the last few years he'd been importuned this way himself, insides beginning to churn with little or no warning, aims in life suddenly constricted to pinning down the whereabouts of the nearest toilet. It must have been a late-flowering gene, later even than the one for the horrendous sneezing fits he had dismissed as recently as ten years ago as just another sad crudity of his father's. But he also, nowadays, blew his wife and kid away.

He quickened his pace. As nuts as they, he actually looked forward to the next hour or two, beginning (when he rang the bell) with their surprised delight. Absolutely happy he had not warned them of his coming.

Born-and-bred New Yorker, he cannily crossed Third A venue against the lights as the traffic roared and lumbered by, walked down St. Marks, glanced into the Five Spot, jazz joint supreme that had been there forever, smiled he hoped in friendly fashion at the young and not so young milling about the street in jeans and greenish orange hair, leftover sixties' hippies crossed with seventies' *anomie,* or some such thing, he had not learned absolutely nothing up there on the Heights in old man Casey's sociology class, glanced uptown along Second Avenue toward St. Marks Church in which W. H. Auden had read his poetry and at a later date Allen Ginsberg his, Sams wary of slighting fellow alumni and contemporaries on their borrowed home turf in the East Village however unsavory their lives and work (how broad had been, at times, the mentor's taste!) appeared to him, walked along Second Avenue past the Second Avenue Delly not Deli with the huge salamis and k-nubblewurst in the window, but also new places to buy of all things tortillas and falafel, but it remained his world, the one he had grown up in, street bums seeking handouts with their shelter still where it had always been on East Third Street between Second and Third Avenues (now the Bowery); crossed Second Avenue and headed east once more.

A Death
in the Family

HE WALKED NOW with caution down the long decrepit block between First and Second, where amidst the ancient tenements with fire escapes running down their blackened faces had been situated since '63 or so what was said to be Hell's Angels' headquarters for the nation, or perhaps (given his tendency toward exaggeration, dolled-up memory) HQ for Angel activity east of the Mississippi River. It was a modest complex, either way: garage-style cavern, alongside and above it a three-story brick building containing (he imagined) both office and living space, the whole once a blacksmith's shop, perhaps, and as usual three or four Harley XQ41's (he invented) standing lonely on the sidewalk, as if inviting an attempt at theft, so that their monster owners might appear from nowhere and pummel your brains out. The unattended bikes were illuminated eerily by a sodium streetlight, with not a soul in sight, but Sams cautiously "crossed over" (phrase from childhood) and kept an eagle eye on the place from the other side of the street while appearing to look straight ahead. He was of course reminded by the uneventful passage of his near-misadventure with a motorcycle club in Woodstock days: he'd been doing some

serious solitary drinking on the patio of the Espresso Tavern
one summer night, only deciding that the wine had lost its
savor when the unkempt and boisterous crew arrived and
took over a couple of nearby tables (not precisely scared
shitless, mind you, simply not yet drunk enough to know
that nothing, ever again, could harm him), and so he popped
into the Toyota, parked right out front, not even his own
car but on loan from his friend Robert Stone, who was in
London (and Stone, superb writer and drinker, at home
everywhere, would have known instinctively how to handle
this, if there was anything to handle), finally discovered
where the key went (not in the windshield), and backed the
car fortunately rather gently into a single shiny motorcycle
which took down the other six like dominoes.

All the tales he'd ever heard of motorcycle mayhem, of
individuals discovered (usually, thankfully, already dead)
with their balls sewn into their mouths (and he fancied he
could tell from a quick glance which of the immense tattooed
wild-bearded motherfuckers carried the needle and thread,
which the bullock blade) propelled him from the car and
around it to the pavement, where too frightened to do any
more than look briefly at the throng — it appeared that none
had moved; they simply stared out at the carnage, as aghast
as he was — he proceeded with amazing strength and grace
to right the seven bikes and dust them off with the bottom
of his University of Kentucky Go Wildcats T-shirt (gift
from his downhome sister-in-law Verline, who understood,
indulged, his poseur passions), quite sure that the symbolic
wiping would not suffice as restitution, but hoping it might
mitigate his punishment.

But all that happened was that two of them gestured
threateningly with their huge arms and an already waning

indignation, made some unflattering remarks (or flattering, for all he knew, or could make out from where he was: he had performed, after all, perhaps in record time, a super-human feat), and hardly believing they would let him go this easily, since among the seven there had to be at least one crazed sadistic freak thirsting for vengeance, and another dying to watch, he climbed back into the Toyota in what seemed to him the slowest of slow motion, took (for cau-tion's sake) a circuitous route back to his summer house turned year-long prison, and once safely there, did not leave its confines and counted his blessings and drank nothing stronger than black coffee for a number of days.

The Angels, too, were law-abiding, it was said, or cer-tainly did not shit where they ate, were not only peaceable but helped the overworked cops in the Ninth Precinct keep at least the street they lived on free of crime and drugs. Jason had never cared to check out the truth of this, à la Hunter Thompson, à la his friend Jack Newfield (also orphaned by Al's sudden departure), à la anybody of the ilk. The role of "J. Sams, Investigative Reporter," willing to get his ass reamed out for his convictions, or just compelled to dig for and reveal the outrageous truth of things, had never par-ticularly drawn him. Contentedly awestruck bystander to unholy Angel din when they roared off for points and ad-ventures unknown.

Near First Avenue he raised his eyes to the crucifix atop the green dome of the Catholic church between Avenues A and B, the guarantor (at last) of safety. He had grown up with one of the church's four enormous clock faces right outside the apartment windows, back in the days when all four clocks worked and the great bonging bells within the tower sounding at seven sharp each weekday morning woke him for school from fourth grade on, dispatched the gangly, pimpled, unloveable thing he had become off to Seward Park High School on Grand and Essex Streets, Seward's Folly, and bonged again at noon when he was rarely there to hear them, and bonged forlornly at seven P.M. all through the winter of his first semester at Columbia College (before his mother convinced his father to spring for the tiny off-campus room), heralding his lonely life, his reading-burdened melancholy evenings.

Vivid still was the smell and feel of fresh plaster in his nostrils when his parents brought him for the first time to the building across the street from the enormous church while the building was still being constructed, the year he was eight, and he thought he remembered that the looming presence of the enemy so close at hand almost persuaded them to look for lodgings elsewhere, but the reasonable rent and the amenities-to-come must have made up for that. Through the 1940s every occupant but one (apart from the succession of black "supers" living in the same ground-floor apartment) of the six-story building had been Jewish — who else could have afforded to live in a building so splendid it came with a name, the Colonial Hall, the four white Jeffersonian pillars at the entrance as well as the brass fixtures on both sets of wooden doors leading to inner and outer lobbies so American and tony as to almost compensate for the sometimes slow, sometimes too-fast elevator that figured in young Jason's nightmares, shooting him at times right through the roof and into space, where the fantasy would end, or as often (in dreams) down to a sub-sub-basement far below the washing machines and the furnace and the bicycle and baby carriage storage room where it would then move horizontally through a chamber of Coney Island horrors, JoJo the Dogfaced Boy reaching for him, Jason obliged now to confront the no-longer-genial Reptile Man. The sole tenants remaining from that early time were his parents, still occupying the one-bedroom on the fifth floor, and the Greenbergs, both of whom were hopelessly arthritic, in the two-bedroom on the third, doughty survivors into the time when Spanish not Yiddish was the neighborhood's second language, and the brass was long gone from the outer doors, and junkies shot up in the vestibules. The pockmarked pillars had long ago turned dingy, gray.

Young Jason, keeping his counsel, had always loved the church, from his particular private clock face and the great hidden bongers on down (the crucifix crowning it all a more recent enthusiasm), loved watching from the fifth-floor windows pagan pageants like Easter and Christmas and the beautiful, decked-out Christians they drew, or conjured, loved most of all playing punchball for years on the long stretch of sidewalk fronting the cathedral, an activity the rugged-faced priests rarely objected to, and he struck many a ground-rule triple into old Rasmussen's cellar, hadn't thought of *that* individual in some little while; he had looked exactly as a mortician should, six feet eight inches tall and sounding like the undertaker sounded on the Jack Benny Show, and far from delighted to discover some snotnosed Jewish athlete in pursuit of a rubber ball climbing down into his cellar.

Jason saw his first corpse through the mail slot in Rasmussen's frosted door, a well-dressed fellow in a blue suit with a little smile on his ruddy face and white hair combed back in waves, not so different from the ones young Sams was trying hard just then to cultivate, guy peacefully supine under a canopy that looked like the one Jason had seen once at a wedding, and if you looked at him long enough the bastard breathed! Breathing corpse wrote finis for a time to all such peering, and, in the nighttime horror show, for a while preempted JoJo in the elevator dreams.

And once there had been an actual *garden* next to and belonging to the Colonial Hall, where you could play after school and bring your friends and explore its narrow recesses around to the rear, a green garden where caterpillars lived, padlocked off and barren now these twenty years, but not entirely bricked in and sealed with concrete until recently when the street his parents lived on became the Drug Capital of the Western World, or was so designated by *Time* magazine, and indeed stretch limos with out-of-state plates cruised down Avenue B and up the block to buy any mood-altering substance the occupants desired through narrow slots in metal doors, until Someone in Authority happening to glance at *Time* despatched squad cars and paddy wagons which in no time at all cleaned the small fry off the street; a sequence that Jason's father, who worked now in a small shop around the corner, and as a favor to the damned changed their tens and ones into fives so they might buy themselves the nickel bags they craved, the people who dealt drugs behind the slots not interested in making change, had solemnly confirmed.

There was no public phone convenient to him now, even if he decided at the last minute to warn his parents of his coming, and he would need he now realized a little bit of luck, since the graffiti-covered door (brass handles not even a memory) leading from the street to the outer vestibule was still often locked these days, preventing access even to the bank of bells that got you into the building, and if it was locked he'd be obliged to find a phone somewhere, or else stand below the apartment's windows whistling up five floors the way his father used to whistle, Johnny's Got the Measles, or what was the lyric that went with the almost tuneless tune, the almost-forgotten family music, but (luck holding, door open, someone having made off entirely with what lock there had been) he had the opportunity instead to give the family ring, three rings of equal duration, not your subtlest signal but it had worked for his parents since before he was born, and it worked more or less now, his mother booming out, "WHO IS IT?" never having come to trust the technology, and Sams (somewhat surprising himself) simplified her life by booming back, "IT'S JACEY, MA," old J.C. himself, Ma, neurotic potted scribe ringing your doorbell without warning as perfect coda to his pointless day, and do you happen to know who it *really* is, rolling down the road to Mama's house? Do you know who that middle-aged drunken loser really is? It's Christ Himself, Ma, ah Ma, Ma, it's Jesus Christ Himself! And Sams knew that had he been tanked enough to act out this charade his mother would have managed to appear unsurprised, hip as she was to the antic literary temperament, remaining at seventy a great reader and indefatigable taker of courses, "The Old Testament as Literature" at the YMHA on East Fourteenth Street, "American Writers of the Twentieth Century" at the New School for Social Research (and why, she would plague the poor instructor, wasn't her estimable son's name on that list?), and she would say with the solemnity the situation called for, "Why do you want to make fun of J. D. Salinger, Jacey (let alone think that at this stage in life I can be baited or shocked by the mere mention of Christ)? Salinger still has a lot to teach us, despite being a slow writer like yourself." And while the imaginary exchange passed through his sodden brain she "ticked back" (translation from the Yiddish? family argot merely?), leaning on the bell long enough to allow ingress to a hostile army, let alone a son.

Passed quickly through the denuded lobby, once furnished like a living room, kerosene-style lamps and carpets depicting scenes from the Revolutionary War and oak sofas with flowery upholstery someone's bastardized idea of how things must have looked in Colonial times, he couldn't even tell you just when it had become this empty shell, but these appointments had been gone for years, vandalized or ripped off or removed by a cautious landlord, and he summoned the elevator (same one now as then, from time to time refurbished) and rode it fearlessly to the fifth floor, expecting her to be waiting there in the hall when the door opened, but she was not, though the apartment door (with its triple locks) was ajar by way of greeting. He pushed it open and entered, staring from the entranceway directly into the kitchen, from which his mother now emerged. Looking right at him, she asked, "Jason?" Confirming to her satisfaction that it was he, she said, "Let me give you a hug," and he stooped to the embrace and to the loving glare, looking beyond her and off to the right into the living room, the china shop, at the endless things accumulated in a lifetime, some few of considerable value, and as always he took comfort in the ones he recognized from childhood, the porcelain man in the nightcap with eyes crossed staring at the fly on the tip of his nose, the round, distorting, gilded mirror beneath its heavy eagle. Once his father's junkshop had been the source of much of this; now it was his father's job in a shop that sold and purchased everything, a cornucopia of crap and treasure, things acquired in bulk from the Bureau of Encumbrances, Dickensian or Kafkaesque designation for the branch of city government whose function it was to collect the goods of people — retired army colonels, obscenely rich recluses — who died intestate and without family, and people whose goods and chattel for whatever reasons wound up on the sidewalk in front of where they once had lived. His father's store bid on these "estates," and more often than not came away with truckloads of stuff, from Modiglianis to busted vacuum cleaners, grand pianos to mooseheads, ur-typewriters, coin collections. Sometimes his mother would drop over to the store to see what had arrived at Harry's. At other times his father (although knowing the risks) brought something home he thought she might possibly enjoy.

How had young Sams lived in that apartment, grown up there? Hadn't been a sign for many years of his nightly presence in the room in which they stood; he supposed you could call it a room, ample, doorless space right off the living room, leading to the kitchen, without a trace of privacy. They called it a foyer, same name they gave to the short narrow hallways that connected other rooms. Bookcases and a highly polished, oddly shaped tan table, chachka-laden, occupied the corner where his bed had once been (disguised as a sofa by day). How had he grown to adulthood, done homework, masturbated, slept, read, thought, written, entertained friends, and, most difficult to fathom, holed up there twice in artistic and spiritual and financial disarray after his return in less than triumph from Japan, and (thirty-one years old!) after his desperate return from Europe, six years later? THERE WAS NO THERE THERE, as

Gertrude Stein was said to have said about Oakland, California; here was the Oakland of one-bedroom apartments.

His father emerged from the bathroom, to the left of which, invisible from where Sams stood, was the bedroom and its twin beds with their intricate mahogany headboards wherein had lurked (particularly at dawn) a zooful of monsters; but the bedroom also contained a "secretary," with a flimsy folddown desk, and *that* had been how he had done it, there at any rate was where he'd done his homework and courted his young muse and made his filthyminded phonecalls on the extension phone and Jesus, ungrateful pup that he was, he must have had two or three times the lebensraum either of his parents ever had growing up, with armies of siblings to cope with, in no more space than this . . .

"Hi, Pop."
  "Hello, Boy."
  "Grabbing a nap?"
  "I was in the can. Before that, I was watching a little TV. What brings you down? To what do we owe the pleasure?"
  You had to be there; or at least privy to his (fifth grade dropout) old man's comelately pleasure (as the writer's father) in his own, his native language: the very father who in his own words had trapassed (traipsed) to Greenwich Village one Saturday afternoon late in '69 after the bad news which he didn't recognize as such was in and bought up every remaindered one-dollar copy of *Slow Dying* he found in the bin inside the store, dickering with Doubleday, as was his custom, so as to also purchase the one in the window, the one that had drawn him into the store, which they would no longer be needing with no further copies in the store to sell; gave them all away to lucky colleagues except

for the pair he kept in the front window of the maroon diesel Mercedes he was driving at the time, kept them there for years, where they flanked his other talisman, the plaque that read "Support Your Local Police."

Which is to say that Julius Sams' remark, *To what do we owe the pleasure,* was born of homage (love), not irony.

"Found myself in the neighborhood."

His father approached, hugged him without a by-your-leave, and, to Sams' amazement, planted a kiss on his mouth.

"Sure. What's Boston, two hundred fifty miles?"

"All right. Came in on a business trip. Had to see my publisher. Then I thought, why not drop down and surprise them."

All business suddenly, his father asked, "So what came of the talk with your publisher?"

"Too early to tell. Let's celebrate anyway. You up for a drink, Julie?" He shot a worried glance at his mother, who sat at the kitchen table, or more accurately at the dining room table (two adjoining alcoves, but he knew what the nomenclature meant to her); she fingered her spent Sabbath candles — the room filled with the burnt tallow smell; he had forgotten it was Friday night — and he was pleased to see that she still beamed, that the thought of the two of them indulging in a little schnaps had not dampened her pleasure.

He wished he'd been there for the ancient ritual, seen his mother put on the shawl and cover her face and pray the prayers welcoming in the Sabbath. He remembered then the older ceremony, her mother his grandmother Molly praying the same prayers in the crowded flat on the vanished street with an enormous doomed carp swimming in the four-footed tub and the baking smells and then or at some other time Molly in some mystic rite swinging the still-living chicken over and around her head, and the strangers his seltzerman grandfather who always smelled of Turkish cigarettes and schnaps would bring in off the street, and how after he died she was able to move into this very building and live on the same floor in a life much constricted and changed, but in high school and after he still went in there every Friday night and watched his grandmother light her candles. And he listened for hours to her stories, of the strange creatures she had not even imagined could exist when already nearly twenty she pursued her husband-to-be to London, and he took her to the zoo. Helped him sell hot dogs from a pushcart in New York on the immigrant-crowded streets of the Lower East Side before their first-born Jason's mother was born, before old Joe even dreamed of having the money to buy the seltzer wagon and the horse that went with it. Loved his grandmother as he loved her young daughter his aunt Lil, who babysat him first, herself no more than eleven or twelve at the time, and he would always be grateful that he was past all his to-ing and fro-ing when his grandmother died, had been there in New York to help her sons his uncles carry her coffin.

And the thirtyish rabbi with the full red wiry beard and gentle face who appeared from somewhere to preside was another of his damnable identical twins, but this time too close to the mark, because Sams knew it could well have been and probably should have been him, sweet alto that he'd been, cantor for the Mosof service at his own bar mitzvah back in the days when he'd loved the old language they taught in Hebrew school and loved reading in it as if for the first

time of the tricky doings of his forefathers and their re-
monstrations with the Lord, awed anew each time by
Ruach, the "great wind," God's own inventive spirit moving over the face of the inchoate waters. Saying in the old
language Let there be light, and there was light, and it was
good! To be one day forever deflected by . . . what? his
poor father's prayers, Julie's faithful mumbling morning
and night in a language he did not comprehend and could
not pronounce, putting on the tefillin every weekday morning, black boxes with bits of Exodus and Deuteronomy
sealed inside, first kissing the things then the mindless precision of the winding? When Jason turned thirteen he had
a go at "laying tefillin" himself, and did not mind until
the old man's fearful mumbojumbo finally stuck in his craw,
just about the time the interdictions of the Sabbath came
into conflict with important softball games, or vital Dodger
games at Ebbets Field. But in a Jewish cemetery somewhere
in Queens in his thirty-third year Jason recognized when
the young rabbi glanced his way and their eyes met and
held a look that told him his twin too had met and faced
down all such trivial obstacles to his calling. Never before nor since has Sams yearned toward his gilded mirror
image with such hopeless passion, although in this instance
the holy man is clearly troubled by having to find the right
things to say about a woman he does not know, knowing nothing of the London zoo, the shame her illiteracy
caused her, nothing at all of turn-of-the-century hot dog
sales.

So he helped lower her plain coffin and watched his gentle
grandmother go for the second time into the ground. He
had been there sixteen years earlier too when with a cry and
an audible intake of breath that would creep into her speech

thereafter she threw herself onto her husband's coffin between the first and second shovelfuls of earth, and these, all these — no addled drunk at seventeen, not yet — were memories he trusted.

"Maybe a quick schnaps."

His father's face, Jason noticed, had turned grave.

"How's Jenny and the kid?"

"Jake's fine. Jennifer's fine."

"I assume you heard the news?"

They stood in the kitchen, Jason in the act of reaching into the cabinet above the ancient fridge where the liquor had always been kept, about to play host to his father with his father's stash, the bottomless supply of wholesale J&B.

"I don't know, Pop." For some bizarre reason he was waiting for a joke, likely one he'd heard before, the kind enjoyed by the feeble chap in Woodstock he sometimes gave a lift into town: "You better keep your eyes open today, Jason Sams." "Why's that, Gerry?" (no killjoy he). Followed by the cackle, the gleeful rubbing together of hands: "So you can *see*, dummy!"

"What news?"

"Your Uncle Abie died."

"He WHAT?"

"He passed away this past Wednesday. You knew he'd been in the hospital for a while." (Jason hadn't.) "But the cancer in his prostrate went out of control, ate right through his body. They sent him up from Florida this morning. We'll bury him Sunday. Your mother didn't tell you?"

Tillie tried to get her oar in, but Jason stepped on her lines.

"My mother didn't tell me. My father didn't tell me. My cousin Eddie didn't tell me. His social worker wife didn't tell me. That's their business, but what the fuck is wrong with *you* people? What are you trying to protect me from?"

"Don't be angry with us, Jacey," Tillie said. "I thought you'd be too busy writing and teaching to come to the funeral, so I didn't see the point in giving you news that might upset you."

"Terrific. And you? He was your twin brother. You also thought I was writing and teaching?" He was not sure why he continued.

"I thought your mother let you know. Anyway, what's the big difference? You're in town now, he's still dead, so you'll be at the funeral. Keep your pants on, Son."

He kept his pants on. He wrote down the address of the funeral parlor, gulped his scotch, which had almost slipped his mind, and opened the refrigerator. As he had feared, there was little in there but the remains of a chicken, boiled unto a second death. Normal fare for a Sabbath eve.

"If we'd known you were coming, Jacey, I would have had Dad shop for the things you like."

"You don't do your own shopping anymore?"

"Only by my grocer on Avenue A, or the kosher butcher down the block. Not in the specialty stores on Essex, or Houston, or Delancey. They're overrun by the Spanish element. I had a gold chain yanked off my neck right outside Russ's about six months ago."

"You never told me that, either."

"Why should she tell you? After you finished worrying about it, what? You would have captured the perpetrator?"

"They never caught him?"

"Be realistic, Jacey. You think the cops are any help? I've still got the red marks on my throat from where he ripped the thing off. Here, let me show you."

She lowered her face to him. There was a red circle, mercifully faded, all around her neck.

"Jesus. Maybe you guys ought to stop bullshitting each other and really move out of the neighborhood."

"You think it's any better anywhere else?"

"Yeah, Dad, I do."

"Well maybe where you are, but not in New York. Crap like that goes on everywhere."

"You think he'll ever move now, when he can walk to work around the corner? The spicks could tear my head off, and he wouldn't move."

" 'Spicks'?" Jason chastened his Bible-studying mother.

"All right, Hispanics. One word comes from the other, doesn't it? He'll move himself down to Florida with a chippy after I'm dead and buried, that's when he'll move."

His father chuckled and chewed on an unlit cigar. "Your mother's a bit nuts," he announced sagely.

Jason knew the ancient drill, setting him up with this third-person garbage not even as some useful arbiter but as more-or-less captive audience, doing it to him even on the phone, his mother on the kitchen phone and his father on the bedroom extension bitching at each other right through him, then remembering he was there, and switching to Your father did, Your mother is, until he threatened to hang up (did so once, to their pained surprise; they learned nothing from the rebuke), but in the present, stuck right here in person, unless he wished to storm out into the night, which he did not, a different strategy would be required.

"All right, listen, back to my empty stomach and the empty larder, I noticed a jar of gefilte fish in there. Some creamed herring. Why don't I just put up a pot of coffee, and I'll be fine."

"No no, let me make the coffee. You never knew how to perk a pot of coffee."

This was true; who perked coffee anyway, these days, when no less an American personage than Joe DiMaggio advocated drip, in a particular machine? But his mother, hip (she called it "hep") as she was, had no reason to pay homage to Joltin' Joe, or to his new means of livelihood: she continued to do magic with her three different-size coffee pots, her own proportions, her own crazy alchemy. She used an ornate three-minute egg timer picked up at Harry's shop and she waited until the last grain of sand trickled through the neck before removing the pot from the stove. Even so, there should have been no way to percolate a decent (an exceptional!) pot of coffee in three minutes flat, except she did it, had done it for years. Sams knew for a fact the feat was unduplicatable; when others, like himself, tried it, even with her beloved Maxwell House, they came up with tan bilge.

"Make me a cup also, Tillie," his father said.

"Not while you pollute my kitchen with that foulness."

"I'm *chewing* it, for God's sake. The thing ain't even lit." As part of his selective observance of the Sabbath Julie Sams wouldn't smoke, from sundown on Friday night to sundown on Saturday. At one time in his life he wouldn't work on the Sabbath, or drive his car, or flick on a light, but those pious days were behind him.

"Why didn't you ask for coffee before I put up the small pot?" she persisted. "Now I have to go through all the mishegaas of changing to the midsize pot."

"So change pots," Julie said.

So long as they railed at each other in the second person, mano a mano, Jason felt protected. He went to the fridge, served himself two elliptical pieces of the fish in the jellied broth (really the broth he was after), found the thin glass bottle of red horseradish in the door of the refrigerator and dolloped it out with the aid of a teaspoon, noticed three bottles of Rheingold beer in there also (hadn't seen the brand in years), and opened one.

"Anybody else care for a beer?"

"I'll have one," his mother said.

"Since when do you drink beer?"

"I drink beer. Why should you be the only shikker in the family?"

"Are you joking, or do you want the beer?"

"Son, she asked for a beer, so open her a beer."

"You want one?"

"I'll share hers."

Jason pried the caps off two bottles of beer and brought them to the table. He brought three glasses. A great time to keep his mouth shut, he knew, but when had either he or his mother resisted a clear call to arms?

"I can't help thinking, Tillie, there's implicit in all of this some kind of moral instruction. I already had a scotch, right? Coffee's almost ready? So why do I need a beer in between? So you'll ask for one, to make your point. Well, I'm having dinner, partaking of food, is why I need a beer."

"Jacey, if you play all the parts yourself, who needs a conversation? You're a novelful of characters walking the streets, no wonder you're in no hurry to write another one."

"A nice observation, Tillie. But you called me a 'shikker,' an ugly Yiddish word for 'drunk,' am I right? I find that offensive." He paused to sip his beer.

"Find it what you have to find it. I can't help what I see. I get the distinct impression sometimes you carry on like some kind of alcoholic."

"There's only one kind," Jason announced, with no idea how he had come by that particular piece of information.

"Maybe she's right, Son," his father chimed in. "Maybe from time to time you drink to excess."

"Well, it's been a difficult day. How's Trixie taking Abe's death?"

"How do you take a thing like that? She's taking it lousy."

"Where is she?"

"She's here, staying with Ed and Helen. Later she'll decide what she wants to do, live in Florida, move back up to New York, or what."

"And you? How are you getting through it?"

His father shrugged, looked away. "I'll be fine."

"What do you take with it, Jacey, sugar, or the thing in the packets? I must be getting senile. I can't believe I don't remember how you take your coffee."

"The thing in the packets."

Without thinking, he pulled a cigarette from the inside pocket of the black jacket he still wore. He knew at once it was a mistake, but not how much of one until his mother made as if to grab it from his hand.

"You still smoke?! Well not in *my* house. And not on a Shabbas night."

"I'll take it out into the hall."

"They're no safer out in the hall. What do you think killed your Uncle Abie?"

"Prostate cancer."

"That spread all over his body," his father said. "She's probably right, Son. He was a very heavy cigarette smoker, your Uncle Abe."

It was very likely true. They had exactly the same genes, Abe and Jules, and his father, chewing on his unlit cigar, looked as hale as could be. His other father had been carried off by bladder cancer just the year before, also merely seventy, always with an unfiltered smoke dangling from the corner of his mouth, even on the memorable occasion the pair of them had taken a leak at the Columbia faculty club at adjacent urinals that differed oddly in style, conventional long marble one next to the douche with the dolphin lip, which of them had used which he no longer remembered, might well be recorded in his journal of the time, but he recalled clearly that even as they voided, the great scholar/writer/teacher puffed blue wreaths of smoke around his head, squinting into the wall, the middle distance. Sams never read a word anywhere to the effect that cigarettes caused or were implicated in bladder or prostate cancer, but he knew.

(Knew also that failing to bestir himself the previous year to travel to New York and lose himself anonymously among the multitudes attending Trilling's memorial service had been one of the great drunken blunders of his life.)

His own smoking had not diminished.

His mom was an ex-smoker, five years clean (so she had puffed away herself — though rarely more than half a pack a day — until the age of sixty-four; gave young son some leeway!), and ex-smokers are intolerant.

He prepared to go into the corridor.

"Sit!" Tillie commanded. "Stay! Smoke! I don't see you often enough to worry about how incorrigible you are. How's Jake doing in school?"

"Tearing up kindergarten two." He inhaled, turned his head and blew smoke toward the doorway. "He's a bright kid," Julie said, watching his only son inhale and exhale, with no envy, no temptation whatsoever, to break his Sabbath vow. "Don't smoke it all the way down," he cautioned. "That's what my brother did, for fifty years. Down by the end's where the poisons are."

"That's what the filter's for."

"Filter don't mean shit."

What was he going to do with this pair? They (often he could not separate their messages) were going to protect him from life, for life! Should one of *them* happen to die (if by some miracle either predeceased him), the other might never reveal it!

And yet their own lives had not been without adventure. He had grown up in this house, crown prince, fifth wheel, yet what did he really know about them? Shocked as they were (or he'd imagined they would be) by his marrying out of the faith, he could not have readily predicted that his mother would be delighted to see him (at the late age of thirty-six) married off at all, or that his father would be crazy about Jenny, but beyond even that, that they would get it together some years later to drive down to Appalachia from Manhattan and then jounce down back-country roads and then down the rutted tractor path into the holler (following behind her father's pickup) in that selfsame Mercedes in late spring his father driving all the way since his mother had never learned how in order to visit and get to know their *machatanim,* great Hebrew word become Yiddish indicating the parents of one's offspring's spouse, and that the four of them would hit it off. Jason's father saying to Jason's father-in-law in the general store in town, "You know how to fight?" when Cletis made as if to pay for a purchase, as the farmer had been doing at that store all his life, and Cletis saying with a broad grin, "I don't reckon I get much call these days for fightin'," and Julie saying, "Well you're going to have to learn how to fight if you try to take money from your pocket," then pulling out the huge wad of bills Jason had never known him to be without and Cletis grinning still more broadly and saying to the shopkeeper, "This here's Julie, my kinfolk from New York; he'll pay," bad Broadway heartwarmer, Neil Simon cleaning out his drawer, but there it was, the two of them bouncing along in the pickup from the general store to the cucumber pickling factory so that Julius might see how it was done and Cletis with a listener at last who cared about the price of beans, and that the women too would hit it off, and that his parents would sleep for four nights without a murmur of complaint together in the sagging doublebed in Jennifer's former room now the guest room with the tickytack figure of Christ on the mantel that blinked on and off and that his davening father would pray there morning and night, and recalling the trip afterward with a humor his son until then had not known Julie (around this subject, anyway) possessed, would say, "Why should a blinking Jesus bother me, Son? When you're trying to talk to God, you take all the help you can get," Jenny's mother Opal discovering early that her daughter's mother-in-law would not or could not eat pork in fact could not abide the sight of it but would eat chicken for four days straight so served her chicken cooked four different ways, Tillie carefully watching the preparation (but from the look of the dried-out bird Jason had glimpsed in the fridge, not much had been learned), appreciative of all the work Opal was doing, while what the two of them spoke of, and they spoke nonstop, remained a mystery . . . that all or any of this would take place he could not in a million years have foreseen, or invented. He might have been able to imagine this: once the trip was done, and it came time for the Samses to return to the Drug Capital of the Western World, and they climbed into the maroon Mercedes laden now with jars of preserves and a bushel basket containing ears of corn and another containing the most succulent of beefsteak tomatoes and enormous but nonetheless sweet-tasting cucumbers, foods both wife and mother loved, Sams' parents would observe that the kind of sadness their departure caused to fall upon the now familiar Appalachian faces of their machatanim was of a kind reserved only for European Jews, survivors of pogroms, or so they'd believed until then.

He lit another cigarette, briefly in awe of them both. The scotch and beer, the recollection of things he had not seen, filled him with warm loving thoughts. But he knew it was fragile; knew he was extremely tired, and would have to keep his wits about him to turn aside the invitation that was sure to follow.

He phoned Boston, but Jenny wasn't home. The sitter answered, a zaftig nineteen-year-old who lived in the university dorm across the street, once a luxury hotel, the very hotel (although, since he'd been no alumnus, no commemorative plaque announced the fact) where Eugene O'Neill had lived his final weeks, and died. So poor Sams could never drive the sitter home, act out or at least imagine himself hip deep in some cheapo literary fantasy. Life was not literature, alas, or Jason Sams' was not. Where the hell was Jenny? The sitter didn't know, but she had a phone number to call in case of emergency. Did he want the number? He jotted it down, thinking he might recognize it, but it meant nothing to him, and he had no plans to call it. He would have chatted happily with Jake, his flesh and blood, but that worthy, the sitter reported, although awake in bed reading, refused to sacrifice his creature comforts to come to the phone and talk with his father. This grieved his dad, amazed him in a way, beyond doubt pissed him off, but he thought he understood the process that took the child from A to B. *You're there, I'm here, my mother's where, so fuck yez both I'll wait it out and make it on my own.* Could be wrong, but bore no grudge. Well kiss him for me would you and tell my wife all's well, he lied; he'd save the news about his father's twin (of whom she had been rather fond) until he spoke to her himself, later that night or in the morning.

"She didn't want to say hello to us?" his mother asked, when he came back to the kitchen table.

"She wasn't there. That was the babysitter."

"You left him with a sitter? Is it someone you feel you can trust?"

The question angered him briefly, since with every sitter they had ever interviewed, and used, he'd asked it of himself.

"Yeah she's OK, Ma, not all of them are crazed killers. This one probably isn't, anyway."

Now here it came: "So, my son, you'll sleep here tonight? We'd love to have you. Dad can run down to the basement for the folding cot, and we'll set it up in the living room."

"Thanks. I've already made plans."

"A hotel? You can stay here and save yourself some money. In fact, if you don't think you'll be comfortable on the cot, you can have my bed. We wouldn't even *need* the cot. I sleep just as well on the couch. What sayest thou?"

He looked beyond her glasses, directly into her wide blue watery eyes, filled now with yearning, a notion of love, and what troubled him most beyond embarrassment was the sense of looking into his own face. He turned to his father for relief.

"You're welcome to sleep over, Son, if it's what you want to do."

"I'm staying at a buddy's loft on Fourth Avenue, Pop. I'll hook up with you down here on Sunday morning, or else I'll go straight to the funeral parlor."

"Which buddy?" his father asked, as if he had a right to know, as if he knew (as once he may have, in the long ago) all of Jason's friends.

"Paul Pisacano. I think you may have met him."

"The wop architect?"

"The very same." And wop painter, land developer, gourmet cook of pasta, wop lover of many women.

"A real character. You put him in *Slow Dying,* am I right?"

"That's him."

"We had a good long talk, as I recall, about buying and selling land. He's no dummy, Jace."

His life is coming apart now, Jason almost said, but realized with relief that it was not going to be his lifelong task to keep his father (or the rest of his scanty readership) au courant with the fate of his fictions as they moved through time.

"Yeah, I remember you hitting it off."

"Was I there?" Tillie asked.

"I don't think so, Ma."

"How could you be there?" Julie said. "You must have been in school."

"You begrudge me my classes?"

"Did I say that?"

"All right, look, before the third-person crap kicks in,

I'll be on my way." That sounded harsh, and was. "If I don't get there soon," he amended (lied), "it's difficult to get into the building."

"A little something to take along? You might get hungry in the night. Why don't I put a piece of chicken and some cherry tomatoes in a bag for you?"

Jesus, no. "I'm not in the mood for chicken, thanks. The tomatoes sound good, and maybe a couple of those hardboiled eggs I saw in there."

"And an apple, an orange. How are you going to travel at this time of night?"

Jason glanced at his watch. It was only twenty past nine, but he shared her terror of the once familiar streets. What he would have been delighted to take was a fifth of J&B, but there was no way to ask without risking a tirade, handwringing lecture at least, although he probably would have left with the bottle in the end.

"I'll grab a taxi on First Avenue."

"I'll cover the cab," his father said, shifting his weight, farting, reaching into his side pocket for his roll.

"Forget it!" Jason snapped. "I can pay for my own cab."

His father withdrew his hand from his pocket, hurt. He put his hand on the kitchen table. It was a rough, laborer's hand, with a backhander or two left in it still. Not that Jason had any clear recollection of ever being struck by his father; but as a child he had been down at the junkshop a time or two when one of the freelance drunks had turned up illadvisedly at the end of the day minus his pushcart and tried to get paid nonetheless, and, well, he'd seen what he had seen.

"Have it your way," Julie said.

"Just be careful," Tillie said. "And remember, whatever

the doctors say, it was cigarettes killed your Uncle Abie,"
a thought for the road.

He walked a few blocks along Avenue A to Tompkins
Square Park, which contained the field where he had hit a
softball homer, once, just clearing the fence, some thirty
years ago, to the delight of the misshapen math teacher,
Miss Eichner, who clapped as he shambled round the bases,
and who'd also loved his mind, and the now shabby Boys
Club was still where it had been, and the public library, and
the Ukrainian restaurants (doing well now as tourist spots),
and there he waited for and caught a crosstown bus, trans-
porting a handful of dreary passengers west, passengers with
lives (it gave him some perverse relief to think) even drearier
than his own. And he wondered, Where had been his father's
grief? Close beyond close that pair of twins; never a sign
that Jason ever saw of the competitiveness and outright
distaste identical twins were said to feel for each other, at
least from time to time. (In a story he had heard more than
once his father as a kid in the nineteen twenties down on
Avenue C which was a mean street even then had had his
head bashed in by a gang of Italians protecting the honor
of the sister of one, an honor somewhat compromised by
brother Abe, but throughout the beating murmured no
word of explanation, or complaint, and appeared to bear no
grudge, at the time or later on.) Not that his father had ever
been in the habit of revealing his emotional state to Tillie,
and certainly not to him, delicate blond curlyhaired oh so
sensitive and gifted son, the pair of them estranged from
each other from day one by his mom's ferocious shaping.
(So, genius, how then explain the volumes in the car window, the hard kiss on the mouth?) He'd liked his Uncle

Abe, hardguy with a sweetness Tillie, for one, did not trust, who became a cabdriver after the fatal fire and the sale by the twins of what was left of the junkshop to a supermarket chain; between his share of the proceeds, and driving a cab, and the insurance on the shop, Abe did not do badly. Eventually he bought a medallion, sold that, made a bundle, while Julie suffered through a service station failure and maybe much else his son never knew about, or no longer remembered, inebriate gallivanter through foreign climes that he'd been during those years. But Julie made some wise or lucky real estate investments, and with his present off-the-books employment, and his social security, and hers, and the rent on the digs in Colonial Hall that had stayed low long enough for them now to be spared by their ages all but minimal annual increase, Jason's folks would be all right.

And just as well! He trembled to think what would have happened and might happen still should either fall prey to some draining disease of old age, or death, or poverty. Middle-aged son, fuckup, virtual pauper, could not even handle (maybe cousin Ed would bail him out, since they now shared, more or less, a father) the sad task of hunting for a decent nursing home, and as for taking one or the other of them into home and hearth, the downside of that he could not begin to contemplate.

At that Chinese restaurant family reunion Abie without the knowledge of either of the child's parents had thrust a hundred-dollar bill into the hands of the three-year-old grandnephew he had never seen before and would not now see again, which Jake (deep into the barbecued chicken wings) forgot all about yet somehow retained all the way to Boston, where he dug the crumpled picture of Ben Franklin out of his pocket and only some shrewd detective work on the part of his parents pinpointed the source. A C-note! From Abe! Who understood such things?

His mother understood such things. Her rage remained clear and constant as a mountain brook. Jason would give one piece of advice to his son, when Jake was old enough to listen: whatever else you choose to do with your life, Son, never marry an identical twin.

But his bookloving mom (his own, let's face it, once-and-always primary influence: how many hundreds of cuddly hours had he spent being introduced by her to A. A. Milne, and Lewis Carroll, and Aesop, and the *Hollow Tree Tales,* learning through unforgettable doggerel in a book called *Tirra Lirra* of horrendous happenings — years before Pogo lived! — "on the banks of Lake Okeefinokee," then one day under her prodding *he* reading to *her* of Munro Leaf's Ferdinand, quiescent, flower-loving bull whose subversive escapades as depicted by Robert Lawson settled the way a *corrida* would ever after look and feel to Sams — in all this the very stuff of literary memory) derived considerable pleasure from the gift he sent her for her sixty-seventh birthday, Galway Kinnell's book of poems entitled *The Avenue Bearing the Initial of Christ into the New World,* which contained as part of its title poem several stanzas on the junkshop fire. Kinnell had lived in those days just across the street from the shop, relatively solitary member of the hip contingent that had found the low-rent district as early as the late fifties, in the easternmost outpost of what came to be called the East Village, Galway occupying absurdly cheap quarters in a rotting building that, for all Jason knew, may once have housed one or the other pair of his grandparents, way back when, and Galway had been home the

night the patrimony burned to the ground, witnessing as
only he could witness:

It was Sams' junkhouse,* the one the clacking
Carts that little men pad after in harnesses
Picking up bedbugged mattresses, springs
The stubbornness has been loved out of,
Chairs felled by fat, lampshades lights have burned
    through,
Linoleum the geometry has been scuffed from,
Carriages a single woman's work has brought to wreck,
Would come to in the dusk and unload before,
That the whole neighborhood came out to see
Burning in the night, flames opening out like
Eyelashes from the windows, men firing the tears in,
Searchlights smashing against the brick,
The water blooming up the walls
Like pale trees, reaching into the darkness beyond.

Nobody mourned, nobody stood around in pajamas
And a borrowed coat steaming his nose in coffee.
It was only Sams' junkhouse.
                        But this evening
The neighborhood comes out again, everything
That may abide the fire was made to go through the fire
And it was made clean. . . .
                        Carriages we were babies in,
Springs that used to resist love, that gave in
And were thrown out like whores — the black
Irreducible heap, mausoleum of what we were —

---

*"Gold's junkhouse" in the original poem. Kinnell, with this noted, has kindly
permitted the tampering.

It is cold suddenly, we feel chilled,
Nobody knows for sure what is left of him.

Whatever her own views on the fire (which appeared for
a time as if it might drive a wedge between the twins, but
in the end brought them closer), Tillie loved the poem, and
owning the book, and (perhaps most of all) her artist son's
thoughtfulness in sending it to her. By and by Sams would
meet Kinnell, at Yaddo, the artists' colony in Saratoga
Springs, and on a stroll with him one night into Lena's, the
coffeeshop in town, where a modest booksigning for the
poet was to take place, spoke of his own connection to
the poem, and how much pleasure it had given his mother,
who had grown up on Avenue C.

The rugged Irish poet had been pleased.

"To Tillie," he wrote, in the fresh copy of his book Jason
bought at the signing; "Everything that may abide the fire
was made to go through the fire / And it was made clean: /
Nobody knows for sure what is left of him." And signed
his name. Tillie spoke of this for many years.

The bus dropped him off almost at Pisacano's doorstep. He
thought he needed a drink to get through whatever lay
ahead. Paul would have gallons of wine on hand, very likely
nothing else. Wine sometimes did the trick, but at the end
of a day like today would probably make him ill. He did
not want to sit in a bar. A few blocks away on Third Avenue was the liquor store that sold Goodmore scotch at four
dollars and change the fifth (the only store he'd ever found
that carried it at all); once or maybe twice he'd bought it
by the undiscounted case, secure in his first impression that

it was one of those "sleepers" he was forever discovering, obscure and inexpensive off-brands that to subtle palates like his own turned out to be better than or at least as good as the major brands, and fine with him and with his pocketbook if no one else discovered this, or agreed with his judgment.

But he was tired, and Third Avenue was a world away. He needed no further adventures. He remembered with delight the can of beer he still carried with him from the train. He'd try to bumble through with that; chug it down, be tired enough to sleep. Pisacano's name was on a slip of paper taped near a doorbell, but Jason knew from experience that the bell didn't work. He pushed at the heavy wooden door and it creaked open, as Paul had said it would, and he began climbing the steep flights of rickety stairs. The first landing was as dark as it had been the last time he'd been there, however many years ago that was, and he groped his way around the bend, still with two flights ahead of him. Small businesses gave way to loft apartments, from one of which, on the landing below Paul's, came sounds of Mozart, signs of life. He rested there a moment, put down his overnight bag, readied himself for the final leg. Paul's front door was wide open, the soft sound of jazz filling the apartment. Every light had been left on. It appeared no one was home, but he called out Paul's name as a precaution. He walked through the huge, high-ceilinged room that smelled strongly of paint and paintings; a half-dozen somber canvases hung from pulleys attached to the ceiling. A new phase of Paul's, or the work of his latest live-in sweetie, whom he'd saved from a fate even worse than Pisacano? On the upper floor of the duplex the architect had built himself, with the permission of the church, back in the days when all was well between them, was his enormous bed and the rest of his bedroom, and right there off the kitchen where Jason stood was an unmade cot with a thick mattress, and fresh, folded bedclothes on the chair beside it. No small thing, he congratulated himself, to have kept up through his years of wandering his contacts in New York, certainly this one, so as to have a place to lay his weary head apart from the apartment he grew up in, and which was not a fancy hotel he could hardly afford or a shabby one with the shower (if any) and crapper in the hall, and gloomy light, and sagging mattress, which, still weary from lack of sleep at six the following morning, the penurious traveler could hardly wait to put behind him.

He relieved himself in the old john Paul had for years talked of modernizing (having long ago installed a spanking new one on the second deck with a Jacuzzi and stall shower and two marble basins), but was unlikely to bother with now; went back to make up his bed, remembered the tomatoes and eggs and creamed herring and fruit and took them to the ancient fridge, and hit paydirt, four lovely dark green sixteen-ounce bottles of something called Ballantine India Ale, and, appreciative drinker that he had always been of quart after quart of Ballantine ale in its tall, light green bottles, wonderful almost acrid taste hardly related to Ballantine beer or any beer, good to get smashed on all by itself or chase something stronger with, cook a stew in, his Armenian flame had once washed her auburn hair in it, holy beverage, he couldn't praise it too highly . . . Ballantine *India* Ale however was a new concept; he opened a bottle, found a clean glass and poured a taste, held it up to the naked bulb in the kitchen before bringing it to his lips and noted the color to be much darker than the ale he was familiar with, more on the order of a British ale, say Watney's, one of those, made perfect historical (empirical?) sense for an India ale to resemble a British ale, but enough pseudo-historical bullshit, Sams, mark one thing well, may you never become too old or jaded to appreciate whatever new alcoholic beverage the good Lord might still from time to time send down the pike, so he took a sip and found it good, dark and heady, and without further ado polished off the contents of the glass.

He remembered Jennifer, his Boston life. He'd make the call on his AT&T card, so that his own number would be automatically billed; not to abuse Paul's splendid hospitality. He'd finish off that first ale and maybe start another, then call it a day (and a long one), not even looking for a way to turn off the lights or Pisacano's jazz, which was soft enough to fall asleep by, and he'd crawl into his cot and sleep to morning. Then he'd find a way to make some coffee to go with the morning cigarette (probably some instant on hand), then go downstairs and buy a *Times* and do a thing he loved, play tourist in New York, look for a pleasant restaurant to breakfast and read his paper in. Or perhaps Paul, back by then, would join him.

"Hello, Jen."

"Oh. Hello."

With the enthusiasm of someone fielding a call from a bill collector at three in the morning. (But what had he expected?) You could never, in these matters, accuse her of duplicity.

"You don't sound delighted to hear from me."

"I was already in bed."

"I tried you earlier, from my folks', but Bev said you had gone out somewhere. Where'd you go?"

"I was visiting Delilah and Sam. They're not doing very well."

Married friends of hers who had the knack of not doing very well. He didn't really want to know the latest details.

"Well, I'm over at Pisacano's now. Getting ready to go to bed. Just called to say goodnight."

"Oh. How is Paul?"

"No idea. Haven't seen him."

"Oh. How are your parents?"

"Still squabbling. Seem healthy."

"How did things go with your agent and editor?"

"Hard to say. I laid some groundwork."

"That's good." She yawned. "Jason, I have to go to sleep."

"Is Jake still awake?"

"Of course not. It's eleven-thirty."

"How is he?"

"He's all right, I guess. Same as he was when you left this morning."

"He wasn't awake when I left this morning. Look, uh, my uncle Abie died."

"Who?"

"Abe, my father's twin brother."

"Oh! How did he die?"

He finally had her attention. He took a long pull on the second bottle, drained it, opened a third. He hadn't planned to drink this much; would have to find a liquor store and replenish Paul's stash in the morning.

"I don't know. Wait, yes I do, cancer of the prostate, spread through his body. Caused by smoking cigarettes, my mother says."

"Well, *your* prostate is enlarged."

"Yeah." So was his head right now. He'd approved of

the way she'd been able to quit smoking while pregnant with Jake, but found himself wishing more than once that she had afterward resumed.

"The funeral's on Sunday. Think you'd want to come in for it?"

"I couldn't, Jason. You seem to forget we have a four-year-old son. Besides, we'd already made plans for Sunday."

"A simple 'no' would have done it." Splendid place for him, too, to let it drop, but, "What plans did we have for Sunday?"

"All right, I don't want to come in. It's not my idea of a fun time in New York. OK?"

"What plans did we have for Sunday?"

"Let it go, if you don't remember."

"When do we outgrow the fun and games? Whatever it is, it slipped my mind."

"I've got to go to sleep. Goodnight."

Incredible. She had hung up on him. He fought off the crazed, enraged impulse to call her back, and opened the fourth bottle of ale instead. It had no taste by now, but would help him fall asleep, and stay asleep, until his bladder woke him.

He doubted he would himself have arranged on short notice to attend his uncle's funeral if he had not already been in town. He'd dropped everything the year before when Julie had the minor heart attack to fly to New York and had arrived at the hospital just in time to watch his father negotiate with a pretty Chinese nurse to soap down his privates, although the nurse on the previous shift had apparently done that very thing not fifteen minutes before: "Now don't bullshit me, Mr. Sams," the Chinese nurse said, as if they had known each other forever.

But that had been his father.

He peed forever, hoping it would suffice to get him through the night, knowing it would not. He rinsed out his mouth; no great teethbrusher at the best of times, which this was not. The world spun, but he took the trouble (although he thought it a pointless, drunken act) to stand the four empties underneath his cot, concealed by the bedclothes. He climbed in and, as the saying goes, was asleep before his head hit the pillow.

Someone was jostling him awake. He tried to incorporate the outrageous intrusion into a dream, and for a time did, but had less success with the raucous voice right by his ear.

"Sams! Famous author! Do not piss away your life in sleep! Wake to morning! This is one of your minor inventions, summoning you to the revels!"

"What fucking o'clock?"

"Ah. He lives. He asks after the hour. It's three in the morning, baby. No time to lose."

"You son of a bitch." He turned away, but knew he was up, would get out of bed. He had already seen that Paul was not alone.

"Nothing of the sort! Contemplate the literary choices offered by the hour! Prepare to fish with Papa, or with Nick Adams, as it were; moon about with F. Scott, popping a brew while you wait for four, which is the truly dark night of the soul; or rise merely to sample an exquisite beverage new even to your jaded palate. And the chance to meet a lady."

"What beverage?" he asked fearfully. His bare feet touched the cold floor.

"First things first, is it? Joan, this is Jason Sams, a writer who missed the sixties, assassinations, moonlandings, civil rights marches, Bob Dylan, Woodstock nation, Vietnam, Nixon, the whole shmeer. He spent the decade going down on his muse behind the shithouse, until she left him for a screenwriter. Jason, this is Joan, a thoughtful artist like yourself."

"Hi, Jason."

"Good morning, Joan." He shook her hand. He was intrigued to see how pleasingly ordinary she looked, how unexotic, not a trace of sizzle, almost plain. Did this mean Pisacano was maturing at last, on the qui vive for material better suited for the long haul? Or was it a further sign of his deep despair?

"Pleased to meet you, Joan."

"Likewise, Jason. He's been talking about you all night."

"What was the gist?"

"I was finally going to meet a friend of his worth breaking out the India ale for."

Fully awake now, watching Paul open the fridge, gently close it.

"Father, can you shed light on this?"

"On . . . ?"

"The mystery of the absent India ale."

"Consumed, Father. And as tasty as you intimated. The moment the stores open for business tomorrow, rather later today, I'm replacing the four with a six-pack."

"You drank the last four?"

"That's how many there were."

"Prick, they happened to be the last four bottles in the city. In the country. In the fucking galaxy."

He did not seem to think he was exaggerating. He was not, Sams observed, going to be jollied out of this.

"What are you talking about? I'll hit every liquor store in the city. I'll make it my life's work."

"I'm having trouble assimilating this, Father. You drank every single one? What time did you get here? Where are the empties?"

"Why don't we have a little wine, Paul?" Joan said.

"Why didn't this fucking lush have himself a little wine?"

"Best you see this side of him while there's still time," Sams said to Joan, still trying. The sudden anger must go with the new territory, Pisacano's new unhappy life. He reached under the bed and produced the four empty bottles, one by one. For some reason, this seemed to have a mollifying effect on Paul.

"That appears to be keerect. You drank all four. I tell you what, Sams, things being what they are, the evening's over. Look, I cut you a key. It's on top of the fridge. I assume you'll be hanging out here long enough to need a key?"

"If it's still OK."

"You baffle me, Father. Stay a month. Stay a year! Make free with the amenities. But I swear to God, I didn't know you were an out-and-out drunk. I thought from time to time you might overindulge. Mea culpa."

"Thanks, buddy. I'll replace the beer tomorrow."

"Ales. Yeah. Don't lose any sleep over it."

He slipped at last into a fitful doze, incorporating movement from above, making use of Pisacano's crazy laughter and Joan's happy squeals, willing himself at least semiconscious so as to avoid not only all indications of third-party fucking, should that distraction be in store, but also any reminder from inside his own racing head of how bruised he'd been and still was by Pisacano's rage; through all the many years, he'd never seen Paul's anger directed at himself, and worse even than the anger was the triviality of what had set it off, some missing ale, his guzzling down (admittedly) the third bottle and the fourth, and for that small indiscretion being termed a lush, a *lush,* which was a long way from his own calm pondering from time to time whether he might be an "alcoholic," or exhibited, now and again, "alcoholic tendencies." Paul's judgment was more hurtful for some reason than his mother's, or even his wife's, shrill and angry as that one could become (thanks to that fucking Al-Anon!), and the conclusion she drew from it, that for him the drinking life was over. His habit had always before been a source of amusement and wonder to Paul, even commanding respect, in the good old days when it had seemed to go hand in hand with spurts of progress on *Slow Dying,* that long-term project redemptive of the nasty jolts administered by life and by his Armenian lady, helping him convert a personal disaster into useful, vengeful art, echoing Sams' own longstanding faith (and far from his alone!) in the union between booze and creativity. Or so he had believed Paul believed.

But all he'd had to do was polish off this (supposedly) irreplaceable elixir to jeopardize a lengthy friendship, and be publicly humiliated for his pains. Before much longer he might well decide that he was more sinned against than sinning, feel a healing indignation rise; but for now he'd settle for the hurt, the need to sleep. And whatever Paul's odd opinion about the limited availability of Ballantine India Ale in the universe (but the worm of doubt had begun to wake in Jason's mind), a determined Sams would devote as much of Saturday as it took to tracking it down.

He woke for good at seven-fifteen, rummaged in his bag for generic aspirin and prophylactic B-12, stomped and coughed around for the company it might bring, but heard nothing from above. Which was OK. Had more luck than he'd dared anticipate on the old commode, found a wash-cloth and treated himself to a GI shower (crotch and arm-pits), enjoyed the luxury of clean underwear, slipped on the same khaki trousers, a fresh blue shirt, a clean pair of socks, his ruined sneakers, lit a cigarette, and creaked down the flights of stairs into a brisk, sunny New York morning. The day was his to squander, or use, find hard-to-find ale in, prepare for a funeral in, watch his thoughts go by (jogged into richness by his native city) and jot the better ones into the notebook he carried in his pocket. He bought a *Times* and a pack of cigarettes at a kiosk near the Eighth Street Bookshop and took them into a coffeeshop with its prices handwritten in the window. As happened much too fre-quently these days, he waited what seemed an interminable length of time before he was served, but remained cool, and finally a thin and pleasant waitress wandered over with the coffee he had not asked for and he ordered his bacon with eggs over easy. Now that he had the coffee he could light his second cigarette of the morning, drawing the smoke deep into his lungs, making a production of it, for he knew it would likely be the last cigarette of the day he would in any sense enjoy.

You bastard (he addressed it), having bumped off my uncle Abe and Trilling too, it must now seem a pleasant irony for you to come after the only living bridge between this unlikely pair. He laughed aloud, almost bringing the

waitress back to his table. The day he could not make himself giggle or guffaw by virtue of his nose for life's crazy
juxtapositions would be the day he . . . cashed it in, perhaps, let the black depression (and whatever might lie beyond it) take over, for apart from the times he made himself
laugh there were not often many consecutive moments in
a day when he inhabited with ease and comfort his own
mind and body. Shitman, too fine a day to start on such a
morbid note. Hyman Hamburg, an old New York acquaintance his age or older, just then entered the joint looking fierce and lorn. Their eyes met, remained briefly locked,
then Jason barely nodded before dropping his gaze to the
day's news. He could not for the life of him remember what
that relationship had been about, why there would be anything to fear and loathe should Hyman join him, and then
a bit of it came back, his picking up the phone one afternoon
and hearing You Jew son of a bitch you went and did it,
somebody besides Mailer finally got right how men and
women live, that *Slow Dying* is people fucking each other
up like no one else has captured it, you bastard! Ah well
ahum, Hy, nice of you to say so, you write like a dynamo
yourself, you know, *Buccaneer* was a terrific book, but
thanks for the praise which God knows I need to counteract
the reviews, or some. I am having a few people over to the
house tonight for no particular reason, a couple of neighbors, an English editor and such, would you be free to join
us?

So there at his New York City digs east of Gramercy Park
in late '69 or early '70 with himself laying on the booze in
the good old days before their relocation to the country
followed by their unhappy subtenant burning them out of
the city for good (she'd painted the walls purple prior to

the accidental fire) had been a party, and sometime late in the evening out in his lovely cultivated garden with the white Ryoanji stones where he sipped Rignes beer and conversed with his English publisher-to-be he saw a serrated kitchen knife being waved around which scared the shit out of him but struck no fear into the heart of Giuseppe Dinelli the homosexual scholar of English letters who lived two houses down, a witty fellow Jenny liked and even Jason did by then, despite Joe's quirk and no harm done or intended of appearing to stare at your crotch at times inopportune, particularly loving to acknowledge acquaintance with new males of whatever persuasion by ogling what lay between their legs disconcerting to more than a few enflaming to others but never to the extent to Jason's knowledge that a kitchen knife as it happened one of his own made an appearance but Dinelli pushed the blade aside and said to the much larger Hamburg You want to wallow in macho garbage do it elsewhere, swine, get out, we don't need that bullshit here, you histrionic putz, out! out! Hamburg's enraged then puzzled then stricken face above the knife fighter's stance looking to Sams for instruction, and Jason obliging, Hy, this ain't really working out, this party, maybe another night for just you and me to shoot the shit old buddy, Hyman dropping the knife on the grass at this betrayal saying thickly Fuck you and your faggot friends together with your phony book and staggering through the apartment knocking over this and that and out the door leaving behind of all things a pair of rubbers item of apparel I had not seen in lo these many years but rain had been forecast, maybe his maiden aunt had rung him up, Hyman, guard your health, and the party if such it was ran its course Sams' black domestic Ruby due over the next day to clean up after his literary doings and Jason was actually at his typewriter still the machine of preference that following day doing some work on the book that would languish on one page one or another for some twenty years putting back snifter after snifter of seventy-year-old Courvoisier when the telephone rang, Listen man I may have fucked you up last night, my memory is shot, if I said or did anything to regret I regret it and when could I drop around to pick up the rubbers I left behind I ain't got the bread to buy another pair and Jason who considered himself compassionate but could not keep the scolding from his voice said Why not right now Hy I'll leave them in a paper bag outside the apartment door in the foyer and buzz you into the building, but I'm working right now and I'll be working when you come and Hamburg thanked him

Could well be a more accurate version of the night's events, and close at hand, but he had no wish to disinter it. Nor did Hamburg, it appeared: he had already found more congenial company at the counter.

So Sams didn't stay as long as he'd intended, relishing breakfast, downing endless cups of coffee, smoking, digging with exquisite pleasure into every section of the *New York Times.* A roaring headache lurked behind his right eye, but if he hit the air and walked briskly it would probably pass. He tried to gesture for his check, and finally caught her eye, but it had taken forever. He adjusted the tip accordingly.

Ten felt too early to begin the quest, so he strolled west to Sixth Avenue and beyond it through the meandering streets of the West Village. He'd lived in the area once, lived in terror one summer in a sublet one-room apartment on the top floor of a Charles Street tenement with a fire escape leading to the roof right outside his head as he slept. He was robbed it seemed once a week, but he stuck it out until one Saturday night he went to bed early and legs appeared on the fire escape shortly after, and someone fiddled with his window, so he reached up and knocked on the window, and the thief was good enough to vanish up the fire escape, but enough was enough and he made the call and his parents came and fetched him back with his belongings to the Lower East Side. He'd celebrated his high school graduation in a defunct nightclub somewhere in these streets, sat in later years in a booth opposite an incoherent Kerouac in the White Horse Tavern, may have glimpsed a loaded Dylan Thomas on the same premises, but was too soused himself to care, but he had done most of his serious barroom drinking further east, at San Remo's and at the Kettle of Fish on Mac-Dougal Street, at Louie's, at that other place whose greatest attraction was the sawdust on the floor, which apparently drew folk for miles around, drank at the Kettle with James Baldwin once, dined with Rudy Wurlitzer and Grace Paley in the Lion's Head in Sheridan Square, drank everywhere with Wakefield, but had never, it still saddened him to think, made any particular place his own.

A place where I have merely to show myself for the bartender to put aside the glass he's drying, say, The usual, Mr. Sams? Make it a double tonight, Jimmy, my wife left me and I've written four perfect pages. Beautiful, Mr. Sams.

Even *editors* were recognized: Maduras at the Cedar the night before, Seamans at Max's Kansas City, to which Jason had tagged along quite happily with Al — "double Dickel, Mr. Seamans?" "And the same again for my friend Jason Sams, Eddie, he's a terrific writer, and a couple of draft beers" —

the beer a touch for his sake, Jason knew, as there had been many such touches in the days when Seamans lived, and before Sams' gift had splashed away

So *nu?* In his time (with friends or by himself relishing Murray Kempton's column in the *New York Post* belly up to the bar in some Irish hole in the wall) he had become as smashed as Papa ever got, in Cuba or the Keys, as creatively looped as Faulkner ever got in his own barn, ah now, *that* bastard, I devoured him, even read *Mosquitoes* twice and tried like hell to read the poetry, then for years wrote just like him, if you believe that, Jewish kid from the Lower East Side of Manhattan playing Ivy League aristocrat way up there on Morningside Heights knowing he would never make it until one day having read and reread all the works of the great William Faulkner published to that time began writing like the mind of the South, struggling toward a style, until one day confronted the man himself, in the American embassy in Kyoto or Kobe or Tokyo couldn't rightly re-member must have been '55 or '56 (by which time already a civilian) heart thumping at my own arrogance as I kept my hand in the air while Japanese kids all wearing the same school uniform were getting the call all around me and asking questions in an English absolutely impenetrable to Jason but no problem to Faulkner until finally the westerner with the weak chin and large nose got the nod and threw out some perhaps profound query about black Dilsey, who'd endured, as all his people would endure, *speaking directly* to William Faulkner who died a year after Hem-ingway a short six years later while I languished in Sweden, Hemingway suddenly all over the bookstore windows in Lund in '61 then Faulkner in '62, and both would endure, and Bill (shorter in stature than Sams had imagined) fielded the question whatever it had been and gave the westerner whose voice had trembled and whose heart was pounding a short measured courteous answer.

He stood in the shadow of the West Side Highway, the truck traffic rumbling along beneath it heavy as well. There were no traffic lights in sight, and he wondered about the wisdom of trying to brave the flow for a better glimpse of the Hudson River. It wasn't *his* river, not the way the East River was, upon which he had cast his bread on more than one Yom Kippur afternoon and watched the holy seagulls swoop upon his sins, and played as a child under the Williamsburg Bridge connecting Manhattan to Brooklyn off Delancey Street no sane preadolescent would try that today and walked the Brooklyn Bridge at dawn to catch a New York sunrise with his great high school friends Joe Pacheco and Charley Marowitz both gone on to sweet triumphs and miserable failures and many years later was driven over the Williamsburg Bridge by Al Seamans to partake with his editor and great friend and sometimes their brides as well of the incomparable rump steaks at Peter Luger's on the Brooklyn side almost directly under the bridge itself luscious thick rare steaks accompanied only by the huge beefsteak tomatoes as good he had to admit as the ones his father-in-law grew or the ones he'd grown himself in his Woodstock garden with help to say the least from his farmer's daughter wife and slices of a Bermuda onion of such sweetness you knew you could bite safely into one whole at Peter Luger's where he had not set foot since Al the son of a bitch died and would probably not set foot again since once you had done certain things with certain people in certain places you did not go there again.

*

No need to take his life in his hands for a better glimpse of Joisey.

Now it was noon of the Saturday preceding the Monday commencing with which perhaps he'll juice no more and the first thing Sams saw upon turning to rejoin civilization was a wiry old fart the proprietor probably unlocking and pushing back the heavy metal gate of a liquor store already surrounded by his first clients of the day a shabby bunch indeed whom he apparently relished treating with the respect they deserved and he could get away with which was none. Pity the poor bums, asshole, Jason silently admonished, offer in an appropriate ceremony a free case of sneaky pete to the millionth customer, why not, these guys have built your empire, but he waited circumspectly nonetheless until the bum elected to do the buying had exited the store and the group in toto had expostulated off to consume the stuff before himself entering the shop. The owner eyed him briefly, resumed dusting off the stock.

"Um, do you carry Ballantine India Ale?"

"Ballantine ale we got. How many quarts did you need?"

"I need a six-pack of Ballantine India Ale."

"You want Ballantine, or what? I don't know from no India ale. You want Indian, go look on the reservation."

"Thanks for your help."

Eight thousand liquor stores to go he cavalierly estimated in Manhattan alone but he would work his way east then north by bus and cab finding what he needed in the posher stores on Madison Avenue or else in Italian Harlem where Pisacano often ventured for true Fontina not Swedish or Danish Fontina, black olives, handrolled pasta, freshly baked bread, going wherever we must fucking well go to locate the brew which hadn't been all that tasty when he thought back on it and which was no longer the issue but had never been the issue must give the lie to the rude fellow lay him in a year's supply or a monthly delivery to his doorstep or some other splendidly vindictive generosity the wop would understand and admire oh yes as he had shaken his head in absolute wonder (and Jason wanted this!) at the story of the book in the mail with its heart cut out, No shit! She did that? Sams, you got yourself a worthy adversary.

But ten liquor stores later all admittedly in parochial Greenwich Village but even there one or two professed to have heard of the stuff and even seen it in days gone by one wag suggesting it was out of print no doubt available in some warehouse somewhere at ten dollars a bottle but not worth his (the owner's) while tracking down if it means that much to you you'll probably have to phone up every liquor store and every wholesaler in the city nay the nation and the best of British luck so

he grabbed a couple Nathan's hot dogs for lunch with sauerkraut and mustard and Dr. Brown's Celery Tonic a delight of his youth available here and there in Boston but only after the same kind of quest he was on now and on a mere hunch wended his way to the Bowery where he'd once bought Goodmore by the case and would pick up a bottle or two now to take back home if home it was.

The guy there bald and bearded like himself sold him the Goodmore with a flicker of contempt and knew nothing of any Ballantine India Ale.

*

It hadn't been so brilliant buying the scotch since he'd have to carry it God knew where so he headed back to the loft to leave it there and maybe even donate one of the two bottles to Paul as gift and peace offering, not that Paul was likely to carry a transient grudge into a new day, at least Jason hoped not, and Paul never drank the hard stuff himself, happy with his wine and beer, but might find himself with a bibulous guest someday, maybe the rector of the church come to evict him would take a tot or two, and in the ensuing camaraderie reevaluate the church's need for space. Good things could yet come of this, serendipity would out.

The downstairs door was locked, but he remembered his key, climbed the flights, and let himself into the apartment. Paul and Joan, fully dressed, reading, were seated at the kitchen table, sipping instant coffee, appearing happily married, which to Sams meant, Not much to say one to the other, and yet (since no issues, no missiles, to zing each other's way) content.

He was relieved to see the girl puffing on a cigarette. Paul did not smoke, and as a rule barely tolerated the addiction in others.

He put one fifth of scotch into his overnight bag and, after a moment's thought, placed the other in the middle of the table. He lowered himself onto a wooden crate. Lit a cigarette.

"Join us in a relaxing cup of coffee, Father. Forgo, this once, the deadly morning drink."

"This bottle's for you, Paul. For the house. A token of my gratitude. Besides . . ." he made a show of studying his watch . . . "it's well into the afternoon."

"Sweetness," Pisacano said, "would you care for a drink?"

"No thanks. Thanks, Jason."

"How about you, Father? A touch of the grape, purveyed by thyself?"

"No, not yet. I need a clear head today."

"For what?"

"I've been out combing the city for your India ale. You're absolutely right, it's hard to find. So . . ." a thought occurred . . . "why don't I simply track it to the source?" He reached under his unmade bed for an empty. "Brewed in Brooklyn, shit. Why didn't I do this earlier? I'll give the brewery a call."

"Sams, are you fucken crazy? I already told you the stuff doesn't exist. The importer's been gone from that address for years. Nobody makes it anymore. I lucked into the last four bottles in the cosmos. Forget it, spare me the holy grail crap!"

"I'd feel a whole lot better if I could replace it."

"Well you ain't gonna replace it! Don't turn into a fucken Jew on me! Find it in your heart to absolve me last night's wrath! You'll wind up out in Greenpoint, trapped for life in a Saul Bellow story! I repeat, the reason nobody imports it is that nobody makes it! So will you let it be?"

"Yeah, OK."

"Excellent! What's left of today is free time, because tomorrow at the crack of dawn we drive out to the Berkshires, to look over some property the syndicate might buy. A hundred-acre farm, Sams. It'll take you right back to your Appalachian roots."

"Wish I could. I've got a funeral tomorrow."

"Whose?"

"Uncle Abe. My father's twin."

"Identical?"

"Yeah. I never told you my father was an identical twin?"

"I don't know. Maybe I read it in your book. But you gave yourself a younger sister in there also."

"Back in the good old days when fiction prevailed."

"How old was he?"

"Seventy."

"Must be tough on your old man. Must be tough on you, even."

"I don't know. I lucked into even being here for it. Nobody thought to invite me."

"Hey, Sams. Families is weirdness. Protocol and self-pity need not apply."

"How'd you get to be so wise?"

"I don't know, baby. These days, just take it where you find it."

"Modest, too," Joan said. "Paul, I'm going to go home and change. Do you want to pick me up or shall I come here later on?"

"These are hard decisions," Pisacano said. "I may be out pursuing my art and/or livelihood, in which case I will fall by your pad, as the vernacular once had it, at a mutually agreeable hour, like between six and nine P.M.? Else, if I don't get off my duff today, why wouldn't I take advantage of the shifting mores and command your presence?"

"Fine. Give me a call when you make up your mind." She rose, went upstairs to collect her things, said goodbye to Jason with what seemed to him a genuine pleasure at having met him, and left the loft. Sams gathered that even this one, who seemed to have the inside track, understood that for all she knew she might be departing forever.

"You going to blow this one too, Father?"

Paul chortled, leaned backwards, hands locked behind his head. He was wearing his round, wireframed glasses this morning, which gave him the look of a political scholar, a biographer of Garibaldi. His black hair was wild. He was, Sams noted (not for the first time), an exceedingly handsome man.

"Father, did I ever claim for myself the ability to read the future? This one, as you also seem aware, is definitely worth the candle. She thinks the world of me; she's even trying to get divorced. But the last time I got serious, Sams, the chick ran three thousand miles. Hey, look what happened to you in Armenialand."

"Ancient history."

"Right. And you even got a book out of it. And now you're happily married, with progeny, the whole package."

"So there might be hope for you."

"Have a drink, Sams. You're not following my argument."

"I think I am," Jason said. But he grabbed at the invitation, went to his bed, and returned to the table with his bottle of Goodmore. He had been wondering for a while now how he might unobtrusively begin his drinking day.

"Your sense of the niceties, especially for an author, is awry, Sams, did you know that? Don't be a prick. Protect your own bottle, an off-brand if ever I saw one, and break the seal on this one, which otherwise, for all we know, might sit here aging quietly for years."

"No, keep it intact. Who knows when I'll be back?" He fetched a glass from the kitchen. He put back a quantity from his own bottle, neat. It was incredible. He might as well be drinking Chivas Regal. He wished (wished, in other words, he had succeeded that morning) there were some beer or ale on hand to soften, yet enhance, the whisky's wallop. Remembered yet again the can of beer he was carrying, and this time popped it open. Sitting with a friend, discussing life, savoring bargain scotch, chasing it with warm beer — did it get better than this?

"I been there. I been married."

"For six weeks? Twenty years ago?"

"Those are the numbers. They make *my* point, shmuck, not yours. What are you nowadays, the Johnny Appleseed of connubial bliss?"

"A new subject. What's happening with the loft? You going to get to stay here for a while?"

"In the lap of the gods. My attorney is not optimistic. He got me six months, now down to five, and suggests that I find myself new quarters. He's trying to get them to pay this and that to help me on my way. But the joint almost certainly reverts to the uses of the Almighty."

"That's a damn shame."

"You go with the flow."

"Get yourself a glass and join me."

"Sams, how long have you known me? Dago red with meals and once in a blue moon a beer, an ale. I can't abide that shit you're drinking. Not even when it costs a buck or two more."

"Well, if you *were* a scotch drinker, you'd see that this is on a par with the more expensive brands."

"Right, I forgot I was seated with the connoisseur of the buck-and-a-half scotch. Listen, Father, let's bust out, drive up to Harlem, pick up the bread and pasta, black olives, pick up Joan on the way back, return here for, I guarantee it, royal dining. Fettuccine Alfredo, Antipasto Pisacano, a jug of your finest California Zinfandel. You'll need nourishment before your funeral tomorrow."

"Sounds terrific. But I'll pass on the shopping. Need to write some letters, make some calls."

"Certainly, Father. Just bear in mind that if you're too smashed when I get back to appreciate the handiwork, you don't get to eat it."

"Fair enough."

"Later."

Some part of him knew it was an error to pass up the outing, the change of air (and the chance to slum in safety) as well as the golden opportunity it would have provided to keep tabs on Paul. Between here and the shops in East Harlem Pisacano's plans might well change a few dozen times: he might wind up across the Hudson in a ritzy bedroom community paying court to some old now-married flame (having screeched to a halt a block or two from the loft and phoned her first; too old — at last! — to seek unnecessary pain), or he might drop in unannounced on his widowed father in the Bronx, moved to this filial gesture by Sams' talk of funerals, and when he was finished with his father look up some boyhood chums who had never strayed far from the old turf and accept the invitation from Gino and his wife to hang around for a dinner of fettucine Alfredo such as even he had never tasted . . . the son of a bitch did not need to be tanked to do a thing spontaneous or irresponsible, but when Jason pondered the prospect of spending the long evening all by his lonesome (which is what happened), he was not dismayed. Paul's threat hung heavier on him than he hoped he had revealed, planning as he did to make some serious sorties into the Goodmore and having no idea where they would take him, into unconsciousness more than likely but perhaps instead this time out of the underbrush and into the dazzling clearing as had already happened once one stonecold sober morning early in their Woodstock time out walking with a buoyant pregnant Jen to emerge suddenly out of thick forest into a sundrenched meadow with way down at the end of it a single gnarled apple tree the same down home view visible from her sister's front porch both knew and loved and Sams and Mrs. Sams giggled at the wonder of it and rolled in the tall grass and through his tears of joy he reached out to warn her to watch how she rolled that brilliant clearheaded father-to-be morning, a once-and-future writer of wonderful novels, blessed nouvelles, essays that wore their learning lightly, passable poems, the same edenic clearing to reach which all good drunks kept right on sloshing long after they were feeling "good" or had stopped feeling good or feeling much of anything but drinking to reach through whatever dismaying and unrecollected behavior might interpose itself before oblivion supervened.

But tonight have no fear, good sense was here, he was going to sip and space these Goodmores with plenty of water on the side, with long breaks for thinking and scrawling notes and before too long if PP didn't show (a happenstance he soon began to wish for) he'd make his way down to the all-purpose deli on the corner for a six-pack or two and cigarettes and dinner, corned beef on rye with mustard of course no mayo on corned beef, fool and infidel, no lettuce nor plastic tomato either, heavy on the sour pickles, side of potato salad, Dr. Brown's Celery Tonic or a can of cream soda failing that and away we'd scurry with beer and dinner back to the land where the soft music played, for while Paul preferred nay insisted that I did not mess with his expensive stereo (having nailed me long before to the outline of my self-appraisal) he had relented enough to show Sams which knob turned down the sound. Not too handy, this writer, not since crawling along the floor of a beauty parlor on Avenue B as a chubby curly blondhaired child around the age

of three waiting for his mother's head to emerge from under
the funny machine and suddenly eliciting a tongue of fire
and shock from an electric socket by jamming in a bobby
pin burning and stunning himself while women shrieked
and mother in her own words to her best friend later over-
heard by him almost had a heart attack so he had no quarrel
for the next forty years with his perhaps unmerited life
sentence of technical incompetence, even after moving to
the country where this and that required minor repair and
troubleshooting almost any normal soul could handle (but
had his wife for that).

Life was peculiarly strange!

Now and again the phone interrupted his reveries and he
busied himself with taking messages, the proprietor's useful
factotum, listening with respect and recording with care the
communications of gravel-voiced contractors and querulous
ladies and ladies with bells for voices and people who said
they were friends but left no messages and after a while he
realized without surprise that he was waiting for the dark
and thrilling voice of his own Armenian bombshell, unheard
these many years, for he had never doubted for a single
moment back there in the throes that this pair too or especially this pair had been gaily fucking (and maintained
frequent contact) while he perfected suffering a few streets
away believing she had fled to Fresno whereas in point of
fact she was lowering her black panties with that curtsying
smile he'd always loved a few blocks south by southwest
for macho wop and holy shit he was clearly believing it
still, a decade later and four years since the arrival of his
book in the post with its ashy innards and infernal message
but that was in another country and besides methinks the
wench is dead or chasing Gurdjieff into the high Himalayas

or breaking some other fellow's balls although no spring chicken so maybe settled finally into the Marin County PTA with two Armenian brats and dark surgeon husband or still unwed and showing in all the right galleries on Fifty-seventh Street right under his nose had he known enough to look but Paul or some other knowledgeable subscriber to *Art News* would have told him if this had been the case so with his own bottle of Goodmore as good as gone he went to work on the one he had tried to donate to the establishment and been insulted for his pains.

He had drunk and drifted by all need for sustenance but as it was dark over Fourth Avenue he propelled himself toward the fridge where he remembered having seen the dried end of a chunk of fontina and half a loaf of processed white bread and a couple of plastic tomatoes, items it had shocked him to find in Paul's larder, so made himself a dinner of sorts with these and what remained of his own supplies then wanted a beer but hardly worth the trip down all those flights made do with ice water and counted ten cigarettes still in the pack relaxed and made the necessary calls

"Listen, I'll meet you guys at the funeral parlor."

"You don't want to come down here first and have a little breakfast together and we'll all ride up in Dad's car?"

"Can't."

. . . message following the tone.

This is Grant Bestwrangler Susan I trust you remember me and the bland fucking we did in olden days but fucking granted isn't everything do you still have those splendid pouty lips and boobs like rolling hills and untrimmed toenails and rococo chestnut hair? Still sculpt those eight-foot plaster of paris cocks with balls attached one of which I purchased in our heyday and displayed for a month in my garden? has marriage to a reformed rabbi (yes I still read the *Times*) relieved you of obsessive, symbolic carnality? the very opposite?

Had he made other calls? Tokyo? Malmö? Fresno? He came awake on Paul's couch at midnight and dragged himself to bed and woke at two to stagger to the john to urinate and again at three-thirty to urinate and drink great quantities of water and woke at five-fifteen with a riproaring pain in the right side of his head he could not wish nor sleep away and threw his back out getting out of bed or had already damaged it curled on the lumpy couch but hobbled to the shower upstairs not really giving a shit if Paul had come back unbeknownst to him but no one there and spent twenty minutes under the powerful spray almost curing what ailed him beating back the headache and loosening his back muscles enough to do his back exercises, which helped, and found to his surprise and genuine pleasure that he had remembered to bring along his back belt as he called it and strapped that on his hips over the clean underwear and under the khaki trousers. His funeral garb was his daily attire, no help for that, a sloppy artist drunk, quotidian mourner, yet another sound reason if one had been needed to proceed straight uptown to the funeral parlor rather than to the ancestral hearth where parents (one or both) might have tried to stuff him into a suit and pair of shoes belonging to his father (Where's your respect, Son? Where's your pride?) when it was going to be tough enough in a bit to remember who he was.

*

He clumped down the stairs at six A.M. into a warm drizzle, the kind of New York Sunday morning with spring on the way he'd loved since a child. The deli/grocer was open and busy, had been open all night. He bought a large coffee and a box of midget powdered doughnuts from a wisecracking Latin, just the junkfood along with cigarettes to get him rolling at that hour, purchased not one or two but three packs of Merit 100's (which were a few cents cheaper than in Boston), tried to resist but left the store finally with the enormous dead weight of the Sunday *New York Times* beneath his arm. Trudged with the booty back to the loft and checked the obits, but uncle Abie loving husband adored father hadn't made it yet, maybe the son of a bitch hadn't died. Looked for academic positions in the rear of section four, News of the Week, where the ads for academic positions had always been for some odd reason, strange place for them perhaps but you heard no complaints from Sams, who required from his Daily Bugle no more than predictability, the opportunity to lay hands on what you wanted every day without an all-points search, which is what you got in the *New York Times,* daily and Sunday, but not in the jumble of the *Boston Globe.* But maybe it was high time he stopped bitching about all aspects of his present life. No one had forced him to live where he lived. If he didn't like Boston why not stop the complaining and get the fuck out, look for a way to get back to New York, as he was doing at the moment, he'd run it all by Jenny later, once she'd loved New York as much as he did if not more, but move with her or without. Don't shit a shitter, Jason, you'd never leave the kid, having finally found in fathering meaningful work, but right below his pencil was a job in the English Department at Hunter College, for a "Creative Writer" of all things, someone to head up the whole creative writing shebang, no reason he couldn't do that, no doubt he was a closet administrator, knew enough famous writers to line up the guest shots, if he could stomach doing that, asking something of the assholes, and began working on the cover letter and sprucing up his c.v. in his head, and remembered his friend the writer and professor Jon Baumbach for years ensconced in the Creative Writing Department at Queens College, been a while since he'd checked with Jon about a possible opening at Queens unless (for all he knew) he'd called him in a blackout and offended him mortally the night before. A touch of remorse and self-disgust and fear, just then, for what he might have done, but stronger than all three a thirst, and barely enough Goodmore left in the bottom of both bottles to combine and add ice and water to for proper perusal of the Book Review (might find his own name in there under Paperbacks New & Noteworthy if nowhere else, *When this book was first issued our reviewer Jason Sams said Supple lapidary what an ear this sucks,* and if his name *was* there, and he somehow missed it, why his mom would surely sniff it out) and the magazine section and section two for Arts & Leisure and the meat of section four, the weekly news. So teased some ice cubes out of the blue plastic tray and emptied both bottles into a squat glass, filling it with water to just below the brim. I don't usually imbibe in the morning, he explained to the questioning hordes, only prior to funerals and weddings, viz. and to wit how completely plastered on beer and brandy while communing solitary from five A.M. with squawking blue jays in the garden — and single hummingbird! — on the morning of his own farewell to bachelorhood.

Fact was he did not often drink upon rising (discounting staring wakings in the wee hours on far from rare occasions when crapped out drunk at seven or eight the night before and required hair of the dog at two or three or four to catch another hour's sleep or two but rarely drank again at first light no matter how lousy partying in dead of night had left him feeling), so weaved a bit along Fourth Avenue, and since becoming light in the pocketbook he vetoed a cab and strolled through private fog toward Fourteenth Street where he would grab a crosstown bus going west and with the free transfer switch to the Eighth Avenue bus for a direct run to the funeral parlor. He studied the faces and demeanor of his fellow passengers on both buses and was pleased to discover or imagine that more than one chap at nine-thirty on a Sunday morning was as glassy and pie-eyed as he.

Yet once off the bus too sober to avoid embarrassment, outside the establishment running into three young apprentices directing traffic all natty in black and appropriately somber despite not knowing Uncle Abie from a hole in the ground, and heard himself lie to the tune of having just that morning learned of Abe Sams' untimely passing, obliged with clothing misrouted by Pan Am to come as he was, and the spiffy youths who could care less nodded understandingly and waved him on his way. He ducked into an empty chapel and did his back exercises on a comfy carpet and adjusted his clothing then found an empty john, where he took a few drags and swished warm water around in his mouth, spit it out, splashed cold water on his face, wished the stranger in the mirror well, and went forth to join the clan.

Saw his uncle's name in white letters on black background, SERVICE FOR ABRAHAM SAMS, and recalling yet again his own name zigging left and zagging right out of his life that final Boston morning, he passed right by the open ledger, had no signature to waste, entered the room and (looking for her) saw right off on a settee against the far wall flanked by son Ed and daughter-in-law Helen huge Aunt Trixie and couldn't calculate how many years had passed since they'd met nor whether he had thought about her in the interval but as he moved through the crowd to pay his respects despite glimpsing from the corner of an eye his own mother standing lonesome and his father chatting farther off he found when he grabbed Trixie's pouchy hand and looked into her befuddled grief that he came near undone by the wave of feeling cresting from the time he'd been the very kid on whom Solomon had passed his crazy-like-a-king judgment, why not just sunder the brat, half to this claimant half to the other mother, real one will be horrified, kind of a dumb tale to the adult he had become but when their paths had crossed down by the junkshop or anywhere else his aunt invariably treated him like some fucked-up offspring of her own, never as Eddie's rival for the dubious attentions of tightwad father-in-law the founder who sat in a chair out front all day looking swell in gold skull cap and white spade beard slashing out with heavy cane at whichever child ventured too close in noisy play and she would rescue both or either and say Jason, Eddie, keep away from the old shit for the filthy penny or even nickel he might one day give you listen to what I'm saying you too Jacey I don't give a shit about the garbage your deepthinking mother fills your head with about what the old bastard leaves to who or the great respect your father and my son's shmuck father too claim to have for *their* father because he used to beat the living crap out of the two of them with all the kids he had running around I doubt he could even tell them apart but pay attention to your fat Aunt Trixie she would hiss and boom from her mendacious depths, the joyous heart of her vulgarity, this had been some woman, and he bent to kiss her on the mouth and mumble Trixie I'm sorry this happened, but it was not quite enough, and for a time he could not let go of her hand.

"You look crocked, Professor," Helen informed him. "Your mother once told me you never touched a drop before noon."

So he bent back down and kissed her too. That way he could whisper, "Don't be a cunt today, Cuz."

"I try to be myself every day."

But she too corrupted kewpie looked as if she might be suffering; had she been absolutely nuts about her father-in-law? Was her livelihood being threatened in the bicentennial year, her lawyers now dubious about the first amendment arguments? He turned finally to fatherless Ed, his cousin, his brother.

"I'm sorry, Ed."

Ed Sams nodded, shrugged.

"What can you do, Jace? The bastard knew ten years ago he had to quit smoking. How's by you? The family well? Your work goes OK?"

"Everything's swell."

His swarthy cousin fixed him with eyes so brown they seemed black (his own today a wishy-washy blue); seeing what? He knew Ed's expression from childhood, made up of admiration (envy?), love even, and profound contempt for this schoolwise cousin with no earning power; there was too much between them, and nothing; so Jason bent again and kissed him too.

"You look older than your father with that beard," his aunt observed. "You came in from where you live for your Uncle Abie? Or you were already here?"

"I was in town. But I would have come in."

"He was a good man, your uncle. He smoked too much."

"I know."

"I told Eddie, if he ever starts up again with the cigarettes, I'll break open his face. Sweetiepie here also. Did I tell you or didn't I?"

"You absolutely told us, Ma," Helen Sams said.

"How about you, Jacey, you stop smoking?"

"I'm closing in on the moment."

"Don't close in on the moment. Throw them away. And don't worry about getting fat. Your own mother quit, and she didn't get no dumpier than she was before. I quit seven years ago. Look at me, am I as gorgeous as I was?"

"Trixie, you are."

There were people behind him. He wandered away. He nodded at relatives he knew he should have known but had no clue, no names, cousins and second cousins and their spouses and even his own aunts and uncles, his father's tribe of half-sisters and their husbands who (the sisters) had been around all his life, yet who usually, when they were all in a room together, ran together in his mind.

Made his way to his mother's side but she was doing fine now without him, chatting it up with a pretty woman who is studying literature at Barnard and is your first cousin, Jason, Hattie and Marcus' youngest daughter, and it just so happens she writes herself and needs your help to pick out a graduate school to study writing in, I just finished telling her how well your own latest book is going, That's news to me, he almost said, flashing a death ray at his poor mom but kept the lid on while he took in this young cousin's pretty face, pulled out a translucent business card on which

was printed name and address and his new (as yet unprac-
ticed) profession, Technical Writer and Editor, and why not,
a man of fastidious verbal gifts cashing in on this lucrative
technical writing thing as soon as he found out what it was,
do give me a call if you're ever in Boston and I'll make time
for us to get together and chat about your academic needs
but as Tolstoy said to the young man who crossed the Russian steppes in order to find him, hoping in this fashion to
become a writer, *Ecrivez!* and she thanked the mother's son
and departed.

"Jesus, Tillie, why? Does this strike you as an appropriate
forum in which to pop off about my son the writer?"
    "I'm proud of you, so what? Don't be so sensitive." She
squeezed his arm. "You had nothing else to wear?"

Made his way to where his father was, deciding to stick
close to him today, whether or not Julie noticed, or appre-
ciated. The man had never asked him for a favor in their
lives, why would he start now?

Julie glanced at Jason and smiled and threw an arm around
his shoulders, but continued to offer what appeared to be
unsolicited advice to brother-in-law Moish Lefkowitz, millionaire purveyor of moderately priced women's clothes,
but Moish interrupted the flow to nod, shake Jason's hand,
and ask how he and his were faring. How many kids you
got now? Still just the one, Moish, so this bereaved bastard
here is going to remain the grandfather as well as father of
only sons, not that myself and the shiksa bride who couldn't
get away today didn't have a go at repeating the miracle,
but had to settle for what God gave us, Moish, as who

doesn't nowadays, since no longer can we bullshit Him like Moses did, reason him out of His revenge, and suddenly unsure if all or any of this had in fact come out of his mouth he grabbed Moish's hand again while admiring his gray mustache and shrewd empty eyes and wondered if the man might not want to head up a foundation for the purpose of distributing excess funds to indigent artists related by marriage if not blood, no doubt a far-fetched notion, but you never knew until you asked, told his dad he'd see him in a bit, made his way back to the street, to upper Broadway, found a just-opened tavern with no other customers in it less than two blocks away and put back a scotch and a draft which did nothing for him, or to him, so ordered a second beer and after only two sips of this was all at once as drunk as he needed to get.

Wound up crammed into the back seat of a silver Lincoln Continental the property of Uncle Sam who was Sam Gould the trafficker in time and space (what did you say Uncle Sammy does? he deals in time and space?), bartering radio time or advertising pages in slick mags for luxury vacations in the Bahamas which he did not (usually) take but traded off for say a warehouse full of Swiss army knives which someone wanted badly enough to part with several speedboats for, save up your speedboats and get yourself a Lincoln, was that the way it worked? Lucre must somewhere enter it, for Sam and wife Matilda the youngest of Julie's sisters (hardly a year older than nephew Jason) lived rather well (he visited them once, why or when could not recall), childless in ten-room co-op on thirtieth floor with own sundeck and closeup view of East River of course plus all the buildings Jason had loved since a kid from afar

and somewhere below a communal pool up there on East
Sixty-third.

Dims on, gray day in automotive queue to Queens into
cities of the dead acres and miles of tombs and yes even
mausoleums in the goyish parts both sides of road but came
a mammoth headache when he leaned across some kin and
strained without hope to see the graves of Bubbe and Zayde
on his mother's side although his dad's dad Chaim Shmuel
lay out there too Shmuel metamorphosed to Sams at Ellis
Island probably alongside the resting place of the first of
Chaim's wives his blood grandmother the mother of the
twins the younger of whom by five minutes they were on
the way to bury. Killed in a fire June of 1907 days after Jules
and Abraham were born. Chaim following whatever was
a decent interval in those times marrying his housekeeper
who did her duty by the twins and other kids on hand then
went on to bless him with a dozen of her own. Gentle
octogenarian living now by choice alone in one-bedroom
apartment in Stuyvesant Town in Manhattan but not feeling well enough today to watch Abe go under, although
she'd raised him, hey, somewhere among the present crop
of tugboat captains and tax lawyers and Brentwood pe-
diatricians and shrinks and badbreathed brokers might lurk
a maximalist to one day put the house in order, put the
Sams saga in workable shape literal rags to riches and such
literary sweetmeats, maybe the very young woman his
mother had been speaking with and he'd been supercilious
to, but it would not be he, crushed among cousins and uncles and at that very moment unleashing a cigarette cough
powerful enough to reinjure his tender lower back (the
American malady), this distracting him at any rate from
vicious headache but fair warning too it was going to take

some doing and a bit of luck to arrive intact at the finish to this day.

Gingerly, then, he squeezed out of the Lincoln and began searching for his father.

Followed Julie up an incline and stood a foot behind him at the lip of the grave. Stared into the loose red earth. Never knew the holes went down that far. I looked away and out beyond the gates, at rows of yellow cabs, and said, "Why all the cabs?" and Julie said, "Your uncle drove a hack for many years, they're here to pay respects."

I put a hand on his shoulder. I couldn't look at him. "Good turnout," I said.

"Hope to do as well when my turn comes, Son. Some business, Jace, lying in your own bed one day, in a hole the next."

Watched cousin Ed file by below sobbing and supporting his mother my aunt with his wife my cousin through marriage the entrepreneur and true fictioneer of the family marching by with her arm through his on his other side. I never saw the coffin going down, never heard the prayers, blind and deaf to happenings on the hill. But I looked again into the hole and Abe sure enough was going to be living in a box in the earth. Gun-toting bastard though he may have been (but who had proof?), nastier twin (in Tillie's view) by far, he nonetheless deserved better. My mother trucked on by below, accompanied only by the life of the mind. I fought back the impulse to join her. Drunk, disabled, I'd probably trip and fall on her while making the descent.

*

And sudden hallucinatory surge: he couldn't be seeing what he saw. Needed a mirror to check out the workings of his own mouth. Our enemy is dead, maman, a toast? circumspectly sharing her Gioconda smile.

"Throw some dirt on him, Jace," Julie commanded.

"Do what?"

He thrust the shovel into my hand. "Do what I just did. Throw a shovelful of earth on Abe."

He'd picked the wrong time to ask me for this favor. "I'd like to, but my back is out. I can't bend my knees."

I watched Ed Sams fly up the hill wearing the same expression he'd worn thirty years before when he'd sprinted across cobbled, heavily trafficked Avenue C to deck the monster who had just decked me. He ripped the shovel from my hand and covered his father.

Jason was driven to the Colonial Hall in a different car from the one he had come in, it being lawful and proper to officially mourn (sit shivah) in more than one household, spouse and twin having dibs on grief but Trixie since now domiciled amid Miami Beach malls and palms she sat in son Eddie's house splendid condo or co-op on Seventy-fourth and Third which struck many if not most as the official place of mourning, which was not to dishonor my father's strong claim, while I, I went downtown where I imagined I would find comfort, be needed.

To watch Julie sit shivah shiver sit with Shiva the Destroyer whatever they were up to here, his dad to sit there on the hassock for seven days without a shave the mirrors covered was it to keep the soul of the departed from wandering into Wonderland or Purgatory or *your* soul from tawdry distraction who knew the ins and outs of such mat-

ters the straight poop was doubtless in the Mishnah and do
not forget reformed Jews and conservative Jews and lapsed
orthodox Jews let alone degrees of lapsing as say he and his
dad along with the meaning of the prayers he recited information he could function without so by the time I arrived
already too late to check out my own distorted image underneath the weighty eagle not unlike the eagles on my
shoulders, mentor on one and mother on the other, watching and clucking as I typed and drank but this time the
possibility of eating well for she or he or someone had laid
in the ethnic specialties missing Friday night the lox and
cream cheese plain and with chives and creamed herring and
sharp matjes herring and whitefish and sturgeon I for one
could take or leave but popular among my father's sisters
mostly and their mates who shuttled from one house to the
other and lovely pumpernickel had our Jewish wake and
pop seemed cheerful for the circumstances so did mother as
I moved between the living room and the kitchen cabinets
downing rapidly and neat the J&B but also ate now and
then in the warm house, not just the steam heat and chachkas
of childhood but piled high with his own early promise
(yes!) and even (yes!) achievement who could forget the
brown leather looseleaf book of poems verse to be precise
of his own devising that sometimes drove him wild there
in the bookcase typed long ago by her loving hand from
second and third grade that she would offer to part with
now and again this should be with you now Jace not with
me I mean for your permanent records sure I would miss
it but after all it's yours That's OK for Christ's sake Ma
may it live here forever not to mention multiple copies of
his corpus and even worse perhaps if any of it mattered as
a kind of centerpiece on the tan hourglass table the March
1960 issue of the glossy magazine she had had bound in

leather embossed in gilt in gilt wert thou embossed my son in guilt shalt thou go what have you written for me lately the name of the magazine and his name writ larger still and the name of the story he had published therein a mere sixteen years earlier that had put them on the map but found himself in earnest discourse by and by with one of his aunts or cousins late in the evening about that too-long story snaking its way through the back of the men's magazine's aftershave and body building ads page after page and how apart from the ads the story had been changed which is to say he had changed it between its first appearance and its subsequent incarnations in anthologies and in his own book and then not giving the matter very much thought (beginning to yearn for his bed) he lent the damn thing to her for her edification (for she seemed genuinely interested in comparing the magazine version with the way it read in his book which she happened to own) just as if it had been his to lend.

When aunt-cousin left you can bet your bottom dollar he heard about it in a sad rebuke and analysis of aunt-cousin's character who borrowed things she never returned jeez I'm sorry Ma I didn't know but at last it was time to go home to Paul's loft and on the morrow home to real life in Boston and his own distress

so said farewells and took a last look around at artifacts of childhood lingering over the heavy crazy mirror in the living room with the sheet over its distorting surface but golden eagle uncovered and he felt its weight again and then the weight again of his own pair of eagles one on each shoulder he had lived with for twenty odd years the Trilling eagle and the Tillie eagle peering into the Olivetti gabbling and stepping on each other's lines *that* won't do and surely not *that* tear it all up and start over you've lost it kid you never had it can't you write anything at all without mocking your kin or your mentors you guys are kidding aren't you this is literature ah but in this instance so derivative Mr. Sams well fuck you Lionel we perch here now in utmost sadness I am tired of explaining your silence my son perhaps Mr. Sams you ought to consider taking an additional five years off sans the otiose effort to perform since neither your mother nor I is able to pretend your more recent volume brought us any happiness not an easy profession you chose for yourself Jacey but do it or get off the pot GOOD LUCK TO THE PAIR OF YOU and he imagined the weight lifted what a feeling although the test was yet to come so grasped Julie's hand and kissed him on the cheek and kissed his mom while patting her back and wishing her luck through the ordeal ahead cutting her short as she asked after his own plans longrange and short putting up with a last lost long look of love and hit the road free at last he thought waiting for the elevator out in the familiar corridor when the apartment door creaked open and his father came into the hallway.

"Where you headed, Son? You flying back tonight?"

"No, headed back in the morning. One more night in Pisacano's loft."

"How you getting there?"

"Cab. Bus. I may even walk."

"Let me grab a jacket. I'll walk with you. I need the exercise."

"Don't you have to sit?"

"I'll be sitting for a week. There's time to sit."

"Fine, I'll wait here."

His father returned wearing a maroon sports jacket and a gray fedora with a feather in it.

"You still scared this thing will stop between floors and you'll get stuck in it?"

"You remember that?"

"How could I not remember, you used to drive us nuts every time you got in it. So how's your back? Any better than it was?"

"Yeah, a lot. I think the J&B cured me."

"Cured you like a piece of meat, maybe. Well, you're grown up, I can't tell you how to drink."

His father lit a cigar as they waited for the light to change at First Avenue. "So what's happening in your life? You become a Boston Red Sox fan?"

"Nah. I went to a few games last year. But you know how it is for me, I'm still stuck back there with the Brooklyn Dodgers."

" 'Dem Bums.' Yeah, you were a fanatic for them, all right. You smoke cigars?"

"No, thanks, Pop. But I like the smell of yours."

"You should. They retail for a dollar each, but I get them for fifteen dollars the box, from Hector, the auto parts guy, he has relatives in Cuba."

"That's great. Are you going to be all right? I know how close you and Abe were."

"I'll be fine, Son. My brother Abie had a good life. When God says your time is up, it's up. I only wish I'd had a chance to see him before he died. Your mother wants no part of Florida, but I should have gone down there on my own."

"For a visit?"

"For a visit, to live permanent, whatever. Your mother,

God bless her, is not always easy to live with. Like she's apt to throw a fit if I smoke in the house."

"I know."

"So tell me how things go with you. You need a little extra cash to get by?"

A grand a week would do it, Jason thinks.

"No, we're fine, thanks. I plan to pay back someday what I already owe you."

Some years earlier at the kitchen table, when he was in for a few days from Woodstock, his father had whipped out a small notebook (as he was handing over a generous check, and with a baby and no job Sams was busted then) and read off the sum of thirty thousand dollars. "That's how much I've advanced you to date, Son," he had said, looking pleased. Jason had been shocked by the fastidious record-keeping, but it had not made him as angry as it had made his mother.

"You don't owe me nothing, Jace. I'm just hoping your ship comes in. I know how hard you work at your writing, and I have no doubt that someday you're going to hit it big. So tell me, how's my daughter-in-law and grandson?"

"They're both fine, Pop."

"Good. That's what I like to hear."

Walking safely now beside his dad through the dark and derelict-infested streets, Sams arrived without incident at the store where he'd bought his junkfood breakfast a century ago that morning. His father followed him into the store. Jason bought a Freihofer's coffee cake and a small jar of instant coffee for the morning, and a six-pack of Schlitz for what was left of the night. He felt a lot fresher than he'd felt when he left his parents' house.

"Let me get it, Son," his father said, and Jason, who had his return ticket in his wallet, and twenty-two dollars besides, and wanted to take a taxi in the morning, and eat something or other on the train, complied without complaint.

"It's four flights up, or I'd ask you up for a beer. I know Paul'd be glad to see you, if he's there."

"That's all right, Son. I'll be getting back to your mother."

"You walking?"

"Nah, I'll grab a cab."

He flagged one down.

"Take this, Jason, will you, as a favor to me, without giving me crap? You'll return it when your ship comes in." He stuffed some bills into my hand. I didn't resist, but he added, "If you don't need it, give it to my grandson. So you flying back?"

"Taking the train."

"Better you than me. I had enough of trains the last time."

"I know."

And for the second time in three days he kissed me on the mouth. He climbed into the back of the taxi; I shut the door behind him. He lowered the window and threw his cigar stub into the street. "The guy says he has asthma." He shrugged. "I knew a guy with asthma, it can be a bitch." The cab lurched forward, turned east at the corner. I watched him go, Julie Sams, survivor, doppelganger-free.

There was no sign that Paul had been back since the previous morning. Jazz still played softly, a trio doing a fifties' version of "Let There Be Love." My kind of music. The apartment was too warm. I stripped to my underwear, cracked open a beer, and sat on the sofa. The beer was to help me sort out the events of the long weekend, unearth their meaning (in the spirit of the day). But the mind remained blank, the stomach grew queasy. After an interval, a cigarette, a stroll, a leak, the dating of an empty notebook page — Ides of March, Bicentennial Year — I opened a second beer, took a long swallow, and remembered to deposit the spare key on the four-paneled door that served Paul as a kitchen table. I should not be needing it again, not on this journey. I climbed to the second floor and showered, stealing a march on the next day's departure. Came back downstairs in my pajamas and laid out my last set of clean underwear. Vast, black reservoir of anxiety churned just below everything I did; I dammed it for the moment with another beer. The last three cans would be there waiting for him in the fridge. Pisacano I give you one can Schlitz even up for one bottle India ale minus one you would have let me drink take it or leave it paisan he'd see the humor in it maybe if humor there was. I checked my Amtrak schedule another time, although I knew as well as I knew my name that I was shooting for the 7:45 A.M. I climbed beneath the covers. The world spun when I closed my eyes, but gently enough to ignore. The next day would see me reunited with my (small but select) family, might I not take some pleasure in that? Yeah but. We should have had another child or two, or done it at a blow with twins. We should have had a dog. I should have married Jewish, or rich, or both. Maybe I should see about having a lock put on the studio door, or rent a separate space, off the premises entirely. One thing was certain: I was going to have to put together two or maybe even three weeks of abstinence so as to launch the book that no one, any longer, thought I would write. Not my new porcine editor, my old thin distractible agent, my long-suffering wife, my clever best friend. (Why, having lived so long, had I no better best friend?) And at the end of the three weeks, with fifty solid pages behind me, I'd re-enter, buy Chivas for the house, and forgive my enemies. I would by then have taken in several Vedanta lectures on back-to-back Sundays to shore up my holy compassion. On such thoughts of shriven enemies, won over and subdued, I slept. And dreamed. A ritual killing and the corpse trapped beneath enormous stone. We tried to move the monolith to give the body proper burial but my boys couldn't budge that rock. So I watched violent television with the wrong woman, lost my way with her or another in labyrinthine restaurants, dreamed away the night it seemed with a glut of unconnected fragments yet by the end had returned to that pisser of a plinth and this time my niggers moved it easily and the corpse rolled free. At the time it seemed a happy resolution; I woke with it, and with cousin Eddie on my mind, not merely the most recent business of ripping the useless shovel from my hand but cousin Eddie way back when, cousin Eddie and his glottal stop, cousin Eddie rich, with a second condominium on East Tenth and Fifth Avenue, cousin Eddie and his spouse out jogging every morning, returning to their doorman and their mile-high television set, then Eddie in the years he brought the necessary toughness to the junkshop job stuck down there before *his* ship came in *Doan fuck wid me yuh black rat-bastard I'll kill yuh yuh nigger cocksucker* keeping order thus among the sometimes unhappy pushcart pushers remnant of that trade survived into the early nineteen fifties or right up to the fire Eddie's managerial style not unappreciated by his uncle Julie and his father Abe. Noted again in his own purview how Seamans might have done something more to spare the world Sams' own obscenities, which on a recent thumb-through of *Slow Dying* seemed to its author to deface every other page.

Or would Jason the purist have bitched and raised a stink had such liberties back then been taken?

Who could tell? Believer in patterns as he was he would not have been surprised to see cousin Eddie's white stretch limo-for-hire awaiting him at the curb with Eddie himself at the wheel as he hit Fourth Avenue at a quarter to seven in the morning on Monday, head and stomach out of whack, feeling strange, more than usually fearful, but the driver of the cab that responded to his hail and veered into the curb drove a yellow taxi from a different era, a rattling piece of crap inside and out, and his face pushed Jason back into his fragmented dream, a burn victim at a guess, half a head of hair with an ear gone and a hole for a mouth from which thankfully issued no sound until Jason under the panicky misapprehension that the freak did not know where the new Penn Station was (having overshot it to the north and west), suggested same, perhaps untactfully, and the guy became so agitated Sams feared he would be asked to exit right then and there from the cab. I'll get you there, the driver said, in a voice that seemed to issue from the bottom of a well, you don't know the weekday traffic patterns, do you, why don't you let me do my job, and outside the station Sams with his dad's gift in his wallet tipped too generously in honor of Dostoevsky and fire victims and all the insulted and injured including the armies of beggars some with signs with long stories on them who had sprung up in his beloved city since last time he was there but the ungrateful son of a bitch picked up a new fare and sped off without acknowledging Julie's money in his hand.

Headed Home

INSIDE THE TERMINAL with twenty minutes to spare he bought a *New York Times* and a *New York Daily News* and a Snickers and a Baby Ruth keeping a watchful eye on his worldly goods while bidding farewell to the metropolis in which if you made it there you'd make it anywhere even in the country to which he'd not moved until the year after the Woodstock Festival about which he had known little other than that it had not taken place in Woodstock and from there still dazed after four years he had moved on to Boston and why, pray, did so much of so much importance happen to him accidentally, while other people seemed to make real choices with their lives? He would have pondered this further had he not had a train to catch and had his heart not begun just then an irregular beat that reminded him of what had happened when he drank on Antabuse distracting him entirely from discomfort in his gut and head and he tried on the move to regulate his heart through deep breathing and prayer to That Which appeared fortuitously more often than not at such moments to be prayed to, absolutely unwilling to endure a heart attack there at that moment among strangers and boarded the already crowded train up from D.C. en route to Boston but found a seat without too much difficulty albeit in a nonsmoking car next to a solid-looking chap with a broad nose and kindly eyes and black curly hair wearing sharply creased khakis and a bulky sweater and loafers and was reading a book, all good signs, but Sams stood up almost at once under the pressure of what had become a pounding in his chest and was already moving about the Minuteman or Paul Revere or Independence I forget when the all aboard sounded and the train began to crawl through the long tunnel out of Penn Station into Queens and he ran into an elderly officious ticket-taker in black suit and cap who asked him for his ticket and berated him for moving about the train without it although Sams knew he had it somewhere on his person but could not be bothered to look as he broke into the man's scolding:

"Is there a doctor on the train?"

"Come again?"

"I'm not feeling well. Is there a doctor on the train?"

"This ain't the *Queen Mary*, Son." With limited time for blithering idiots, the man moved on.

Seems odd that in close to forty-four years of sometimes hectic living Sams had never before experienced a full-blown anxiety attack so couldn't easily identify what was happening to him if that was indeed what it was rather than withdrawal from alcohol since he had not had a drink that morning but jeez not that many hours had passed since the beers of the previous night let alone the aggregate of everything consumed during his three days in NYC which was more than he usually drank in a fortnight or it may have been merely his intention not to drink that day even after the club car opened so that he might arrive back in the arms or at least the general area of his not-these-days-so-loving wife that caused his heart to pound its disapproval, and, well, that plan not to drink was subject now to reassessment, for it did not look like breathing or praying was having any effect on what was going on in his chest.

But had the presence of mind to stoop and peer out an unsmeared window and watch it go and say adieu from the Bronx to the bunched Manhattan skyline, Empire State and Chrysler Building and even Metropolitan Life on Twenty-third and Edison on Fourteenth stepping down to his father's house and nothing but contempt for the inverted pair of trousers one leg shorter than the other still being constructed down at the end of the island. The Sams clan planned to avail itself of the opulent facilities at the top of the tall pant leg for their next family reunion some six months thence, he'd heard, and he might be persuaded (he and his) to come back to New York for that, should he live, for the free booze and the vista, but the Empire State would always remain for him the grandest structure in the world as it had been since childhood even now when they colored it pink at night and the Chrysler Building with its lance poking skyward the most breathtaking so don't fill his head please with talk of change or progress as God intended certain things to remain what they were.

As he moved shakily through the cars he took in the faces in the manner of a *New Yorker* reader flipping through for the cartoons, cadaverous Charles Addams creature here, Thurber eyepatch there, caricatures no doubt but "of all ages and sizes from all walks of life of all religions and races" as he remembered having infelicitously phrased it in a prize-winning essay in junior high school on the wonders of democracy (and scarcely a single political thought had passed through his mind in the eons since), but unlike faces in cartoons some of these disconcertingly returned his glances, took in his weaving progress to nowhere, while others slept. The doors at the ends of the cars seemed to slide open for him most reluctantly, as if he were not quite there for them to sense, down there where the tiny toilets were, smelling none too fresh, not cleaned since Washington, one for men and one for women, Amtrak not yet unisex, interrupting his journey briefly for a few puffs at the far end of the smoking car which set off a fit of coughing so violent that he stubbed out the butt, fearing again for the condition of his tender back. He blundered next into the club car, where minions in white jackets took his arrival unkindly, figuring him to be jumping the gun as would a very hungry man or an alcoholic, since they did not begin serving for another hour, but he threw the pair of them a needier look than was his wont, required neither food nor drink you see, no sandwiches or chips or soda or beer, all he wanted was for his heart to stop pounding, but his appearance and condition elicited no sympathy from dreadlocks and ebony, so he assured them in a voice the calmness of which surprised him that he was merely passing through and they told him authoritatively and gleefully that the engineer's cab was next, he had come to the end of the line.

So reversed himself, observing with something like gratitude that he had not even noticed when the threat of diarrhea had passed, and even his head felt a little better, everything was dandy point of fact except for the breakaway ticker, and the word "tachycardia" came to him just then, along with "infarction," causing him to wish he had learned some Greek and Latin but he had what he had, "infart" and "utfart" popping next into his head, jolly Swedish words for entrance and exit, giving him something to do, at last, find in less than thirty seconds the words for entrance and exit in Japanese, exit came quickly, "deguchi," but entrance was elusive, ending also in "-guchi," mouth, but what the devil was the prefix, and what a waste all that had been, knowing even on the boat going over he would never use it crazy wastes of a life You likee me GI we go now my house didn't need a language school for missionaries in lovely Shimogamo in northern Kyoto for that nor the University of London afterward where good old Mr. Yanada expatriate for thirty years with strong British accent could not help saying "In yenny case" and "Its depend" and where Mr. Beasley the Oxbridge history professor woke him up one afternoon with talk of "feudal Jews," those feudal Jews, might have guessed they'd had a hand in it but it was "feudal dues" he'd heard, ahah, and why such thoughts now and of the many half-pints of scotch he'd bolted in University of London toilets during the dreadful hours from two to five-thirty P.M. when the pubs closed down. Spanish, now, was a mere year at the University of Barcelona in 1959 using up what remained of the GI Bill, but "entrada" and "salida" came when called, not bad on short notice for such an indifferent linguist let alone outright fraud on many counts but fraud me no fraud give me a bit of a break why don't you Jason let me live in peace for another couple of hours and I will show you such sincerity and authenticity as would have pleased the master unhappy as he may have been over some cheap satire aimed apparently in his direction in *Slow Dying,* if, in the latter days, I figured in his thoughts at all.

By the time he got back to his seat, upon which the young man had thoughtfully placed the slim volume he had earlier been reading, Sams (very unlike him) having forgotten to protect his space in any way, he felt hale enough to risk: "Excuse me, I'm not feeling well, how do I look to you?"

The handsome chap dissembled his surprise, fastened his

brown eyes on Jason's face, took some time with the scrutiny.

"You look OK. What seems to be wrong?"

"I don't know. I thought a while ago I might be having a heart attack. Is my face a normal color?"

"A bit pale, perhaps, and you're sweating, but . . . do you have any pain in your chest, and down your left arm?"

"No pain anywhere, just a very rapid heartbeat. It's an odd request, I know, but could you keep an eye on me?"

"Sure. Maybe you ought to sit down."

"Thanks. Thanks for saving my seat. What's that you're reading?"

"*The Empire Builders.* It's a play by Boris Vian."

"Don't know him. Is it any good?"

"It's a great play, I think. But I'm playing the lead, so I may not have much perspective."

Truly crazed, what passed next through his mind: abject, sycophantic fear of what looked like a stranger's success.

"On Broadway?"

"No, no, it'll open in three months, downtown at the Astor Theater."

"I know where the Astor is. Maybe I can get in to New York to see it."

"That'd be great. If you give me your address, I'll see if I can send you some comps."

Jason fumbled in his wallet, handed over one of his translucent business cards.

"You're a writer?"

"Trying to break into technical writing."

"Pays well, they say."

"That's what I hear."

That stopped the conversation for a while.

Finally the stranger said, "I thought of becoming a writer back in college."

"Yeah, so did I," said Sams. "Anything come of it?"

"Well, I wound up an editor for fifteen years, at Holt, Norton, and a couple of other places. I just quit that about a year ago."

"And became an actor, just like that?"

"Fell into it, really. Seems to be what I want to do."

"Did you know Al Seamans?"

"I'm sure I heard the name. He died, didn't he?"

"Yeah, he did."

"He edited a lot of fiction, I seem to remember. I did mostly nonfiction books."

"For fifteen years? You're probably older than you look."

"I'm pushing forty."

Sams noticed that his heart was slowing down, but it picked up its pace under his scrutiny.

"Jesus, I can't sit still. Maybe if I had a drink I could get some relief. Hair of the dog, you know? I had a rough weekend. You don't happen to be carrying any liquor?" he asked without hope.

"Sorry. I don't drink."

"I guess I'll try the club car in a bit. You don't drink at all? Did you quit?"

"Never really started."

"My name is Jason Sams."

"That's familiar, too. Any reason I should know it?"

"No."

"I'm Dick Allen. Not the ballplayer. How far are you going?"

"To Boston. End of the line."

"I get off at Providence. Anything I can do for you? Call ahead? Have someone meet the train?"

Sams considered this. "My wife, but no, she might freak out. If I make it to Providence, I should be OK the rest of the way. I'm just jumpy as hell right now. Maybe if I glanced at your play?"

"Oh, sure. Here."

Jason fondled the Grove paperback. "I don't know if I can concentrate. What's it about?"

"A French family of three — a father, mother, and a young daughter — whose lives keep constricting. They keep fleeing upward to get away from a mysterious, terrifying noise, always winding up in a smaller space, always with some valuable possession like a radio, or a clock, left behind. There's a creature wrapped in dirty bandages, called a 'schmürz,' which accompanies them, or is already there when they arrive. They use it as a punching bag, but only the daughter even admits the schmürz exists. The father usually denies that they ever even had the things the daughter says they lost. Gradually people begin to drop off as well — the neighbors, a maid, the daughter, the wife — so in the final scene the father is left alone in the attic, the noise suddenly very loud, with no place left to go."

"Reminds me of my life," Jason joked. It didn't much matter what he said, so long as he got back to Boston in one piece; he had a terrible hankering suddenly to lay eyes on his son.

"And you play the father."

"Right. 'The father,' that's all he's ever called."

"I think it's amazing, you know, to decide one day on a complete career change, and go out and do it."

"Take a look at Vian's bio. *That's* amazing."

Sams glanced at the back cover. "Boris Vian has been called 'a legend in his own lifetime,' " he read, usual dustcover flatulence. "A novelist, poet, playwright, singer, composer of more than three hundred songs, jazz trumpeter, translator, and engineer, his reputation in France grows steadily. He died in 1959, at the age of thirty-eight, of a heart attack." So he had outlived the son of a bitch already, no matter what happened here on the train. Hell, he'd written songs back in high school with his old buddy Charley Marowitz, entire musical comedies in fact, he'd sung Hebrew melodies and fantasized a crooner career, he'd planned to trȧnslate *Don Quixote* into Japanese but never gained enough proficiency in either language, turned his back on piano lessons in the long ago, something might have come of that, but how had the Frenchman come to be a goddamn *engineer,* that alone bothered old eggs-in-one-basket Sams who had allowed them somewhere down the line to talk him out of his love of mathematics, some asshole of a high school teacher who should have known better convincing him he'd have to choose, and impressionable shmuck that he'd been (or only young) he hadn't even tried to have it both ways but loaded up his eggs, and when the basket went blooie . . . he thought he remembered suddenly the day it happened, had just won the English prize and the math prize too and some teacher he respected said Too bad Jason now you'll have to choose one or the other for career plans and he had chosen and as things had gone he might die here on Amtrak as the single thing he had not (assuming he had ever even become it) remained, how sad, but at least the dying thing had come to seem less imminent, and as he finally began to read the play and got deeper into it while his heart sounded background music he was transported again as he had been all his lucky life whenever he wandered into the presence of a master and knew it this guy Vian whatever his other gifts was absolute master of conveying rank moral cowardice and foul self-delusion and there were probably more than a handful of writers laboring out there these days he knew nothing of who could astound him into keenest pleasure, as Beckett had, but he was just not reading much these days, but if he survived this little jaunt he guaranteed You he'd read his ass off for the rest of his life however long that was, in a nut house if necessary, and recalled his obligation to the *Boston Globe,* negative review wet with crocodile tears he would shortly produce which would not be so different in tone from the one *Slow Dying* received in the *New York Times* in '69 the one he had not recovered from yet, I cannot do it lady with the gravel voice, not in the best of shape right now to trash anyone you see, thus reading and making small decisions he whiled away the time.

Once or twice he rose and walked the other way (for sweet variety's sake) to find a place to urinate. Once Dick Allen went to the club car and asked him if he needed anything, not an easy moment. But in a split second he had thought it agonizingly through and asked for a cup of coffee and a ham and cheese. That, after all, was what he needed, if not what he wanted. What he wanted he would want in half an hour, and tomorrow, and the day after, and next week, and in a year, and five, unless he made it through this moment.

Yet he was a bit disappointed when the actor returned bringing him exactly what he'd asked for.

"Thanks. How much do I owe you?"

"Three dollars even."

"It's a hell of a play. A terrific part, yours."

Allen shook his head in wonder. "So many layers of meaning."

"How much of them do you need to comprehend to act it well?"

"I don't know. I just know the texture becomes thicker every time we rehearse, or when I read the part to myself."

"I envy you. Maybe I should go off and find a theater to join. Start as a stagehand, learn lighting, work my way up."

"Are you married?"

"Yeah. Might be an obstacle. But my wife was an actress before we married. If I took off to join the circus, she might be pleased. How about you, you married?"

"I was, for seven years. Divorced about a year."

"Kids?"

"No. A kid might have made the difference."

"Well, they say a kid is not the best reason to stay together."

"They say a lot of things we're probably better off ignoring."

You sent me an angel of mercy to get me through the ride. So please let him get me through the ride. Water on both sides of the train, sun glinting off sailboats and cabin cruisers moored out there on Long Island Sound, he was going to get through Connecticut it looked like, You gave me the courage to live with my terror, How odd of God to choose the Jews, Dorothy Parker or Ogden Nash, the time had certainly flown, seemed a whole lot less than four and a half hours to get to aptly named Providence, a city he had always intended to explore, but the place now where he must lose this great new friend he would almost certainly never see again. While not entirely sorry to see him go.

"I'd be glad to phone your wife if you wanted, have her meet you, or just to let her know you're OK."

"Thanks, Dick, I'd rather let it go. Thanks. Thanks for letting me sit with you. Thanks for saving my ass."

"You'll come see the play?"

"Absolutely. If you can't send tickets just send the dates, I'll make it in."

Dick Allen waved at him from the platform. The train picked up speed. In three quarters of an hour he would be home in the Hub, but three quarters of an hour suddenly seemed long, nothing to distract him now not merely from worrying his heartbeat but also from a brand-new sensation of having to keep his body parts by an effort of will from flying into space, for the command post apparently had broken down when Allen left, he was due to lose his limbs and privates and probably his head as well, an absurdist fear a quick trip to the club car would eliminate, and he started off that way, knowing he was about to blow the money in the bank, painful hours so far invested in a dry day. He did an about-face and walked back past his seat, discovering four or five cars down another club car, which did not really surprise him, just as it had not surprised Vian's French family to discover at the top of the stairway in each new smaller apartment that the schmürz had preceded them, if not their own schmürz then another. He might just as well give in and have the drink, it would taste great and restore him to one piece and do no permanent injury and he would begin this nondrinking thing first thing Tuesday morning. There were four people already in the queue; he would join it while he thought the matter through. The snack bar might close for keeps before he reached the head of the line, or he might just order coffee and a bag of salted nuts when he got there WHO YOU SHITTIN basso profundo stentorian going right through him along with the large rough open hand that smote him just then between the shoulder blades, shot like huge Mrs. Mack had given him in fifth grade when he wouldn't stop gabbing, she'd sneaked up behind and whacked him one and by the time he turned around still trying to catch his breath she was already lambasting from the front of the room smart kids who thought that smart gave them the right to break the rules but no one stood behind him now and he asked no questions, headed back to his seat and picked up for the first time the newspapers purchased that morning, got into the fortunes of the New York Mets and this bucktoothed Carter character who grew peanuts and was governor of Georgia, scheming to be nothing less than president of the United States, all walks of life all right, if he ever managed to look an inch or two beyond his own nose it might yet be an interesting year, thought Sams, looking up in time to see out there in the far distance the blocky Prudential and the Hancock Tower, harbingers of home, Boston's "loffly skyscrappers" as il papa had referred to them on holy visit to Beantown as inebriate Sams and spouse (how could she say he never took her anywhere?) part of the surging multitudes on the Boston Common digging his holiness high on his jerrybuilt platform, the impossibly thin blue glass Hancock with the habit of losing its windows stirring in him now for the first time a rush of affection and if his ersatz pedagogical career was truly kaput (a prospect he was ready to accept, even embrace) he might check out the possibilities of employment over there, as a "technical writer" of course, insurance company must have its newsletters and other dreadful prose needing to be generated or "impacted on," but healthier outdoor employment as well, signing on as one of the individuals who stood below in Copley Square with binoculars all day long looking up for signs that a window was about to blow, have to learn what the signs are, of course, but even Mrs. Mack had admitted he was a quick study, so enough already of this heartbreaking teaching the unteachable, if he lived, at UGB or anywhere, and enough perhaps also of writing the unwritable, although this was an uneasy afterthought. Things might work out, one way or the other: enter a dry season, pump some iron as in his youth, eat sensibly, put in the hours, delight us all.

Waste not, want not: packed the daily papers he had not had the chance to read much of in the KLM overnight bag his father had left with him on his parents' last trip to Boston, came from the shop where his father worked, of course, and Jason was fond of it, part of the estate perhaps of some important Dutch person's former mistress herself obscurely dead in Tudor City, her worldly goods redeemed from the Bureau of Encumbrances by his father's boss who let Julie make off with this and that now and again to eke out the meager pay, Julie saying to his son, "Can you use an overnight bag?" and only the boor that he'd been more than once in his time, as when he'd once asked his dad for a rag and some polish to shine his shoes with, and Julie had produced *an entire shoeshine box* for him to take home and he had refused it, would have once again said no. "Yeah, thanks, Pop, looks like a nice piece of luggage." "Did I ever give you any shit?"

A rhetorical question.

He detrained at Back Bay Station, in Copley Square. Back Bay was nearer to where he lived, but he hadn't trusted the rinkydink station as point of departure. He caught a cab in front of the station and it took him home.

It was one in the afternoon. Had he told Jenny when to expect him? He couldn't remember.

The handsome, overgrown, university-owned brownstone in which he had lived since October of 1974 in a three-bedroom apartment up on the top (fifth) floor, more than ample for their needs, with a formal dining room, large kitchen, two johns, a reasonable rent, since the Samses had brought their own furniture, even their Sears fridge, cutting all infernal Woodstock ties, trucking on into their new life . . . the apartment had resulted from the kind of serendipity and luck that seemed to befall him no longer, the three of them living in a motel and traveling here and there with active two-year-old in tow to look at flats, all unsuitable and overpriced, when he happened to mention their plight at some university function he had untypically attended for the reprieve from family, at which he happened to wryly mention his situation to the wife of the vice president for academic affairs, not crying about it, mind you, just putting it out there for inspection, here was the Visiting Creative Scribe at UGB with more or less prestige without a place to lay his head, and the next morning he was wakened by a phonecall from the vice president's office and two hours later he was resident in the overgrown brownstone in a small — but no small improvement over hotel living — VIP apartment and the rest of it consisted of sniffing around to see what else might be free in the building, and finding the gem, and calling the university rental office, and persuading them to let him have it for the time at least in part because of his promise to provide his own furniture and the assured brevity of his appointment. Back then he'd had some clout! Had lived in the apartment by now two years longer than he'd said he would, but needs change, including UGB's, and rental office personnel and policy had turned over several times by then, but he wondered all the same as he rode up in the ancient elevator whether now that he had lost the job he would lose the apartment as well, insult to injury, assuming they really wanted it enough to come after it, and had the legal means to evict him once his lease expired.

Did he need to ponder all these woes-to-come, now that his body and head were at last slowing down? He rang the bell to alert her of his coming, if she happened to be home — knew she didn't like surprises. No one responded, and he let himself into the apartment.

The sound of thundering hooves. A flying hug, not an everyday event.

"Hi, Dad. What did you bring me from New York?"

"Hello, young son."

"I'm not a young son. I'm four."

"I know. Sorry. How come you're not in school?"

"I went, but they had a fire. Mom had to bring me home."

"Where is she now?"

"She's in the yellow bathroom."

One of the johns was canary yellow, the other sunset pink; this troubled them for the first six months, then became part of the landscape. He took his bag into their bedroom, briefly annoyed that the bed wasn't made, looked out the window at his piece of the unruffled Charles River and mysterious Cambridge right behind it, peering then at the nearby two-story redbrick Hindu temple and the fenced-in enclosure on its roof, white, crosshatched widow's walk, glimpsing there again a blond out of Fowles peering anxiously at the river, shielding her eyes, leaping for joy as her husband's ship came round the bend. He returned to the living room and sat on the couch to wait.

He watched her emerge. Joy had always been easy to read on her face, and sadness, likewise confusion and rage; eight and a half years down the road from the day they had met, imagining he knew her features better than his own, he thought he knew what was happening now, the brief flick of happiness, as if she had believed for an instant that he still was who he had been, or (since he had never been it), as if she still saw him as she had in the beginning, with a love so intense at times he couldn't stand it, knew she was misguided, farmer's daughter actress he undoubtedly cared for but she lacked judgment here, then that vestige vanished from her face and the rage of being married to a drunk remaining longer, and finally (reflecting, for all he knew, his own exact expression) the negative neutrality that had served them both for some time in lieu of separation, fearsome prospect that (in his cups) he'd threatened often while fearing *she* might leave, bug out and take the kid, and then she said Hello and he said Hello, Jen, knowing that in the movie of someone else's life he would be smiling now with all his crooked yellow smoker's teeth rather than (as always) grimacing tentatively, mouth closed, and gather her up in his arms la di da, wondering again what his own face might be doing in his sudden and absolute neediness.

"Any news from New York?"

"Yeah. I'm really fucked up."

"I meant about your book."

"You were right. There isn't any book. Is there any coffee?"

"I'll make some."

Did she look (from the rear) triumphant, vindicated? But

there could be no payoff for her in his failure. He trailed behind her down the long corridor.

"Jake said there was a fire at the church."

"I said at the preschool," the child said, bringing up the rear.

"Was it a big fire?"

"I don't think so," she said, grinding the beans, releasing the terrific smell. "But the playroom was smoky, so they sent them home."

"Listen," he blurted, "I had a rough trip."

"How come?"

"Well . . . Jesus, my uncle died."

"You weren't that fond of him, were you?"

If he responded in kind it would be finished, and he would be desperately alone. "I need to talk, Jenny, please. Can we sit in the dining room?"

"You go ahead. I'll bring in the coffee."

He went ahead, sat in the captain's chair at the head of the large oval table. Jake remained in the kitchen with his mother. Sams felt very weak, finally about to come apart, in the safety of his own apartment. He could not predict what the next ten minutes held, but knew that the dining room table, whatever pleasant associations of good food and warmth it also had, had been dangerous turf in its time, beyond such drunken idiocies as the night he made Fiona nice and comfy in his chair, more on the order of countless conversations with his wife that escalated to crazy intractable argument during which they each smoked half a pack at least and sloshed themselves with caffeine or he himself with booze and beyond that was the unforgettable conversation with his mother the same weekend his old man had pushed her off the train, Jenny and Jake and his father close by in the kitchen his father enjoying her company and cramping her style while she labored lovingly or otherwise over the roast chicken and fixings she knew they enjoyed and his mother, reaching for his hand, letting it drop: "We hardly ever have a chance to talk, Jason." "So, let's talk." "You know I take pleasure in your writing, Jacey, in everything you write," and he, "You don't have to tell me, sometimes to excess," and his mother, "But since you've written nothing (apart from your wonderful book reviews, they're marvels of their kind) more recent than *Slow Dying,* I've been rereading it, and again I had to wonder, much as I admired it this time also, did you have to say what you said about me the way you said it?" "What do you mean, Ma?" he said with dread. "Granted it was not as bad as what that *momzer* Philip Roth had to say about *his* mother in *Portnoy's Complaint,* and that putz is a millionaire no less, while you still struggle, forgive me, Jace, I know the man's a friend of yours, but . . ." looking at him now, her eyes wet . . . "They were unkind, Jacey, the things you said about me! Did you have to be so unkind?" And Sams, scalp crawling, "Jeez, Tillie, Roth writes fiction and so do I! It was a novel! Fiction! You know what fiction is!" and she, "That's what I told my friends and neighbors, and I hope they believed me. Your father, of course, is so ignorant he was *pleased* by what you did, 'Ah for Chrissake, Tillie, it's only a book the kid wrote,' but you and I know better, Jason (like my own father knew), we know that words are magic. I was in pain for a long time, and I'm tired of not telling someone," and tears in his own eyes he ran quickly in his head through all the bullshit theoretics and said nothing, knew she was right, wished only she had found someone else to tell, and they both let it go after that, sufficient distractions through the rest of the short visit, food, hectic visit en masse to the Gardner Museum, a story in itself, but he did not thank her for her insight, at the time or afterward.

Perils of the dining room table.

His son came into the room.

"Hi, Dad."

"Long time no see."

"I saw you a few minutes ago."

"You're one literal guy."

His wife came in with two cups of coffee.

"I already put in your saccharin."

"Thanks."

"What'd you bring me from New York, Dad?"

"I forgot your present, Jake. I forgot your mother's too. There was too much happening . . ."

He began to cry. There was an instant when he thought he might have choked back the tears, but he let it pass. He did not look at either of them, and in a matter of seconds could not have seen them anyway. When he began to suck air and blubber he took off his glasses and laid his head on the table. His body heaved.

"What's wrong?"

She did not sound concerned, or compassionate, or anything else he could put a name to, but he didn't let it worry him.

"I b-b-b-backed m-myself into a corner long ago, Jenny, and I can't get out. I'm a worthless shit! I'm alcoholic! I screw up everybody's life!"

"You just had a tough weekend," she said quietly.

"Thanks, yeah, b-but everything I touch turns rotten. I'm sorry I'm c-c-crying, but I can't stop!" Her hand was on the table, and he covered it. Her fingers moved slightly. He did not need much more by way of affirmation.

"Listen! I love you! I can't drink! And you know, I don't have to! It just came to me! I can't drink and *I — I don't have to drink!*" He raised his eyes to the ceiling fixture. "Th-thank G-God! I'm f-f-free not to drink!" His face fell apart again, he couldn't speak.

Jake, at first aghast, now touched his arm. "Don't cry, Dad! You'll bring me something next time!"

"I'm not crying, Jake! I'm very happy! Everything I need is already in my life! You, your mom! D-Do you understand me?"

"Yeah, Dad."

There was a napkin on the table, and he wiped his eyes. When he thought he might start blubbering again, he stood and went to the near (pink) bathroom, where he doused his face with cold water, then washed it thoroughly. He looked into the mirror over the sink. The beard needed trimming. The eyes were damp and red. The lips, unlike his own, were thin. For a split second it was the face of his familiar, not the face of Jason Sams. It belonged to some lucky bastard not obliged to drink. Whosever face it was looked good: vulnerable, home after a long absence, stripped of guile.

He borrowed a Valium from Jennifer and went to bed. His mind raced madly, but his heart was calm, he was in one piece; by and by he slept. He woke after two hours, sweating, in a panic, afraid to be alone. He called her name with no response, called Jake's, then thumped the length of the apartment. Jake was asleep in his room, Jennifer was out of earshot in the kitchen. He needed a drink; opened the fridge, found the Diet Pepsi, drank it straight from the bottle. The bubbles soothed him going down.

"Can you spend some time with me over the next few days?"

"How do you mean?"

"I don't want to be by myself."

She shrugged, her back still to him, putting things in the oven, preparing dinner.

"I don't have too many places where I have to be. Dry-cleaning, take him to school, pick him up, that sort of thing."

"I'll drive you both to his school."

"Fine."

"What's for dinner?"

"Shepherd's pie."

"Fantastic."

"If you stop hovering there behind me, maybe I can get it made."

He sat himself at the kitchen table. Smoked. Planned. Got up and went to the yellow bathroom and washed down an Antabuse. Returned to the kitchen. In a few moments he would call the departmental secretary and cancel his Wednesday class; however well physically he might feel by then, he doubted he would be ready to assume the role. He doubted anyone would mind. Today or tomorrow he would phone the *Globe* (or ask Jenny to) and beg off the book review. The thought of having to write it gave him the dry heaves, and he was learning this time around that the painful retching, once triggered, was slow to depart. (He nerved himself the next day to make the call, and the raspy-voiced woman was not in, to his relief, but he left his message, and in due course his friend Shaun O'Connell did the chore, said more or less exactly what Sams would have said.)

Early abstinence was crippling: some days I felt as meek and helpless as a babe. At other times (unloved), incensed — as on the night she went out to see a friend. I understood, I said, why she needed to do it, but could not be expected to approve. After pacing, unable to read or even watch the tube, thinking of waking Jake, looking out the window every ten minutes awaiting her return, I saw with relief her friend's red Volkswagen roll up in front of the house. But nothing happened: no movement, no exit from the car. After about half an hour I could stand it no longer, ran down the flights of stairs and yelled something in at the window, but waited until safely upstairs to let go the brunt of the self-pitying rage. She took it quietly; kept her cool all through those murderous, unsexed days.

From time to time I pondered the sayings of my fathers.

"Must it always be adjective noun?" Trilling asked, smiling, as we strolled from the faculty club (where I'd had two martinis around a chef's salad, and half of a third) to his office in Hamilton Hall. I'd gone up there to see him after I finished *Slow Dying,* or rather after Al wrested it away. What was this magnificent scholar, teacher, writer, silken-haired Jew trying to tell me, how much of it was I missing, as we walked along Amsterdam Avenue? A mild rebuke (but he had written, and one presumed named, *The Liberal Imagination, The Opposing Self!*) for the tedium of my titles? If he was joking, what did it signify? I was my usual obtuse, addled self, walking there beside him. Covering up, I promised him a more substantial (wordier, at least) title next time out, which would surely be published in his lifetime.

"Until your ship comes in," my father liked to say, and sometimes write, when he mailed the checks or stuffed the cash into my hand. And if it did, I often thought, when that treasure-laden galleon finally hove into view, I'd be scanning the skies at the airport.

Scenes from
a Dry Season

BACK IN THE AUTUMN of '75, on the afternoon of a morning spent pursuing an unruly Jake through the apartment, apprehending the foulmouthed speedster outside his own room and banging his ass hard a couple of times and flinging him across the room as incentives to obedience (making a seer of Wallenda), Sams had been "caught short" as his father liked to describe it fortunately at no great distance from the UGB Science Building and its decent toilets and found in the stall a somewhat dogeared AA meeting list, which he accepted as a sign. Knew for a fact a former resident of the building he lived in, pleasant chap with neat red beard now gainfully employed as assistant curator at the Museum of Fine Arts, was crapping in an outhouse in Avila, Spain, where all he could turn up by way of toilet paper was a neatly squared UGB graduate school bulletin which he read with interest before employing as intended and years later wound up performing summa cum laude at that same institution; so surely (if the tale was true) there was meaning in our movements. Proceeding with all deliberate speed (the day being Saturday), Jason flipped pages to see what might be available on the Sunday and found what was described as a discussion meeting scheduled for ten A.M. and located less than a mile down Brookline Avenue. The pocketsize publication was not all that tattered; it did not occur to him to check when it had been issued, which would have told him, had he done so, that the book had been around since 1970, so meetings might no longer be situated or scheduled as once they were. He did not confide his plans to Jenny, he did not confide much to Jenny in those times, but in any event the idea of himself with his sour views on the subject of AA well known taking in an AA meeting even if only from curiosity and Godgiven coincidence must remain private, which was easily accomplished, his wife he knew planning to take his son across the street to the Vedanta service at about the same time the AA meeting was scheduled to unfold. As soon as he saw them disappear into the temple (having watched from the living room window), he went downstairs and climbed into the Valiant which in those days apart from having its loose front seat propped in place by two plastic crates (leaving little legroom in the rear) had developed a cantankerous mind of its own, zooming off at high speed when you started it up, as hard to control as a bronco, clearly dangerous to life and limb beyond even actuarial tables obtaining to drunk driving. But he had no more idea how to get rid of the car (had that been his inclination) than he would have known how to dispose of some hopelessly crippled or otherwise defective child.

Favoomed down Brookline Avenue to Longwood parking between a couple of two-story buildings one of which bore the address he sought and climbed a flight of stairs to what was identified on the door as an American Legion outpost, entered, found four old men playing cards, all of whom registered astonishment at his arrival.

"I heard there was an AA meeting going on here, at ten?"

"That meetin ain't been held here for years, son."

"Oh. My mistake."

He turned to go. If not for the risk of straining something in his groin, he might have tried to click his heels.

"Wait a minute," one of them said. "You came here for a meetin?"

"The one that used to be here," he said, with a sense of foreboding.

"Nobody looking for AA should be turned away. What does Bill Wilson say? Whenever two drunks get together for the purpose of sobriety, that's a meeting. Come on, guys, let's put on a meeting."

"You don't have to go to any trouble . . ."

"No trouble, friend. We'll all drunks here. Just that the meeting ain't usually held here no more."

So he was sitting around a card table with four old men hearing the AA preamble for the first time (one of them knew it by heart), and before long a black woman walked in wondering if she could get some help here for her alcoholic son. She had heard there was an AA meeting here.

"Odd fucken day. No one's been up here lookin for a meetin for years. Now we got two of them."

She was invited to sit even though she was not an alcoholic or said she was not, but the deviousness of the alkie is profound, the old men knew, and they overcame her reluctance to join such peculiar company by assuring her that if she listened carefully to what unfolded she might hear something useful to her son.

But not much unfolded at all, Sams in no mind to contribute to the "discussion" and the old men a bit creaky regarding the sort of confessional mode and memory re-

quired and failure was in the offing until whatever cosmic
error was afoot produced a couple who did not so much
arrive as blow into the room bag and baggage out of some
play by William Inge, looking for an AA meeting, and when
they found one in progress with the life gone out of it,
provided remedy.

"I was a beserker," the young guy said. Somewhere in
his thirties, black jacket, patched jeans, boots that had seen
the road. "I'd walk into a bar with nothing on my mind
but getting a beer and I'd have a beer, then another, and a
couple more, and next thing you knew I was flinging chairs
and tables across the room and once or twice the jukebox,
and if someone tried to stop me, however big he was or
whatever weapon he carried, I'd bust him up, except for a
few tough hombres who leveled me, and I got twenty-eight
stitches across my pelvis from a knife one time. I don't even
know why I'm alive if it ain't the grace of God protecting
me even back then before I found the program and a higher
power, but I'm sober now seven years and my woman and
I just got here from Maine and I'm here to tell you I ain't
a beserker no more."

"I usually just sat there on the stool," Sams found himself
saying, "drinking in peace."

The young man's thin, grim companion, a woman in her
late twenties with stringy hair, wearing granny glasses, had
been doing needlepoint and nodding emphatically during
his peroration, a juiceless individual Jason had excluded
from his life even before she took to aiming glances at him
so personal and baleful he could not imagine what he'd ever
done to her, in this life or any other. He tried not to let
it worry him, enjoying the rap, the "beserker" coinage,
warming to one of the old fellows whose face seemed to
say that what we had here was a couple of absolute loons,

but once he'd surprised himself by piping up she fastened wild eyes on his face and spit out at last her raging thoughts, her plan for Jason Sams.

"IDENTIFY, you, do not COMPARE. You're going to have to get down on your KNEES, you, ask for help morning noon and night to pray and receive the program on your KNEES, you, or you'll never get sober, you'll DRINK! You'll drink again! I hear it in your voice!"

"Ease off, Mame," the young man said.

"It's OK, she's absolutely right," Sams said. He sensed that one of the ancients put a hand out to him as he rose, touched his arm, but he had his opening, still afflicted maybe, cursed, but free, an AA veteran, tried it didn't like it, too much of a freakshow out there as it was, I am a Jewish person, *loca,* Jews don't generally do knees. His crazed chariot barely made the U-turn but got him safely home where awaited cold imported beer and a fresh pint of Harvey's scotch, old Harvey's better known for its sherry than its scotch but there it had been on the shelves at Golden's at a far better price than almost all the rest except of course for the thin gruel of Clan MacGregor about which even he could not delude himself, and sure enough Harvey's turned out to be another Goodmore, better than potable, but he shoveled in some breakfast first and with his family still absent prepared to sip and gulp and contemplate and make good use of solitude.

By the time Jenny returned he was deep into the World Series, hearing the roars live some fraction of a second after they issued from the tube, true stereo here; he lived close enough to be able (tippytoe at his kitchen window) to see into the rightfield stands. She'd dropped young Jake at the home of a friend, and hung out there a while herself. Ennobled still by Swami's morning message, by her son's delight in friends, the sun sparkling off the Charles, she reached around behind his chair and stroked his cheek and brushed it with her lips.

"Who's playing?"

"You're kidding, right? It's the fucking World Series!"

"Oh sure. Boston and Cincinnati. What inning is it?"

He watched Tiant twirl and break off a beauty, an unhittable curve, and saw Pete Rose slam it for a triple (another man's double) high off the green wall. "Look, you don't give a shit what inning is it, or who's winning, why bother pretending?"

"I've always liked baseball."

"News to me."

"Must you always be a drunken asshole?"

"Smoked you out at last."

That had been his first AA meeting, and its aftermath. Eighteen months would pass before he attended another.

By mid-April of 1977 I had put together a year and a month of abstinence from alcohol, thirteen consecutive months of nodding off in midsentence, falling prey to spells of imbecilic rage, and daily perfecting a scheme to exit through my fifth-floor bedroom window. (Strictly on business: I had $60,000 in term life insurance, with the suicide rider satisfied; five-year-old son and briefly mourning spouse could get a running jump on that.) On a day not otherwise distinguished by its clarity, it occurred to me that J. Sams, Prop., had lined the shelves with a dubious brand of sobriety. If the funk I inhabited was not what I would later hear described in AA as the "insanity preceding the first drink," I had only Antabuse to thank for that, and lately I had taken to misplacing my bottle of the pills.

All I did was hint around these doubts and fears one evening within earshot of the better half and an AA meeting list came flying from her purse and I was out the door that same Friday night, en route to the bowels of Trinity Church in Copley Square. Therapists and friends had nudged me toward AA for years, but I was an adept at what *Alcoholics Anonymous* (the book of that name), citing Herbert Spencer, calls "contempt prior to investigation." I knew there would have to be a God involved, at least some "higher power," and lapsed observer that I was, having neither seen nor smelled the inside of a shul since rousted by my father on some ancient Sabbath morning, it pained me nonetheless to think that in *this* Catholic/Brahmin town, He was not apt to resemble the chatty, hard-nosed God of my fathers. Which was surely just as well.

I'd heard too that I would need a sponsor, which I took to mean some Kiwanis sort of nondrinking drunk to back-slap me into the general freakiness. But my state of mind was such that April night that I resolved to crash the event, and take things as they came.

The people at the oblong table, the seedier ones around the room, were as odd as I might have predicted, and a few — it seemed to me — appeared alarmed by my arrival, but none rose to say me nay. In fact an older gentleman seated at the table turned and gestured to the empty folding chair next to his. I took it. The seat at the end of the table was already occupied by a woman in thick glasses, her body outrageously twisted, her crutches parked nearby. At the crack of eight-thirty she called us to order, asked for a moment of silence, read the preamble, identified herself as an alcoholic and addict, and launched into her tale.

It featured a car crash and a malpractice suit, with an emphasis on painkillers and medical travail. But she had boozed in her time, done pot and coke and smack and pills, not just in the years and seconds prior to the disfiguring accident but more so afterward; had she not stumbled when she did into "this God-given program," she'd have been dead long before now. In AA she had learned to "put the plug in the jug," and how to cultivate "an attitude of gratitude"; the program had saved her ass, but now, spiritually speaking, she was obliged to "grow or go." Proud as she was of her eight sober months, her main concern lay in not picking up a drink *today:* "Yesterday is history, tomorrow is a mystery."

The room applauded, and a coffee break followed. My neighbor asked after my tastes (milk and Sweet 'n Low), and brought me the brew in a Styrofoam cup. Following this, the people at the table read aloud from *Alcoholics Anonymous,* which they called "the big book" — and it was a tome indeed. I mucked in for a paragraph myself, extracting little meaning from the sound of my own voice, feeling back in fifth grade, declaiming Kipling's "If." Another break followed the reading. Twenty-five-cent raffle tickets were sold for a chance to win the big book, or some other. During this interval I found myself, to my surprise, describing my theological reservations to my neighbor, Colin R. He nodded warmly as I spoke, pointing out finally that the God I would in all likelihood require would be a "God of your own understanding," whatever he might have meant by that. Then he told me a story. When he first came to AA, sometime after his service on an aircraft carrier in the Pacific Ocean during World War II, he had heard "higher power" as "Hayakawa," yet his desire to become and to remain sober so far outdistanced his patriotism that for six months he had turned his life and his will over to the care of what he took to be a Japanese admiral. I forced an answering smile. As early as this, my first meeting, I saw that if I ever managed to get by the doggerel at the door, I would encounter still greater perils within, the humor not the least of them.

The pretty young woman who won the raffle presented the big book to me. I fretted: was I that obviously a beginner? Not wanting to be beholden to I knew not what, I brought forth a check and anted up for the companion volume, *Twelve Steps and Twelve Traditions*. Perhaps I might *read* my way to sanity, and as early as my very first meeting be shut of the clubby basements.

Yet I was back at a similar gathering the following night, wending my way to Coolidge Corner, searching for what the AA directory listed as a "Young People's Meeting"; and while I was not the only codger in attendance, the group as a whole did seem to generate a towel-snapping, lockerroom atmosphere. Thanks, however, to the round-robin format of that meeting, I got to say a word or two, having captured the fancy of a bearded giant in a leather jacket who used his five minutes to say that while he was no unadulterated pleasure to hang around with even now, had you run into him in an alley during his drinking and drugging days he would have killed you for the pittance in your pockets. For some reason he pointed at me before shambling from the podium. I answered the summons, but had little to say. I mentioned my newness to AA, my thirteen freelance months; of course I mentioned Antabuse. Later, during the break for the raffle, a skinny, sallow kid approached and limply grasped my hand.

"Good to hear your story, man. You want to get off that Antabuse as soon as possible, you know? They used to shoot it into me in the navy. It's nothing but a goddamn crutch."

He was some twenty years my junior; too old nonetheless, I decided, for the horseplay I'd watched him at moments earlier behind the coffee urn. Advice, in my experience, was tough enough to bear from people with some knowledge of your life.

"Sometimes you need to use a crutch so you don't fall on your ass."

"Ah, sure, man. Don't cop an attitude. I was only sharing my experience, strength and hope, like the preamble tells us."

"Man, don't share at me, man, like you know, just *talk*."

(I wish I could say that by and by this youth and I became companions in sobriety; it didn't happen, but AA provides for that contingency as well. "Principles," the literature cautions, "over Personalities.")

And the next afternoon, a Sunday, I was back in the basement of a church, this time on Newbury Street, in the shadow of the Ritz-Carlton Hotel, where, damn it, I'd never even *thought* to twirl the stem of a martini glass and gaze thoughtfully through tinted glass at the public and the Public Garden, with who knew what eminence comporting itself in similar fashion at a nearby table. And in the chaos of the Midtown Meeting (now defunct), I somehow discovered that a sponsor was someone you shopped around for from within, a person whose manner of staying away from one drink for one day you had come to admire, along with the cut of his jib, and who, for reasons of his own, agreed to share with you (what other word would do?) the nuts and bolts of his own sober life. In due course I latched onto John Y, a Catholic, a Harvard and family man, who had (in the parlance) "not found it necessary to pick up a drink" for fourteen years. He was forty-eight that year, my senior in that respect as well. That fall of 1977 I was a newly minted forty-five: one life was over, and I had but the foggiest notion how to start up another. But daily, as I began to take notice of my sharp-eyed son, financial planning via the bedroom window beckoned less. I phoned John as often as I dared, crying the blues, demanding exegesis of the texts, and he made time in a busy life to have dinner with me now and then, squired me to his favorite meetings, introduced me to his friends. He was still around, still available, a year and a half later, by which time I'd gathered strength. At that point we had a falling out over matters unrelated to sobriety. Still later we became good friends.

Then Antabuse, one day, quit taking me. I hadn't planned it. I simply "forgot" to take a pill one day, and then the next. I had become active in the AA sense of making coffee for a meeting, sweeping out a hall. I developed a fondness for the Saturday morning twelve-step meeting that unfolded in Old South Church in Copley Square. "Be careful you don't trip over God on your way out the door," John advised me, and I took his meaning well enough: excessive involvement with AA meetings and spicy individuals therein had split up a hearth or two since the program was founded in 1935 (including, for a time, his own). Yet despite some difficult and high-decibel moments I remained married, and was even doing a spot of fathering. Besides, Jennifer and Jake were both fast asleep at eight on a Saturday morning. I was down in the Square at that hour, breathing in the season, giving a wide berth to the stumblebums already afoot searching out "corners" (the drop or two left in a can or bottle following the previous night's disco and frat house revels), litter to launch a day by, especially useful in winter if you hadn't found an empty (some abandoned or unfinished structure) to bed down in the night before. I rarely felt obliged to "carry the message" to any of these far-gone juicers; I was on my way to where a (more receptive) boatload could be found.

A quick stop at Warburton's for a Cornish pasty and a medium-size coffee, then onward, a spring to my step and the key to the basement in my hand. The brown and yellow room beneath Old South Church resembled, in its contours and odors, the shul beneath the shul much favored by my father in the orthodoxy of my youth, with even a drunken goy or two camped on the library steps across Boylston Street to flick on the lights, should that degree of piety ever again descend upon me. Found his metier at last, Reb Sams, sexton of a surreal synagogue.

"Jay, my man, can you spare a little change?"

Gap-toothed Jerry G awaits my arrival at the top of the staircase leading to the basement. Listing to starboard, back from another stay at Bridgewater, mysteriously lame these days, sporting a scraggly goatee if "sporting" is the word, he is in no condition to help me set up a table, unfold a chair.

"The liquor store's still closed, Jerry."

"Too true." He flashes a dazzling grin, which just as quickly vanishes; it's a problem with affect he'll carry to the grave. "Did you know that Jesus Christ and Cassius Clay a.k.a. Muhammad Ali were one and the same person?"

"How do you figure?"

"The *straight* left jab, the *right* up from the floor . . ." With ominous skill he demonstrates upon the air. "When He cleansed them moneychangers from the temple."

"My New Testament's a little shaky, Jerry."

"Of course! *Pardon* me, Jay. You are fortunate indeed to be of that ethnic persuasion, instead of a poor drunken nigger like myself. Did you know, by the by, that there be *no* Jewish alcoholics?"

"No shit?"

"Inoculated! A gallon of Manischewitz now and then is a ceremonial must for your people, ain't that so? Or it may well be you were shortchanged on the proper enzymes, like them poor Oriental Chinese."

"I think I'll go for a second opinion."

"*Trust* me, Jay! When them liquor people gave away all that study money to Harvard, who you think the Harvards hired to do the research? Ain't you got a *little* change? It be imperative I get me a jolt of white port soon's they open."

"I've just enough on me for the coffee supplies. I'm sorry, Jerry. See you later at the meeting?"

"You don't never know." The sudden grin, the somber visage. "This here be a disease of the spirit, you hear what I'm saying? As well as of the flesh."

And suddenly, as I descend the littered steps, push beyond the iron door into the dark and airless room, soon to be fouled by cigarette smoke and unwashed bodies (for no matter how many windows I throw open some shivering freak will insist on his right to slam them shut again), I'm sorely depressed. I'm thinking of how much that hundred-cup coffee urn is going to weigh once I get it filled, and no way to fill it, either, except lidful by lidful from the basin in the ladies' john. Then one by one the crazy complement will arrive, some "active" in the other AA sense, as in actively drinking, and all of them, drunk or sober, locked into their own heads and griefs, with scarcely a nod of acknowledgment to their *éminence grise,* the hardworking, humble guy who made it happen. Ah, Christ, my mama didn't raise me up to be an alcoholic, at least not here in the Hub; perhaps in Manhattan, where every third AA meeting, I couldn't help but notice while down there on a visit, seemed to unfold beneath some well-appointed synagogue.

And as I glumly throw the switch, bringing on the naked, fluorescent glare, my higher power appears, blessed be His name, the God of my own peculiar understanding. He has evolved through the years from a chip (and then an organ grinder's monkey) on my shoulder. At the moment he is a somewhat shorter Jesse Jackson, with a touch of Oscar Levant. With his cane he raps my shoulder from behind and when I turn He does a fast shuffle down the length of the empty room, vanishes, rematerializes at my elbow.

"How goes the window of vulnerability, Mr. S?"

"Sealed off."

He winks, raises His top hat: "Good-o. Defenestration harms the nation. So how come the long face, amigo?"

"I'm weak on compassion this morning."

"Compassion ain't in fashion. Look out for the *why-me's* and the *poor-me's,* is all is all. And let me give you some further advice. Spring for the Chock Full o' Nuts today, the two-pound can. Forget Star Market's own. A touch of class for My hopeless rummies! Let the wild rumpus start!"

"Tell me one thing, Sire."

"You're My main man, Sams."

"For how long can an individual maintain sobriety on tight-ass cynicism and ironic merriment?"

"For about as long as he or she don't pick up that first drink," He says and, spats gleaming, fandangos onto Boylston Street.

My double drinks when he can get the price together, never straying far from where the purchase is made, hitching up his pants and extending the pint of white port above his head and chugalugging half, a two-fisted macho drinker blocking the sidewalk near the university bookstore in the square. There is something not a little ostentatious, something literary, in the way he takes his booze, a touch of how it must have been when Hemingway was young. He lends to the recently opened book-and-doodad place (an "innovative vertical mall," they like to call it, reinventing the department store) a touch of real ambience to go along with the balloons.

Sometimes I drop a quarter into his blackened palm, although he less often actively panhandles than mutters asides, or shuffles to and fro. We never speak; on winter days, all you can see of his face are the red, raging eyes. When he vanishes mysteriously for weeks at a time, he leaves a sad gap in my experience of the square. I imagine him dead, succumbed at last to demon rum, or hypothermia, or mere natural causes, for he has already lived, as near as one can judge, between forty and sixty-five years.

My son does not understand what makes my double my double — the man's beard is the wrong color and scragglier than mine, he is thinner, never clean — but I know what I know. "Identify, do not compare," they tell us in the AA basements. Recently, after a three-week absence, he reappeared across from the Bank of Boston, sharing the traffic island with the trim Valkyrie who keeps a gimlet eye on the bank's front door from eight-thirty to nine each weekday morning (she did not seem distracted by his presence). Dressed in clown's trousers, slippers, and a ratty topcoat over nothing, he advanced and then retreated from the curb like a zoo animal behind a moat, knowing there would be no payoff even if he spanned it. Years ago, between drinks and foreign cities, I paced that way myself, on streetcorners in Kyoto, London, Barcelona, Malmö, with no compelling reason to move anywhere. In Boston, in the bicentennial year, my luck changed and I put down the drink. But my double stayed the course. No "coffee and conversation" under blue and yellow banners, no "grace of God," will bring those braincells back.

R cut a fine, tawny figure last night, summoned to the podium with only four minutes left and so reasonably certain (as she said) that she'd escaped the call, yet mucking in ebulliently to re-create the eight-day binge that got her here, her "last drunk," on a brutally hot day in August 1980, by the end of which (behind closed windows and drawn shades in a South End furnished room) her skin hung as loose as the sky-blue Angora sweater she pinched between thumb and forefinger to indicate to us what looseness was, the whites of her eyes had turned yellow, and she was close to "shut down," in her own colorful phrase. As a black woman in Boston, her advanced degrees have so far availed her nothing; she still slogs through each day minus a (melodically italicized) "meaningful relationship." But twenty months down the road from that near-final week, her priorities remain vivid and unconditional: sobriety as an unqualified blessing, and Alcoholics Anonymous as the way to maintain it.

On a fair day, if you look skyward on the street leading to the square, there above the post office you will spot Bobby Z, swaying on his "stage," a slatted platform/rope contraption that appears very flimsy from below. A craftsman and an artist, he's just now painting over the 7 & 7 billboard with three mammoth bottles of Myers' rum, inserting tiny freehand skulls and crossbones here and there, eight years now without a drink or a toke or a pill, splashing giant booze across the sky. I heard him speak a few nights ago at a meeting in Quincy, recalling a dream in which a lovely woman picked him out of a crowd and conveyed him to a "space platform"; they were about to transport all the intellectual geniuses to some better place before the planet self-destructed, and Z was consumed with worry: what would happen when they found out he really wasn't all that bright? He rehearses: "Would you tell them for me, honey, it's not like I'm stupid, I just haven't discovered my particular *gift?*"

In the detox down Brookline Avenue, in the dimly lighted recreation room, some in robes and paper slippers watch the fish tank, others study the cartoons. One rises suddenly, gestures in disgust, and shuffles from the tank: "Them fucken nature shows."

The stairs leading down to the basement of Old South Church are covered with Burger King wrappers and sui generis debris. The air is acrid in the bilious yellow room. But every folding chair is filled. I lean against the rear wall and tune in to Manny M, who holds forth from the front of the room (no podium here). I greet five Bobs and three Janes and two Mikes, and know them all. Will Manny, who looks like Zapata, be relatively sane tonight? Or will he veer into his Jesus rap or his "You Americans are just like children" rap, or home onto "We sober drunks must band together, arm ourselves, and off the owners of the liquor stores"? No matter — eventually he'll warm to his main theme, that we all have a "killer disease." And this will remind me that I won't see Tim S down here again, squinting through the smoke, trying to get the hang of it. He went from Yale to an ad agency in New York to living on the streets of Boston, and came partway back. But he checked out ten days ago, age forty-one, drinking nonstop in a room in South Boston for the last two weeks of his life, yet (an AA member to the end) staying on the phone. The only time he ever called me sober was two years ago, to shyly ask if I would be among the speakers at his first anniversary, and I was glad to say yes. Days after celebrating that event he went out for further R & D, then stopped drinking for a while, but never did make it back. His drunken calls went on until you hung up on a poor joke, a meaningless ramble, an insult, a maniacal guffaw. The worst of them for me was the night I picked up the phone and heard a strange voice say, "We have your son." And while I knew in an instant who it was, and while my kid was at that moment almost underfoot, raiding the fridge, I prickled in outrage and terror for days afterward.

Yet I forgave him even that, once he sobered up, although I don't think he ever believed it. Now we'll see him no more, quizzical and burly in the Brueghel Room.

"They did some psychological testing," the woman following Manny says, "and I tested low reality."

"My daily sobriety is like the doings of a duck," says the last speaker, Pasquale of the North End. "Up top I glide along serene, but underneath I'm paddling like a bastard."

I spoke at length for the first time in the basement of the Church of the Advent on Brimmer Street, hunched over the lectern with my back to the worn tapestry on a Saturday night in July of '77, regaling the motley assemblage from a three-by-five index card which held, as I imagined then, the relevant fragments of my life. What better place to break in than at the Beacon Hill meeting, the Broadway of Boston AA — an enormous room filled to the brim every week with comptrollers of Fortune 500 companies and Mass General surgeons, on the one hand, and streetfolk with scrambled brains on the other, the latter not even always alkies but people who knew how to keep warm in winter, and how best to stash a slab or two of someone's anniversary cake in a Star Market shopping bag.

". . . and so I learned to like my sake cold, as did the more sophisticated Japanese. But a large quantity of cold sake is no less potent than the heated brew, and after I'd downed a couple of dozen thimblefuls in the kiosk by Lake Biwa I staggered into the off-limits section, only partly by design. There I, well, leaving my next port of call, I was surprised by an MP jeep just then cruising down the street, and on drunken impulse tore back inside, fled up the stairs, and wound up clinging to the chimney on the roof of a whorehouse.

"I lost a shoe up there, scrabbling around on the tiles, and very nearly followed it down. Since the place was out of bounds to the MP's as well, one of them had to go off and find a native cop to escort me down. But wait, that episode occurred while I was still in the service, and I didn't learn to like my sake cold until after my overseas discharge . . . looking back over twenty-three years, I seem to be confusing my civilian with my army experience, but what does it matter? By the end of my time in Japan I was the same falling-down drunk on Kawaramachi-dori in Kyoto as on Otsu country roads, as gone in my guise as ersatz student of the language and culture as I'd been in my army days. I left Japan in 1956 for no clear reason and made my way to Europe via a nine-month stopover in New York, remaining in Manhattan just long enough to rev up the GI

Bill and deplete my father's liquor supply, and then I was off to the University of London — and this may amuse you — to resume my study of things Japanese. I became familiar with most of the pubs in Bayswater and Chelsea and up and down the Finchley Road, learned to love warm scotch and beer, developed a broad familiarity with hookers from all corners of the empire, but never stopped searching for the one softspoken, stunning, no doubt moonlighting English streetwalker I ran into right off the bat, my first night on European soil. It was too early in the evening for me to want to cough up the pittance she was asking; I still had some pints of bitter ale to swallow, and something even better, I deluded myself, was sure to come along if such a prize had turned up early on. But Soho was an outtake from Hieronymus Bosch once the pubs had closed. She wasn't where she'd been, of course, not on that night or any other, and I've mourned her ever since.

"I graduated with an upper second in modern Japanese and a fading interest in Japan and I took what was left of the GI Bill to Spain. Fooling around with the language of Cervantes, I walked into a plate glass door at the University of Barcelona bright one morning, already smashed on brandy Fundador and San Miguel beer, and fractured my nose. My off-again on-again Swedish friend — or haven't I mentioned her yet? — was there to nurse me back to health, then made the mistake of inviting me to Malmö, and I went. While she was off earning a day's pay I queued outside the state liquor store for my aquavit and a cheap white wine called Fragal. I was supposedly hard at work on my second book, but in fact I was partying with its characters, drinking daily until I blacked out or slept. On some days I'd manage an aimless stroll around the city, or I'd grab the ferry to Copenhagen and sauce morosely in the bars. My most vivid memory of that time is glancing pie-eyed from my window one winter afternoon and watching a pair of policemen maneuver a chess game in progress down the snowy street . . . they belonged there, I didn't, and in the summer of I think it was 1962 I . . . am informed by the chair that I use too much time, and we have two fine speakers yet to come. So let me finish by saying that I earned my place here, am grateful to be sober, and glad to have strung together the ninety days of unbroken abstinence that give me the right to stand up here and speak. In fact, with an assist from Antabuse and dread, I'd already put together thirteen dry months before ever coming to my first AA meeting. But the program, as it does, has smoothed the way, given me new friends and a higher power, and I'm glad to have tacked on the ninety days. Thanks for listening."

Not that they'd had a whole lot of choice. Nor could I get a fix on how well I'd done by gauging audience response: the applause that night (as on all other nights) was hearty, the smiles warm and broad; people I knew and some I didn't extended their hands as I ambled self-consciously back to my seat. And after the meeting a grizzled old tar, who remembered Yokohama fondly (as did I), somewhat delayed my journey home.

It's hard to bomb at an AA meeting. We tend to look for the best in each other, concentrating on those portions of a "drunkalogue" that echo our own worst years, and on that part of an AA recovery that provides a roadmap for our own spiritual journey. Over time I came to envy, without rancor, certain Irish bards from Southie, several honest Injuns from the Tremont Street tribe, a number of ex-bingers on vanilla extract (mousy women with wills of steel), and any number of others who could give their stories shape and in so doing move me, strengthen my own commitment to staying straight.

Yet I doubt I was the only alcoholic in the hall who found it difficult to muster the required degree of fellow feeling (on a different night) for a portly gent who was able to admit to a roomful of mostly strangers that once, three sheets to the wind, he'd held his five-year-old daughter's face in a bowlful of gravy a little longer than her conduct warranted, and the child died, as did, understandably, the marriage she had issued from. But "thanks to the grace of God and the gift of Alcoholics Anonymous" he had re-married after doing some time, and was now the father of "two beautiful little boys in sobriety." Such tales could tax your yea-saying capacity.

Or take the redhaired Scot sober in AA for two years when his wife ran off with her bartender. He proceeded to get tanked and go looking for the pair. "God," he reported having thought that night, "I'm gonna send you a coupla people." An eerie eschatology. Yet *some* power had inter-posed itself, for there he stood, still carrot-topped, once more two years without a drink, to report on the outcome: I was weaving my way across Blue Hill Avenue just as a convoy of bikers went roaring by, and as I had on my kilt that night about six of them stopped, took away my dirk, roughed me up and raped me." The places booze can take you! The outfits it can clothe you in!

There was nothing this tasty in my own doggy bag of anecdotes. Just twenty-three years of murky, accelerating loss, lunatic decisions, blighted relationships, marked by the spastic continent hopping of my youth, then various ill-considered uprootings later on. AA describes this as a "geo-graphical cure," the alcoholic's doomed attempt to leave himself behind. But I hadn't heard the phrase, or not yet acknowledged its pertinence, the night I stood behind the lectern on Brimmer Street and delivered myself of a travelogue (subhead sexalogue).

You can still find me several nights a week with my ears open in the smoke-filled basements. But I never grew more adept than I was that first night at fleshing out with art the bare bones of a drunkalogue: how it was, how I got here, and the things that happened then. My gifts lay elsewhere. I worked with newcomers, brewed up an urn of coffee, swept out a meeting hall. Besides, there were other types of meetings one might attend. There were discussion meetings. There were step meetings, at which, after one individual had told his story, one of the twelve steps was read aloud, paragraph by paragraph around the room, and we then addressed ourselves to how well or poorly we'd been able to "work" it, apply its precepts to our daily lives.

This "working the steps" kept us in touch with the heart of the AA enterprise. The alcoholic had to make some changes in his life beyond mere abstinence, or it was more than likely he or she would drink again. Yet it was only the first half of the first step that had to be perfectly mastered: "We admitted we were powerless over alcohol — that our lives had become unmanageable." By the time a good many of us walked in the door, admitting our inability to drink was more a relief than a hardship. As for the practice of steps two through twelve, the goal remained "progress, not perfection." The belief in a higher power. The habits of self-scrutiny, meditation, prayer. The extent to which you "carry the message to the alcoholic who still suffers." Many of us had the greatest difficulty with the eighth and ninth, the so-called amends steps: compiling a list of all people we had "harmed" in our drinking lives and trying to atone to them all. I loathed these steps on first encounter, and am not crazy about them today. But early on I had perceived that if I "worked the program as it was laid out," "followed the suggestions" (however repugnant they might sometimes appear), I could tap, through this very surrender and regardless of outcome, a source of hidden strength.

The glosses for eight and nine made clear that the response of the people you approached was in no way the point of the exercise: "[negative] reactions will not deflect us from our steady and even purpose." And sooner or later, beyond good intentions, these steps had to be taken: "Let's not talk prudence while practicing evasion."

So I gave it a go. I knew that back from Japan in 1957, or from Europe in 1962, I sat with my father in the kitchen of the apartment I grew up in and (propelled by strong drink and self-pity) I blew him out of the water. He may have been nursing a beer while I gobbled down his J&B, as baffled as ever by this anomaly before him. "So now that you're twenty-five [or thirty], Jace, and have rested up a while, what do you plan to do with your life?" The question was so old, so dismissive of my ambitions, that I felt the ancient rage kick in, only dimly aware that most of the anger was not my own.

"You never loved us, Pop," I let him know. "All the love you ever had to give went to your brother Abe. Shit, you even had more for his *son* than you ever had for me. So give me a fucking break. It's a little late for you to start worrying about my life."

Through the alcoholic haze it seemed to me that *he* was drunk; he was grinning a lopsided grin, his face on the point of dissolution.

"You're drinking my liquor, Son," I heard him say. "You're sleeping under my roof. I've bailed you out of tight spots a hundred times. Anyway, hell, it was just a friendly question."

The phone rang then, his twin brother on the wire, and my father's face lit up as they got into matters of moment. I threw up my hands in elaborate despair and stormed (staggered) out of the house en route to San Remo's or the White Horse Tavern.

In June of 1979, right after he turned seventy-two and some three years after he put his twin brother in the ground, still bemused by his own survival but beginning to take real pleasure in it, my father visited Boston with my mother, and on impulse I brought them on a Saturday night to the Church of the Advent on Beacon Hill. Uneasy in a church, my mother admired the threadbare tapestry and commented on the large number of well-dressed social workers in attendance, along with such interested observers as ourselves — when did the real alcoholics arrive? My father put a five-dollar bill in the collection basket (a quarter was the more usual offering) and waved off the attempt to give him change. Later that night, my mother and wife and son in bed, my father on the verge, I steeled myself to make amends. I didn't expect him to cooperate. I imagined that I'd have to jog his memory, or reinvent the thing from scratch, to profit from its expiation. But I was wrong. He remembered more than I did.

"That little exchange was right after you got back from Europe, Son, in 1962. I'm very happy you gave up drinking, seeing how badly you always handled it. I hope most of the lousy things we heard about in those stories tonight didn't happen to you in your travels. As for that little piece of ancient history between you and me, don't let it bother you. It never bothered me."

"Thickskinned?" I asked him.

"Your mother likes to think so, but that ain't it. You want to know the reason?"

"Sure," I lied.

"You were a shikker, Son, a drunken bum. Nothing you said made any sense. You didn't know shit from shinola."

I nodded agreeably and later that night, drinking coffee with my higher power, I got the green light to put the eighth and ninth steps behind me.

Sober for six years by 1982, I thought it high time AA gave me back my sword, restored some semblance of the old magic. The gifted Jason R was still Jason Robards, following his final fling; Betty F, popping no pills, had become a winner at the intricate business of being Betty Ford. If *my* higher power had some change of vocation in store I wished he would get on with it, although, having turned fifty that year, I was not really dying to hear the news.

"How goes that old novel, Jay?" Larry N would ask from time to time. A North Carolinian who had once caddied for Sam Snead, Larry wound up running bucknaked through the back alleys of Miami, wondering on the move what sequence of events had brought him to this pass; later, apprehended, clothed, it took what remained of his mother wit to lose at cards to a six-foot six-inch cellmate who appeared not to have all his marbles. Larry's star had guided him north, and sobered him up, and now he was the proud manager (at his belt a ring of keys a warden might envy) of several handsome buildings at the Public Garden end of Commonwealth Avenue.

"Or should Ah rather say, 'How goes the *new* novel?' "

"Developing slowly, Larry."

"What if you just snuck in some fast-moving tales from mah own particulah lahf? Hell's bells, Jay, if Ah had yo' kahn o' leisure tahm, Ah'd write me one o' them buggers all bah mahself."

"Buzz off, N."

"Well mah, mah. That indeed does 'Keep it simple,' as our banner suggests. Ah'm raht pleased to see you making progress in sobriety."

I had sounded off plaintively at enough meetings to have invited such chaffing, but as the years kept rolling by I'd come to feel (alongside the rage and self-pity) a touch of guilt for letting down the side. We measured our own sober progress, after all, by the achievements (and not the spiritual ones alone) of our fellows. The fear was this: you could stay dry and occupied with AA itself for years, stuck fast like flamehaired Rita R, accomplishing nothing, surviving out there on your wits and the dole, laying at the doorstep of that pernicious entity, your "disease," every stray happening and failing. "This disease is a *mother,* and mine is definitely *on* today," she'd say, great bosoms heaving. "On the way over here I almost *crushed* some fag ticket-taker on the T, who had the balls to want to check the date on my disability pass. But did that give me any relief? Not on your life, not with *this* disease. I'm *still* in a frame of mind to tear a few faces off."

Yet for Rita too there came (as one's own time accumulated) acceptance, and not just because she was perceived to be extremely helpful to any number of female addicts, hookers, and Combat Zone hoofers who were trying to break away from the life and death in the streets, but simply because one became, with sober time, more tolerant of the foibles of the folk one sat around with, and listened to, and opened up to, three and four and five times a week in the same set of rooms. You didn't wind up liking (and surely not, as some had it, "loving") everybody in the room, but you soon stopped questioning anyone's right to be there, even the bullshit and ripoff artists (who were infrequently one and the same). "The only requirement for membership," as the preamble said, "is a desire to stop drinking": whoever decided he or she belonged, and did not cause mayhem on the premises, was "in the right place"; "nobody ever gets to AA by accident." Sometimes a familiar face vanished, and you might not even miss it unless it reappeared. A drunk might switch to different meetings, or try to stay straight without the program, or, in the phrase, go out to get a better story. Some people vanished for good, and we didn't always know the reasons. Some turned up on the obituary page, and we generally knew the reasons then.

So I learned to roll with the teasing, and even appear serene in the face of unsolicited commiseration concerning my dammed-up or vanished literary skills. Bookish Sam B, aspirant intellectual if ever one was, offered condolences, chiefly through the mail. For two years we engaged in correspondence, although we lived three streets apart. He was one of the people whose unlikely presence at intown meetings nourished me in the early slogging. I was cheered by his oval, fearful face, fastidious enunciation, involuted commentary on the twelve steps, and I credit him for my earliest perception that you needn't have wound up in the gutter to be welcome in the halls of AA. He liberated me also from my early keen discomfort at listening to people who continued to intimate the need to "get down on your knees" in order to properly communicate with your higher power; a Boston aberration, he assured me, "recovering Catholics," some not recovering rapidly enough. Similarly with my disinclination to say the Lord's Prayer at the end of a meeting (or respond well to other New Testament jive; *my* Messiah, She was still on the way), Sam was the first to assure me I could stay clean and sober without this overlay. Often he would turn up at meetings with a cumbersome pile of newly purchased books, a French Rumanian dictionary, perhaps, cheek by jowl with Gregory Bateson's essays, or a fat biography of Martin Buber nestled against a paperback of some volume or other of *Remembrance of Things Past*. He was forever reading Proust, or rather continually re-enrolling in the same course (PROUST) at Harvard Extension, in the hope that he might one day be moved by someone's chance remark to crack open a volume.

Most nights, back from a meeting, I would jot its coordinates into my journal, against that great getting-up morning when my higher power would give me the nod to pull it all together:

June 1978. Damion L seemed happy in his swishiness at Beacon Hill last night, chairing his fifth anniversary: "All I ever wanted to do as a small boy was *culuh!* Give me crayons, give me the heavy outlines, I was *happy!*" Once, he said, he was arrested for public drunkenness in old Scollay Square. They put him in a cell with a tattooed giant. L breaks the ice: "What you in fuh?" "I smacked a homo in the chops. How about you?" Damion, basso profundo: "They busted me fuh child support."

September 1979. Bailey G described life in his first furnished room, after twenty years in the streets. He nailed his curtains to the window frame. Then, as he was getting relatively comfortable: "They condomized me! They was going to let me buy back my own apartment! 'It will have an exposed brick wall,' they said. 'Shit,' I told them, 'I been living with exposed brick all my life.' " He returned, a year sober, to a halfway house, much relieved.

February 1980. Tom N, around thirty, rangy Irishman, deep blue eyes, ex-con, decked three people at Trinity Church last night. A moral avenger, not sober at the time. "If you don't get AA, AA will get you," we like to say, but this seems not to hold for Tom. He's been "around the program," as he puts it, since 1968. He came beaming into the room last night, then spotted the sleaze in the ponytail. He weaved over that way. "You're here to scoop chicks, animal, you're after skin, *you are not interested in getting sober!* Move in that chair and I'll pulverize you." To me it seemed the sleaze didn't stir, but N popped him anyway, then floored the two who tried to intervene. Someone called the cops, who came, but Tommy was long gone by then. We are told to be wary of our "self-centered fear," but you'd have to be nuts not to fear some of these people.

December 1982. Tommy N is back among us. With a straight face he quotes the conventional wisdom at me: "Jay, I'm here to tell you, there ain't nothing worse than a headful of AA and a bellyful of booze."

He found me at the Sunday meeting on Brookline Avenue. The place was jammed, but there was one empty seat in front of me. "Sams, watch my back." "Got you covered, Tommy." He sits, spins around. He's shitfaced. "Hey, didn't you once bring me in a cab to detox one time?" "Yeah, it was me and Frenchy, two three years ago." He winks. "I'm still in a slump." "Maybe you ought to close up your stance a little." He roars appreciatively. He seems oblivious to the heads that turn our way. "You old fart, you ever write that book?" "Not yet." "Procrastination is a bitch, ain't it? But you wrote a couple already, didn't you?" " ' "In my youth," said the sage . . .' " "That's Lewish Carroll, ain't it? That Father Williams what tried to rip off his own son?" "You read much, Tommy?" "In the jug I did. You know what it was, Jacey, I was trying to get educated so that dude Norman Mailer would bail me out. Hey, listen, you know what AA really needs, that might be up your street?" "What's that, Tommy?" "A Damon Runyon kind of wacky writer to capture all the variety. Or a

Mark Twain. I ever tell you how I walked away from MCI Concord with a black guy, we walked away and boosted a canoe and sailed off down the river? His name was Eddie Grace, but after that I called him Nigger Jim. Me and Nigger Jim sailed off down the Concord River. Have you read *Huckleberry Finn?*" "Not recently." "I heard they found Eddie dead with a spike in his arm." People are shushing us now, some looking quite irate. For their sakes I say, "Why don't we lock into some meeting, Tommy." "Sure, old timer, hear something we can use. You don't have to ask me twice."

The journal has suffered neglect over the past several years, the pipe dreams grow hazy. But Jason S, working his program, retains an interest in his fellows. Just last week I was at the Travis Restaurant on Newbury Street, following the Saturday morning meeting, and there as usual sat Kevin P, deep in the *Boston Herald.* Kevin directs the East Boston halfway house where Sam B, Proust-lover, is now employed. He no longer attends the Saturday morning "zoo" as often as he did, but can generally be found over at the Travis when the meeting is over. With his snow-white hair, ruddy complexion, air of being privy to amazing secrets, he bears some likeness to the other Kevin, Boston's former mayor. But P radiates a kind of moral health, despite a recent liver flare-up (a "residual," he called it) that very nearly carried him off, although he hasn't had a drink in fifteen years.

It was mid-November, but warm enough to set up shop at the rickety tables outside. The Travis, with its dull, unchanging menu, endless wait for an overpriced grilled cheese, is as close as I need to come, these days, to the wine-and-cheese jostles conducted by and for the literati at the nearby Harvard Bookstore Cafe.

"I haven't seen Tommy in a while," I said to Kevin, grabbing an ice cream parlor chair.

"N? He was cooking for me at the house. He phoned me just this morning, stoned out of his skull."

"I didn't know he cooked."

"He doesn't. You toss a hundred franks in a pot and you saw the lid off a giant can of beans."

"How'd he make out?"

"He was doing good, until last week. Then he drank, and I had to can him."

"You booted him out?"

"That was the deal we put together. If he drank, he was gone. He threatened to kill me this morning."

"How'd you handle that?"

Kevin chuckled. "I was tactless. But in the event he remembers what I said, or what he said, he knows where to find me."

He swept his hand across the *Herald*. "Jason, you have the advantage of a few years on me, if you don't mind my saying so. You ever read the Irish sports page?"

"Read the what?"

"The obituaries. Take a gander at this. They're dropping like flies. Even a second cousin of mine just went belly up. It moves me to contemplate my final resting place. Yourself, you have a plot?"

"Not yet," I told him. "A hint of a theme. A handful of characters."

He was utterly baffled for a moment, thrown. Then there issued from his chest the splendid, phlegmy roar.

"Sams, you're a hot shit. Did you happen to see in your *Boston Globe* where it says alkies sober five years or more can drink all day Monday?"

"How come, Kevin?"

"It's Veterans Day!"

Eight-year veteran of happenings in Boston basements, perilously jaded, he went to Montreal in July of 1985 to lose himself among the multitudes celebrating AA's fiftieth anniversary, as well as try to get a sense of the foreign city under happier circumstances than when he'd gone twenty years earlier (as a drinking drunk in the company of petite redhead Hubert Humphrey lookalike to terminate her pregnancy, not a story in its nuance and aftermath he's been able to "share" at AA meetings even yet). For three days he attended meetings and seminars and giant rallies, mingled with drunks of every stripe, bumped into a few old friends and made some new ones, but was moved most profoundly by their numbers.

Affirmed, headed home, shopping for overpriced gifts for Jenny and Jake at the airport, gratitude welled up in him for his unmerited blessings. Somehow, through years of daily drinking, and through the rough years of early sobriety, in and out of AA, he had managed to retain a wife, a son. Gratitude was followed by a rush of self-congratulation, tricky turf for an alkie, but, old hand that he was, he knew which memory to tap to ward it off. Just the afternoon before, a woman from AA's General Service Organization in New York, presiding at the "Around-the-World Callup," had tried to locate in the packed auditorium the nuns and soldiers and authors and shopkeepers who had been designated standard-bearers at the farewell bash at Olympic Stadium that night. (Once the man from Japan blew in, she thought she had before her representatives of all fifty-four countries in which AA flourishes, or has a foothold.) "Ladies and gentlemen," she told them, "if I may make but a single suggestion. When you march out there tonight, it is best you do not imagine that you represent your country, and certainly do not be deluded into thinking that you represent AA. You will just be a drunk, carrying a flag."